THE GIFTED CHILD

JOHN'S SAGA

Berlena!
thank you for your
Support

28, Jun, 06

Tonie J. Short

ABOUT THE AUTHOR

Tonie Short grew up in the Deep South at a time that challenged and pushed him to prove to himself that he had the right stuff to make it in the world. With religious conviction, he believed that for every door that was closed to him, God would open another.

Meroe Publishing

This book is in dedication to Mrs. Dorothea Brinson, a woman that saw something in me when no one else did.

TABLE OF CONTENTS

Prejudice Cuts Like Glass

I come from a strong, proud heritage in a far away land,
My ancestors were manipulated, beaten and then drug in American sand;

This hatred is documented in films, movies, books, and oral speech from
generation to generation,
For too many years, because of race, people were educated, fed, and even lived in
separation;

Time has healed some things and enabled some people to move forward,
But with hate crimes still being committed, we must continue to call on the Lord;

I love ALL people and life, so much that I try very hard to be strong,
But sometimes because of the actions of others, I'd rather be alone;

How do I move on? How do I get past…
The things they've done, the words they've said, when they continue to cut like
glass?

How do I grin and bare it? I forgive, but I can't forget,
The things they've done and the words they've said, when they continue to cut like
glass?

Oh God, help me leave everything that's happened to my family behind,
Show me how to gain the peace that I want in my heart and mind;

Please help me get past, the prejudiced things they've done, the belittling
Words they've said, so they no longer cut like glass.

A poem from Heart Felt words by: TERESA MITCHELL

The Gifted Child

Prologue

It was a warm September afternoon and I was headed home after I received a bit of good news. I had just landed my first management position at a distribution center. It had been a long time in coming and I was relieved that my job troubles were now at an end.

My excitement was still high when I saw my cousin, Rachel. I parked my car in an abandoned store parking lot, hopped out, gave her a hug, and shared my news with her. She hugged me, congratulated me, and told me she was on her way to pick up her mail. She asked me if I minded walking with her. I told her "No problem," and we began the short walk to the post office.

We had hardly walked ten feet when suddenly there was a screeching of wheels, and a truck roared around the curve of sleepy, downtown Cusseta, Georgia. It should not have been traveling that fast. The speed limit was only twenty-five miles per hour. The vehicle was obviously speeding and out of control. It was headed right for us.

I was still elated and did not see it coming and a surprised Rachel jumped back into the grass. She saw that I was unaware of the danger and reached forward and tried to grab me in almost the same motion, but it was too late. I was swept away as if the current of a swollen river had caught me. I was knocked sixty-five feet down the road, crushing the front passenger side of the truck. I bounced upon the windshield and completely shattered it.

My battered body was now impaled with shards of glass and rolled over the top of the truck and hit the pavement hard. My head bounced off the curbstone and the impact lifted my body vertically, and it collapsed violently back down to the asphalt and I barely moved again. I was seriously hurt and things didn't look good for me.

Everyone ran about in disarray and it was hard for anyone to believe what had just happened. People appeared out of nowhere. The apparently empty streets were now packed with concerned observers.

Charlotte, Rachel's sister, arrived on the scene and assessed the situation. She quickly gathered everyone together and they began to pray in the street, holding hands while emergency personnel tried to stabilize me.

She then called my mother, Barbara, at work and told her to get there as quickly as possible: A truck had hit me and I wasn't doing well.

The people who saw the accident had told Charlotte there was no way I could have survived. She wisely withheld that part from my momma as if she was a seasoned spokesperson.

Upon hearing the news of the accident, Momma rushed off the job and up the road. By the time she got there, the ambulance had already taken me to the hospital. She slowed down at the accident scene, took a quick look around, and instinctively went there too.

When she arrived at the hospital, all of her daughters who lived in the immediate area were there and in deep distress. My siblings had already called for my brother who resided out of town. It appeared everyone had given up and was preparing to read me the last rites.

After several hours, the doctor came out of the emergency room and told them I was going to make it. I would be taken to a room soon and they could visit me there. He said it was incredible that I was responsive and even cognizant of my immediate surroundings so quickly after the accident. It seemed that I was in extraordinary physical condition and that probably saved my life. The doctor asked if I played sports and lifted weights a lot because there was hardly any fat on me. He said I was in the best condition that he had seen in a while.

For some reason, three months ago I had a strange desire to start working out. It was as if someone or something had prepared me for this exact moment. This intense desire for physical perfection appeared to have been an omen to prepare me for my greatest tribulation.

I was allowed to recuperate in the hospital for a few days, but when they found out I wasn't insured, they kicked me out. They rolled me to the door like a pile of garbage and left me to my family. I wasn't able to stand and almost collapsed to the ground. The world was spinning, and I couldn't focus on anyone or anything. My life had become a mess and was free falling out of control.

Things got worse when they told me the truck wasn't insured and the driver was a young guy who had neither a license nor insurance. I would not be able to get anything out of him because he had nothing. It wasn't even his truck that he had driven.

That information pushed me into a stupor. I refused to think about anything anymore, including that coveted job I had just acquired. Because of the severity of my injuries, I never called to inform the company of the accident. It was as if success and I were two trains destined to pass in the night.

To add to my problems, after several months of being in a daze, all of my friends abandoned me, and my robust body began to waste away. My dark black skin and lean muscular frame had lost its entire glow. My weight dropped off and it looked as though I was living in the worst drought-stricken area of Africa. I was going through my own personal famine. I looked frail and pitifully weak. I was a man broken in body and mind.

My confidence was all but gone and any pride I had left was completely eradicated in one brief thoughtless moment. The wheels completely fell off my life, and I fell to the bottom of my personal abyss when my nephew and niece ridiculed and disavowed me because of my color. I had never done anything to them, except try to help them. They repaid me in such a way that it brought back bad memories. I thought that a black person thinking like this had gone the way of the dodo, but obviously it had not.

The harsh words they spoke echoed over and over again in my bowed head. I was shocked the issue of color had once again come to this. My own nephew and niece had disavowed me because of the hue of my skin.

9

I was now at my all-time lowest point. I was simply destroyed. The water swelled in my eyes as the silent tears of pride trickled down my face. I knew who and what I was and I knew they had been brainwashed about color, as so many had been before them.

Robert, another one of my nephews, heard them as they spoke their troubling words. He came over and hugged me because he could see that I was so distraught. He told me, "Uncle John, I don't care what anybody says, you are still my uncle."

At that time those words sounded so good to me that they took the place of the echoes of the previous statement. Still at my lowest point, I broke down and knew the Lord again. I picked a spot in the center of my house and began to pray. I asked God to let me live up to a little of the ability that He had bestowed on me. A good and wonderful feeling enveloped me, and I knew at that time that something or someone was telling me everything would be all right. I was reinvigorated and felt as though a great burden had been lifted off my shoulders. I easily rose to my feet with no pressure on my stressed frame.

I just had a couple of life-changing experiences and found out who really and truly cared for me. After that initial tsunami of concern had passed and the dust had settled, there was only Barbara. She was there offering salve for my battered body and bruised ego. She would not give up on me and was determined to stand by me. She supported me, even when I could not support myself. My weary momma stood by me when everyone else abandoned me, except God.

The Almighty had blessed her abundantly and she was now doing very well for herself. It was hard to believe that she had come so far, and against all odds, she had made it through. She now allowed her blessings to fall upon me by taking me in.

Her life had changed so much, and at the same time, she still did most of the things she always had done. Momma still scavenged at the recycling center, even though she didn't have to. She was a little packrat at heart and knew the value of things that people threw away. It just so happened one day when she was there a philanthropist placed a computer on a table. She plugged it in and it came on. She brought it home and gave it to me. I managed to get it to operate in safe mode. It was an old out-of-date model, but the program Microsoft Word worked on it just fine.

I smiled because I knew God had answered my prayers and smiled on me once again. I was inspired to write the story of my life that seemed to flow from my mind like the sands through an hourglass. And, thus, began **The Gifted Child: John's Saga.**

Chapter One: John's Arrival

America was still smoldering with pent-up emotions immediately after the civil rights movement. Regardless of the rapidly developing situation on the ground, life went on for both black and white. And on the 17th of June in 1969, somewhere in the midst of the quiet after the racial storms had passed over, I, John Johnson, came into the world. My life had an inauspicious beginning. I was born on the floor of a house where the ground peeped in everywhere. It was a joyous time for the family. The word soon went out all over the community that I was born.

Neighbors and relatives streamed into the little wooden house. The old floor ached and moaned to support the weight of the guests that ventured in to see me. I looked like any other Negro. My skin hue was fair in the beginning. It is common knowledge to most people of this era that most Negroes are of a lighter complexion when they are born. It takes a little while for the melanin to kick in and give us our final color.

Birth was also the time a Negro child received his first inspection and confirmation visit. Upon the occasion of my birth, three behemoths of womanhood slowly rocked into the room. There was not a lot of fanfare upon their arrival, and there was not a lot of space left in the small room once they ventured in. They took up everything except the air, and it was stretched very thin. They greeted Momma and talked much about nothing.

After about fifteen minutes of babbling, I was given to the women to be examined. I was only a few hours old when they scooped me up from Momma's side. I gave a lot of protest, and rightfully so. I suffered the callous inspections of the old matriarchs of the family.

Before the modern blood and DNA testing came about, they were the ones who gave their seal of approval to the paternity of the child. All the mother could do was wait and be as polite as possible. These rituals of courtesy did not bind the child. This was obviously true, because I took advantage of this loophole and was not being understanding. It has been said a child can sense the negative energies swirling about him; this has merit, because I was hollering something terrible.

The old biddies had their noses in the air the whole time they looked me over. They knew exactly what to look for to determine the physical traits of a baby. It was like a science, or so they called it, which was taught and passed on through the matriarchal line.

"Oh my, what a set of pipes he has. I think he wants you," they said to Momma, as they proceeded to turn me this way and that, finally acknowledging my calls for her.

All the noise I made did not stop them from finishing their examination. They looked me over from head to toe and everywhere in between, literally. After all this was over, they begrudgingly gave me their seal of approval of being my father's child. They eased me back into my mother's arms and continued their conversation amongst themselves.

Momma didn't say much. She was tired. She was somewhat hurting too because there were no spinal blocks or pain medications available during this time when a woman gave birth at home. To further complicate her problems, the old women had passed me around like a trophy, and I still had not quieted down. The only thing Momma hoped would happen was they would leave. She was not going to ask them to go, because this was not how things were done.

She listened as they heaped their praise on me and paid her the familiar compliments: "Oh, what a wonderful child. He is so handsome. He's a precious little thing. He is a fine child."

These phrases came standard when a baby was born. Momma had been around enough to know that the compliments that they gave her were sometimes different from what they actually thought or said when they were alone.

The old harpies still grinned as they finally excused themselves from the room. It was not a bit too soon for Momma, because she could see right through their smiles that were as false as their teeth.

They began to congregate outside and round up the little kids that had made the trek with them down the long, dusty red road. After several minutes, the crowd started its journey. About half an hour and a quarter mile up the road, they began to let loose with their laughter and jokes.

"Did you see his ears? He is going to be black as night, an old oil can…"

14

Laughter rang out even louder when a yellow woman chastised the darker one by saying, "Ain't that the pot calling the kettle black?"

A brief hush fell over the crowd, and after a moment of silence, laughter rang out again. One of the little girls accompanying them up the road was curious, and asked them how they knew what the baby would look like. She was told, "You tell the final color of Negro children by the crown of their ears and their fingertips. You also check the toes and in between their legs. Pressing and shaping can change the shape of their head and nose," they told her, "but color on the other hand, is pretty much what they have to deal with all their life."

They looked down at her and smiled. The girl was not of a fair color herself. So they added, "Unless you bleach your skin," with a wink.

Chapter Two: Struggles

Daddy was standing in the door, using the doorframe to rub an itchy spot in the center of his back that he couldn't quite reach with his hand. This was a typical weekday in the Johnson household and he was about to leave to do some tough construction work in Columbus, Georgia.

"Barbara," he said while putting on his boots. "I am going to have to get another truck. I think I have just about worn this one out."

"Another truck? Can we afford another truck right now?" she said rolling over onto her side to look at him.

"Whether we can or not, I have to get one. I work on this job and you know I am trying to run my own business on the side, a good truck is something I have got to have."

Daddy looked at Momma and the look of disappointment in her face. He knew it bothered her that he had not broken ground to lay the foundation for a brick home for us like he promised, and now he was talking a new truck.

He shook his head and said, "Don't fret, baby, I am going to build us that house," and leaned over and kissed Momma on the forehead, and turned to look at my sister, Diane.

"Come here, Poot. Give Daddy a hug before he leaves."

Diane was bright-eyed and bushy-tailed; she was a morning person and rushed toward Daddy's arms at the first sound of the invitation. Before she could get to him, a bottle ricocheted solidly off her head and caused tears to flow. Daddy knew the routine and started to threaten me at once.

"Come here, boy! I am going to put this belt on you!" He shouted as he fought to pull his belt out of his trousers.

I ran around the old potbelly wood-burning heater in the center of the floor and crawled frantically over Momma, who held her hand up to shield Denise, my newborn sister, as I clumsily scampered over her, fleeing from my Daddy. I bounced over them in between the wall and bed, trying to find a safe haven. Daddy was determined to give me something I didn't want.

"Come here, boy!" he shouted. "I am not going to tell you again!"

Threaten as he might, I was not interested in what he had to offer and started to bawl loudly. Momma finally stood up and placed her hand firmly into his chest, blocking him from getting to me.

I was safely tucked away on the other side of the bed. My refuge was buffered by Momma, and she pointed out something better he could be doing by saying, "Jay, go to work and leave the boy alone before you are late. I don't feel like hearing all this noise this morning."

Momma had grown tired of our game. She knew I was active, but Daddy was always a little too eager to get me for any little thing. She wasn't willing to turn him loose on me just yet. She turned and scooped me up from my hiding place that was in plain sight, and laid me beside them in the bed.

Daddy paused for a minute and looked at me peeking and grinning at him from over Momma's shoulder. He looked at her, and then at me again. He looked at Diane, who was still crying with tears locking together beneath her cheeks. His temper was barely held in check as he took the time to point his finger at me and shake it vigorously, but he could not get his words to follow right away. It was obvious the thought of me making it to safety was about to give him an aneurysm.

With one eye still on me, He scooped Diane up and rubbed the spot where the bottle bounced off of her head, and then promised me all kinds of butt-whoopings I would carry for the rest of my life. This caused my smile to widen into a mocking grin, irritating him even more. I was only two and this is what two-year-old little boys do.

Daddy knew there was no way Momma was going to let him hit me, so he was resigned to find gratification in making empty promises and wasted threats as he threw a few more my way, reminding Momma of the offense I had just committed.

"Barbara, he hit my baby upside her head with that bottle and I am going to beat his little bad butt!"

"It didn't kill her, Jay. Leave the boy alone and go to work before you are late."

Daddy looked at me again, said some things to himself under his breath, which were probably a few more resolutions as he stomped out of the house in a huff. I was working his nerves and he was determined to live up to his promise, if he ever caught me straying far enough from Momma.

I heard the exterior door open and Daddy walking outside into the early morning darkness. Dawn had not the strength to loosen the fingers and break the grip of the lingering shadows that still inhabited the earth. I was a little anxious to get down, but I had not heard his truck crank yet, so I wisely stayed under Momma, knowing Daddy had gotten me a couple of times by doubling back and catching me before I could make it to safety. I was resigned to waiting him out, listening for his truck to start. I listened and I could hear him stumble clumsily about in the yard, falling over things and cursing more about Momma spoiling me, then him banging his foot.

He tossed his masonry tools into the air and I could hear them crash angrily into the bed of his truck and the door open and slam shut. The engine turned over and then died. The door opened again and the hood could be heard opening, crying out in the stillness of the morning air.

A short time later he tried to crank it again. And again the truck engine just barely turned over as if it was saying, *I don't want to move this morning*. He struggled with the engine a little while longer and cursed a few more times, because now he was officially going to be late. As harbingers of day, the first rays of light, peeked over the pines he pulled out of the yard and was gone for the day.

With the coast all clear I climbed out of the bed and started antagonizing my sister again, giving her the business by wanting every toy with which she wanted to play. It would do her no good to protest because I would cry and pout until Momma would finally say, "Give that boy that toy and sit down somewhere, Diane."

"Larry, I am going to have to put one good butt-whooping on your nephew. In order for me to do that, it looks like I am going to have to go twelve hard rounds with your sister"

Larry laughed and Sonny, Barbara's cousin, who was working nearby and overheard the conversation, also laughed and said, "He acts like you when you were young, Jay. You are getting some of the same stuff you put on your parents. He is just going through that stage. He is going to be all right."

"Yeah, well, I don't think I was ever that bad. And he is going to be all right because I am going to get his little bad butt in line, you can believe that."

Sonny wiped his face and looked up into the sky and leaned back, stretching his back, saying, "I have to find me another job. Man, it's hot here. Is it hot enough for you?"

Wiping his face with the forearm part of his white long-sleeve shirt, Daddy said, "Yeah, this heat has whipped me all day. It's almost break time. I am going to finish laying these last few blocks and I am going to stand in the shade and cool off. Larry, you playing baseball with us this weekend?"

Larry was a little hesitant and he thought about before saying, "I don't know. I doubt it, Jay."

"Why? Don't worry about what those guys are saying Stretch. I'll tell you; I struck out when I first started playing for a longtime, without even fouling a ball, and made about six eras. You just got to stick with it man."

"I doubt it." Larry said.

"Stretch, we can talk about it when you finish up. Like I said, it's almost break time. I am about to sit down and cool off for a minute."

Larry picked his pace up a little and said, "I'll join you soon. Sonny, can I get you to give me a hand with this cord? I have to get this and some of these tools around the building so I can just start up after break."

While Larry rolled the cord up, Sonny grabbed some of the tools and they disappeared behind a wall, taking the equipment to a spot where he would need it when they started up again. On the way back they stopped by the cooler, drank some of the water and headed to the shade of the building to cool off with Jonathon.

Disbelief rushed into their eyes and their legs grew weary. Their hearts almost burst. Jay was gone in the sound of a crash. He was buried beneath a large steel door as a pile of dust greeted them with its testimony and left them stunned.

People moved frantically to get him free quickly, but his injuries were too severe. It would only be a matter of time before his life force expired, and he would leave behind a widow and a large family to carry on without him.

It was a time of sorrow. I didn't really understand what was going on. I don't think any child has a concept of death at my age. I just remembered seeing Daddy lying in the coffin in a suit and people talking about how nice he looked, and how Momma had given him a nice burial.

When they lowered him into the ground, I think this was the beginning of an existence that would see Momma fighting a war for our family survival. She had no time to cry and reflect on what could have been. She looked in all of our faces and knew that she could not break down. We needed her and she could not wither away from a great responsibility.

Initially, she was given many assurances of aid. People were making promises and pledges to stand by her like they make at all funerals, I suppose, but they were soon forgotten.

Our entire family would suffer without our patriarch. But I was hit especially hard. I was young and my struggles would come early and often without my Daddy. When he was laid to rest he took with him a protection and a comfort for our family that could never be replaced because we were his and his alone.

I would be about five when I started to wander away from Momma to explore. Initially, everything was fine, even though I was a scraggily looking child that wore hard times upon my person. After two years of being given a free pass, I started finding out the hard

21

way that my road in life would be filled with many bumps and bruises. All the benign feelings toward me evaporated, and exposed the scorn and disdain that would cut me like jagged rocks.

Unfortunately, or fortunately, however one would look at it, I was going to have to fight hard to make it in my community, and harder to make it in life. Nothing would ever be given to me, and many things denied, including a fair chance to blossom and prosper. Adversity reveals character, or so it is said, and whatever I was made of would be revealed early on.

The horn to start the raise of life had started for me. The two years of roaming freely over the community were over and my venturing away from home would be rewarded with a maelstrom of rejection. I became fair game and often found myself dodging all manner of primitive missiles hurled at me with deadly intentions. These included, but were not limited to wild plums, dirt clods, sticks, and an occasional rock. I managed to avoid all the debris with an uncanny ease being that I was agile, mobile, and uncannily fast.

The acrobatic feats I accomplished were not easy, and this was a somewhat serious game in which I refused to let them deter me from entering their domain. This routine quickly became par for the course where I was concerned.

After penetrating the uneasy security of my cousin's yard on this day, they started a game of freeze tag that I tried to force my way into. The crowd ignored me and drifted around the corner of the house playing their game in a zone instinct told me was forbidden. Something didn't seem quite right, and I wisely stayed in the front yard within sight of the indifferent eyes of adults.

I pulled out my jack ball and tossed it as high into the air as I could, drifting this way and then that, trying to make the catch. I was okay with playing alone, passing the time away in a relative safe area. I had no intentions of turning the corner of the house because of the

22

bad things that could happen. I had gotten the message when they threw things at me and fled as though I was leprous, that they didn't want to be bothered today.

Soon after they vanished into the backyard, an ominous quiet engulfed the area. I didn't know what was going on. All I knew at the moment was there was no birds flying or chirping, no squirrels chattering, nor were their laughter and shrill screams present as is typical in the game they played.

I stood in the open no longer playing with my ball, watching the corner of the house, and wondering what was going on. I had no idea they were hatching a plot in which they devised the best way to punish me. Whatever plan they conceived was about to go into motion because they soon returned with an open invitation for me to join in the fun.

I unwisely ignored my sixth sense and became a fly trapped in their web of deceit. I chased them around the corner of the house into the forbidden zone an all-out hot pursuit. To my dismay, Jimmy, one of my older cousins, stepped out of nowhere and tackled me as hard as he could. I went sliding across the earth that was sparsely populated with grass, pebbles and a lot of wood chips, coming to a stop a few feet from an old log. I laid there not wanting to move, marinating in ignominy.

"Tag, you are it," he said laughingly.

Jimmy was a Neanderthal and had given it to me good. He delighted at the anguish that manifested itself within my face. He had not restrained himself in the least with that crushing tackle and it hurt. I got up with tears beading in my eyes and he gave me the usual speech of, "We are just playing. We are making you tough. You a man, right?" He said while walking over and taking the time to assist me in knocking the dirt from my clothes.

I chose not to answer that question and lumbered back to the front yard, upset with myself for falling for their scheme. The only part of "being a man" lessons like these taught me was to watch out for myself and keep my head on a swivel.

There was only so much anybody could have taken, and I soon reached my breaking point. Pulling myself to the front of their yard to find something else to do, I walked upon the porch and pulled my jack ball out of my pocket and started to play a modified solo game of racquetball, by slapping it against the porch wall time and time again.

Brian, a cousin that was a couple of years younger than I, approached me in a foul mood and sucker-punched me. My day just kept getting worse. This particular incident was awkward and caught me completely off guard. Not believing what he had done I watched him bounce around a few feet in front of me like a boxer, shouting taunts as if he were Muhammad Ali.

"You ain't no Johnson with your black ass. You ain't my cousin," shuffling his feet to complete his routine.

This seemed to amuse everyone, including Aunt Sharon, who watched the action from the living room just inside the porch door. She laughed excessively at the antics of her baby boy. But I didn't find it funny. The things he said were not called for. He was probably only mimicking what he heard some grown-up say. Children learned by imitating adults; this is just a principle of life. Brian had simply taken in their poison and now regurgitated it out on me at this very moment.

After he finished his provocative boxing dance and it was apparent that his tactics to start a fight had failed, Brian walked over and let loose a flurry of blows connecting solidly to my chest. The barrage of punches forced me to stagger backward. I looked into the house at my aunt, who was barely visible through the screen door of the living room, to see if she would quell the situation. She would not. The joy and laughter showing in her face confused and infuriated me.

I was so angry it looked as though a thunderstorm was approaching as rage and intensity flashed within my eyes. I quickly heated to the boiling point and walked over and grabbed my chubby cousin by the scruff of his neck, and hurled him across the porch as though he weighed nothing. The frightened boy appeared to bounce about two yards on the old wooden planked floor, coming to a unceremonious stop at the corner of the porch under a bar stool. I then slowly moved in for the kill, determined to give this little demon the beating he deserved.

His confidence was shaken to its core. He cowered in fear under the stool, as if it would give him some kind of protection from me. He had realized too late the dangers and the rules of picking a fight: If a person started a brawl, he had better be ready to finish it. Brian didn't know it at the time, but he had hit a hornet's nest. I was going to take all of my frustrations out on him.

I moved closer and closer, in a Clint Eastwood-type fashion. And at this moment, all of Brian's previous bravado had taken flight, and he pleaded with me for a mercy that I did not have for him at this time.

Before I could get to him, I was interrupted by a firm grasp of my arm. Aunt Sharon quickly came out of the living room and onto the porch, and was suddenly against everything that was taking place and started preaching nonviolence. She reprimanded me about fighting and told me to take my little bad black ass home. I snatched my arm away and stomped down the path, yelling back, "I will."

I had been down this road before. I knew the tricks and taunts they used to get me to curse or disrespect them, just so they could call Momma and say, "John did this or John said that."

Most of the time they openly lied, but at this present time it was irrelevant. On this day, I decided to have a revolution. I had made up in my mind not to take one more butt-whooping willingly from anybody. I had had enough of this, and the expression on my face told them I meant it.

I turned around once more and warned Brian that I would beat his fat butt if he messed with me again. I intentionally walked across their cornfield, knocking as many as the sturdy young plants down as possible just for the heck of it.

Looking back over my shoulder, my eyes glistened as I took pride in my work. I had managed to cut a large path that merged with an old trail that lead back home in retribution for my ill treatment. I stood in the old path for a moment feeling a little better about things. This old trail was seldom used after Daddy had died because for some reason unknown to me our relations with my Dad's side of the family had quickly become estranged.

Happy with the stand I took, I found myself talking to myself, saying, "There is no way I am going to stand there and let Brian get away with that. If that is the price I got to pay to hang around their house and play, then it was to high. Um mm, wrong answer today."

There were limits to the amount of abuse I would willingly take, and Brian had crossed the line. My temper still simmered as I walked down the overgrowth-filled trail. Suddenly I heard loud noises behind me and looked back to see the cornstalks giving birth to two big guys. It was Brian's brothers, Jimmy and Ricky. They meant business.

The bullies exploded from the cornfield and quickly mowed down the tall grass and were bearing down hard on me. They had received their orders to deal with me for Brian's lumps. The determined look on their faces told me it was time for me to get out of the area as expediently as possible. My bare feet dug into the soft soil, trying frantically to catch traction. Dust flew from the ground as I accelerated rapidly, trying to escape the two henchmen.

Sand spurs grabbed my flesh as though I was crossing a minefield. I ignored the pain and continued on, knowing the greater peril I faced. I quickly reached top speed, knowing they would be upon me in the blink of an eye.

My house was about fifty yards away. This was the good news. The bad news was that my cousins were now only ten yards away from me, and closing fast. I did not know if Momma was around, so my only option played out in my mind: Should I turn and fight the much bigger and older boys or continue on my course to the yard and hope Momma was there?

Twenty yards from my house, I knew I would never make it. Knowing I would have to face my aggressors, I hurried to a clearing in open view of the house and prepared to put up a good fight. I was praying someone was in my yard and would see me because I was out-gunned on this one.

I knew the obvious outcome of the pending fray, but I had made up in my mind to make them hurt too. Once I reached the open area, my feet dug into the soft earth. In their effort to halt my progress, they left furrows about three yards long behind me. I whirled to face the two assailants, who had slowed to a cautious, stalking stride.

When they were only four yards from me, I heard Momma around the corner of the house singing those old Negro spirituals that black women made famous. In the blink of an eye, as if I was a swift deer, I was off again. They gave pursuit as best they could, but did not catch me. I made it into the yard as Momma turned the corner. Jimmy and Ricky pulled up at the edge of the yard, turned, and slowly started to retreat up the path they had just made.

Momma asked me what was going on and why Jimmy and Ricky had been chasing me. I didn't say a word. She asked me if I had been fighting again, to which I chose not to reply. If they didn't tell, then I would not open my mouth either. I was neither a tattletale nor a crybaby. In my mind I was a man, and men just did not tell things when the going got tough for them. I had my own sense of honor, and telling adults about my problems was not my style.

I walked into the house and sat down at the foot of my bed, frantically trying to catch my breath. Sweat poured down my face and into my eyes. It was a painful, stinging sensation that I wiped away with my forearm. I was glad to see Momma on this occasion, because the goons were at least two years my senior and, without a doubt in my mind, would have beaten me easily.

Momma didn't really ask me anything else about the incident, because she assumed we were only playing. It just seemed to her I was always roughhousing with somebody. I was one tough little fellow. My skirmishes were legendary and many, and my battlefields were all over Brooklyn, Georgia, my little country hometown.

Brooklyn was a beautiful place, with hidden natural springs and beautiful ponds. It had gorgeous canyons that appeared to the eyes as if a person were looking through the glass of a prism. The roads were made of Georgia's famed red clay, which was pretty to look at but as tough as ink to come out of the clothes you wore. After a good rain the air always smelled fresh and it yielded mind-blowing, appealing fragrances to the nostrils. There was almost no better place to grow up than this country paradise. It was almost as if white people had left this place as an enclave for blacks by mistake.

Upon one occasion late in the summer, a foray into the deepest part of a local boxed canyon was planned. It seemed every boy in Brooklyn had made arrangements to be a part of the adventure. We hurried through the woods and made our way to our natural playground. We ventured to the edge of the canyon wall and leaped over the rim of the gorge without hesitation. We seemed to be leaping to our sure demise as a gleeful sound escaped our breath. It was our method of descending the quick way into the canyon.

One by one we landed on a large ledge and the loose, multicolored sand received us with a soft thud. Our legs went knee-deep into the moist, sandy dirt. We hustled to the bottom and returned to the top to do it again. This was one of the things we did to have fun.

Everyone knew what happened in the canyon. The events were as if they were etched upon a bulletin board or some drill sergeant had given an operations order for the day. All the leaping activity was followed by a game of tag. There was only so much we could do and these were our two favorite things to help us get through a lazy summer day.

All morning long we played on the slopes of the canyon. Around noon, we pulled out a loaf of light bread and a package or two of bologna. We sat down in a small grove of trees for a quick lunch and drank fresh water straight from the trickling spring. We sat, talked, let our lunch digest about an hour and a half, and went back at it to play.

The next event was tag. I had not been touched and we were already an hour into the game and I was having a blast. Whether I knew it or not, I was in bad company. The canyon was also a place where old scores were settled.

Only two months earlier, I had handled Brian, who was now afraid to come out of the house because of the threat I made to kick his butt. Jimmy and Ricky had plotted payback for Brian since the day I embarrassed him and escaped them. They picked this moment to settle the score.

Jimmy gave his brother the eye, and a quiet signal was passed just between the two of them and it put something into play. Ricky allowed himself to be tagged, and he quickly gave chase after me, but I easily evaded him. I scampered up the wall like a little squirrel. I easily out-maneuvered the apparently exhausted boy, who chased me to no avail.

Running up the slope to a sandy ledge that was just above an old oak tree, I leaped back and, by grabbing a sturdy branch, dropped safely to the ground. All the kids performed this stunt, but this was my specialty--I had invented it.

Pausing at the bottom of the hill, I looked up to see if I was still being chased by the disenchanted boy, who appeared to have long since given up and was merely half-way up the ledge.

I laughed at Ricky's futile effort to tag me. The instant I finished chuckling, an unexpected force impaled me from out of the blue. A sound escaped my throat and sounded like a comic book "umph." I had walked into a set-up. Jimmy had been waiting at the bottom of the ledge and plowed me straight into the old oak tree.

Bouncing off, more stunned than physically hurt, I collapsed to my knees into the cool sand. My wind was gone and so was I if I didn't suck it up fast. The bounty hunter stood over me as if he was a prizefighter, ready to administer some more punishment. He pleaded with me, begged me to get up so he could knock me back down.

Never bothering looking up I knew it was time to pay the piper. I hesitated briefly, trying to gather my composure and plot my next move. Knowing they intended to give me a good beating I had nothing to lose.

30

As the apparent victor stood over me, I erupted upward with a clenched fist, sinking my powerful right hand into Jimmy's private area. The blow forced the bully down to his knees.

I knew Ricky was on his way and landed a quick kick to Jimmy's head, allowing me an avenue of escape. At this point the vanquished foe was no longer an obstacle. He was lying on the ground, reeling from my counter-assault. I managed to pull myself over him by painfully crawling, and at times almost slithering, trying to get away.

Still sucking wind and no longer gliding effortlessly over the sandy ground, I managed to get to the back of the canyon and began to slowly ascend the wall. The other kids watched and seemed to be amused by the whole thing, and laughed at the fight taking shape in front of them.

I was desperate and frantically scratched and clawed my way up the hill, as if I were in quick sand. I was about halfway up the slope, when a vise-like hand grabbed me around my ankles. It pulled me down, back into the canyon. Ricky had caught me and now towed me hollering and screaming for help from any of the on lookers who were unwilling to act on my behalf. There was no escape for me this time. They were going to teach me a valuable lesson.

Once Ricky got me to the exact position he wanted me, he began to prepare me for a sacrifice. He picked me up off the ground and spun me around like a top. The much bigger boy then pushed me hard against the old oak tree, forcing me to bounce off and stumble forward. He then caught me with a devastating blow to my upper body that forced me to fall over onto my back. I was hurt, and I quickly curled up into the fetal position.

Ricky then proceeded to punish me further. The beating was so easy for the bully he began to talk to me about my transgressions. He let me know exactly what the thumping I was receiving was for:

"You want to fight Brian, huh? You wanna beat somebody's butt? Who you gonna beat, dummy? Beat me, you little nappy-headed oil spill!"

Blow after blow he landed to my chest and abdomen. He kicked me with his feet and hit me with knees, elbows, and closed fists. He even unloaded a couple of striking combinations he had picked up watching Kung Fu movies. Moan and groan over the atrocity was all I was able to do.

When it looked as though Ricky had tired of the routine, Jimmy, who had gotten himself together, started his assault. They pummeled me until I felt no pain. I only heard the licks as they bounced off my body.

Everyone in the canyon watched in amazement, as the beating went on until it seemed to me like forever and a day had elapsed. None of the other kids helped him. It appeared to be my last stand. My name should be Custer, because this was my Little Big Horn, and I was being scalped.

When it seemed I had all but given up, a trumpet-like voice echoed over the canyon wall. It commanded us—I mean them to stop what they were doing.

My uncle Larry, who had been working on the line for his water pump, had heard the commotion. All the noise had alerted him to the fight taking place. He came upon the scene like the 7th Cavalry, warning Jimmy and Ricky to back off and let me go.

They looked up on the edge of the canyon at the towering adult figure and backed away a few steps. This brief reprieve allowed me time to crawl away from the scene while nursing my wounds as best I could. I managed to skirt a shaky, sandy, seldom-used ledge, which contained a path that took me safely out of the canyon.

I looked back over my shoulder to see if I had left any body parts behind, because the two goons had tried to dismantle me. I took a quick glance at the bottom of the canyon at Jimmy and Ricky. I was relieved to see they did not pursue me. Evidently they had had enough fun with me for the day and were content to let me escape. The only things that took flight behind me were the words, "Black mother @#$%!" Black this and dumb that.

I made the long journey home by myself. I was grateful for my uncle's intervention, but I could not thank him for his kind deed. He was on the other side of the canyon rim and I dared not try to cross over to him.

Visibly shaken and upset about the whole situation, I knew I could only fault myself. I knew I had to be aware of those two and had let my guard down. Momma had told me, "Those people will come back twenty years later to get you, if you turned your back on them."

I had not listened, and it seemed to me at this point that Momma did know best after all.

The episode with Brian had been only a couple of months old. I had foolishly let my guard down and unfortunately I learned the lesson my momma told me the hard way. I was tired. The fighting thing was no fun. I was hurt and my body now relinquished its pain in the form of knots and bruises that had begun to emerge from my battered frame. Too hurt to cry, I limped home with my feelings in tow. I didn't know it at the time, but I had just begun my ordeal, and my life was about to be much worse.

Time went by, and Momma needed a little more help around the house. It was time for me to start earning my way. It may even have been her way of keeping me out of harm's way. I was growing older and was learning there was a stigma attached to me because of my color.

It permeated the entire fabric of American society at a time that was supposed to be equality for all. I think black people actually bought into the "dark people could not think" theory. This meant nobody expected much from me outside of physical labor. There was a possibility that this thought even crept into Momma's mind. Even though she loved me dearly, I had drawn the shortest straw and was expected be the one to run the farm.

The chores I was assigned were the most grueling and tedious that could be imagined for a boy of my age. I struggled initially, but my body quickly came up to speed on the tasks that it was presented. It was really hard on me, but I never said a word. Complaining did no good because when she told me of the things she had to do growing up, and I knew she had it harder than I did. So I just accepted my assigned role..

I struggled to deal with the emotional and physical strain on my life at an early age, but reluctantly I came to grips with reality. Hard times were snuffing out the light of any dreams of a better tomorrow for me. My life should have been simple, but somehow it was complicated to the point where all thoughts of an answer to the problems plaguing me were lost somewhere beneath the struggle to survive.

I didn't have a male to take time with me, teach me the things I should know to make it in this mixed-up world. My grandfathers were already in heaven before I arrived. Daddy had joined them a couple of years after my birth, involuntarily leaving me to make it without life's blueprint. I wanted and needed him so desperately. If

God knew how much, then surely He would give him back. I asked myself many times, why had He taken him? There could be no good reason for this horrible deed, unless he didn't love me.

With heavy burdens and solemn thoughts, I became reclusive, detached from everyone, including my own siblings. I began to seek out my own little quiet place, and this cloistered behavior was another reason people thought less of me. I had a personality barren of any joy because I realized I was a scapegoat.

I was being conditioned to accept the low road because of my color. Even the winds seem to whisper to me, telling me, "You are too dark and too dumb to do certain things."

I was being taught a hard lesson because I was forced to see things through a prism. It was bad to be black at this time, but it was almost a crime to be dark black. I honestly felt a secret deal had been struck in some smoky back room to throw my kind from the equality train. The only reason our fellow Americans could possibly have was that we were not "anglocized" enough.

The shame of it all was that my own race was intent on not letting me forget who I was and where I came from. The words washed over me as if they were a powerful tidal surf, eroding away my self-confidence. They sent shudders up and down my spine when they labeled me a "field nigger." I had to come to grips with this classification because I looked as though I just stepped off the boat.

I don't know if Momma ever heard these words spoken to me because she was wrapped up in surviving. Reality had hit her, out of all these children she was raising; there was no way she could bat one hundred percent. The most promising of us received what little time she had. It just so happened by a strange natural selection process, I was the black sheep of the family--literally. And the one to be sacrificed to the wolves.

She had ceased to stress so much over me. She had children other people had given rave reviews. She was told they were so talented. It seemed they didn't have a problem with them.

"But that John…," they told her.

They always paused to warn her of the pending storm on her horizon with me.

"He's a character and you are going to have your hands full with him. Barbara, that boy is bad!"

The sad thing about their poor commentary was that it was being made with tainted eyes. The only thing I needed was a little nurturing to bear my fruits. If only Momma had the time to give to the labor of love and aerate my roots, it would enable me to grow and develop and yield nectar to her that would be sweeter than honey.

She never suspected the heralds of doom and gloom had their kids fighting me for sport. If I fought back and won, then they called her with their lies. Her phone would ring off the hook and she would receive a full report as to the follies I had committed. Not about them telling their children to "beat the tar off that boy," but how I fought with Michael, Brian, and David, or anyone else for no reason.

Momma always listened, sometimes pulling the phone away from her ear, because overzealous parents often talked so loud they could be heard all the way in China. She no longer said anything, probably thinking I was a lost cause. She would sit patiently and allow them to finish and then say to me, "I have told you to stay around this house. I don't have time for you picking fights and throwing rocks. I work to hard too put up with this stuff, John!"

After she finished verbally chastising and threatening to physically give me a whooping, she would close her door and start singing gospel songs really loud. I think it was her way of praising the Lord and hoping He would lift her burdens. I think she missed Daddy more than I did, and although I was not privy to her prayers, I think she asked God for him back because dealing with me was stressing her out. She probably regretted not letting him get me when he was after me, even though I was only two.

Eventually, I stopped listening to her warnings of the follies I would face. She was a woman and there was only so much she could tell me before it started to fall on deaf ears. I was missing a bond that she couldn't give me no matter how much she tried.

To complicate problems around the house, Momma was struggling financially and was a grouch on most days. Life had slapped her around every since Daddy died. She was now mother and father and every day at the crack of dawn saw her working hard, trying to earn income as honestly as possible.

And those people who promised her support were doing everything but that. She was a proud woman and never thought about asking for a handout or a hand. This was a burden she was determined to bear, so everyday from sun up to sundown, Momma did jobs men would not do just so the family could make it and stay together. She wanted us to be able to compete in school and have a chance at a better future. She often said in a pleading voice, "The least y'all can do for me is to complete high school and get your diploma. I wanted to learn and didn't have the opportunity. Y'all got the opportunity and don't want to learn. Y'all don't know how good y'all got it. When I was growing up we had to walk forty miles just to get an education. We had to beg and plead just to sit in a classroom, and y'all don't want to ride the bus, and fighting not to open a book. It don't make sense."

Momma knew education was key, and she told us she learned everything put in front of her. She only had a fifth-grade education, but she was willing to bet no one could cheat her out of her money.

"I am far from slow."

She would throw this in when she finished giving us her little pep talk. If it didn't look like this was working, she changed directions and antagonized us by saying, "I guess we marched for nothing. If the white people knew the only thing they had to do was let black people vote and voluntarily learn, and they would not want it anymore, then they would have given in to those concessions a long time ago."

I didn't know about the struggle and I could not fathom anything being that bad. I was fighting my own battle with society and never realized the price that had been paid for equality. Upon hearing some of the things she said, I initially smirked, and she told me, "Don't laugh, I grew up around the time of the great depression. We could not vote and we lived in constant fear. Y'all don't know how good y'all got it. Just be glad you didn't come up when I did. Some of you wouldn't be here today."

Some of her children listened. Margaret, my oldest sister, was one of them. She was a senior in high school and doing great. She had always taken the little speeches Momma had given to heart. She was a dedicated young lady and had her eyes on the prize. She was headed to college.

She was a true scholar and athlete. My momma was so proud of her and was willing to make a great sacrifice. She urged her on with a promise she would reward her with something she would need for school.

Momma really didn't have to do it because she was already an "A" student, but when she did, Margaret seemed to shift into a higher gear with her schoolwork.

Trying to be true to her word, Momma made arrangements to get Margaret the gift for school she promised. We knew it was going down because every so often a strange white man came around. He was selling something; we just didn't know exactly what it was. No one could get close enough to hear what was going on because Momma didn't like children hanging around, looking grown folks in their mouth when adults talked. "Children should be seen and not heard" was a motto she lived by.

It was private business, so the only thing we knew was Margaret was getting something good. Momma had saved a long time, and constantly made payments on whatever it was her little scholar was going to get. Finally she told the man she would have the rest of his money next week and he could bring it by.

Everyone in the family was extra nice to Margaret because we thought she was getting a car; however, no one knew for sure besides Momma and the salesman.

When the books finally came, no one's eyes were as big and bright as mine. The gift she was giving her daughter was a set of World Book encyclopedias. She really didn't have the money for them, but if one of her children was serious about school, she would find the money for certain things.

Margaret, on the other hand, almost looked disgusted. The encyclopedias were not a car. Her demeanor and body language changed from exuberance to a melancholy state at the sight of the books in no time flat.

She didn't really care for the books, but I tore through the pages like a child opening a gift at Christmas. I devoured the words on those pages as if they were candy, and I had an insatiable sweet tooth. Those books quickly became my comfort zone and I hid out amongst them.

I enjoyed reading because it took me places I had never been and probably would never see in all my life. By reading, my imagination took me all over the world, and I learned many new and wondrous things. I visited the Acropolis and the pyramids of Egypt, South America and the rarely discussed pyramids in the Sudan.

I took mental excursions to the Colossus of Rome, the churches that the Ethiopians had cut out of stone, and the Great Wall of China. These books were the best things in the world Momma could have put here for me.

My budding imagination seemed to blossom and I imagined myself being a world-renown archeologist and historian. I was everywhere, excavating and studying strange texts. Times like those were really good to me. I could now stay in the house away from the delinquent kids and read my books. I never wanted anyone to touch them because, with the mentality of a fifteenth-century explorer, I had laid claim to them first.

Once I even told Margaret to leave *my* books alone. She looked at me, laughed, and informed me they were her books. She then asked me if I liked looking at the pictures or something because, as she put it, "You cannot read."

She didn't know it, but that last part was not true. I could read, and very well. But I never told anyone otherwise. I let them believe what they liked about me.

Chapter Three: School

While all this was going on at home, I had already been in elementary school for four years. I hated school from day one. I felt I had a bull's-eye on my chest from the moment I boarded the little yellow bus. My unsteady footsteps and coy demeanor signaled me out to be prey.

The little children were so mean and unforgiving. They were always dressed up and looked so nice and they always got the benefit of the doubt, especially when dealing with children like me. Almost everyone had a preconceived notion of who and what they thought we should be. Their opinions of children like me were not too flattering. We were seen as lazy, roguish, fabricators and dumb.

An important theme to come out of the equality push was the content of a person's character and not color of skin. One of the most beautiful things about America is supposed to be, "It doesn't matter where you've been, but where you are going."

People like me were the ones who tested the meaning of all the little corny mottos that were coined to mean something. Instead of sacrificing me to the pack, I should have been defended like a newborn foal. I was shaky and lacked composure, but I had a heart of gold. I was everything but the stereotype people had picked out for me.

"If a lie is told enough times it becomes the truth." This was a slogan effectively used against me. The publicity campaign waged against me as being terrible had worked. My reputation preceded me and it dug into me like a tick. I could not get rid of the stigma even though I tried. I did the best I could to get along with everyone. But the sight of me dressed in my garb seemed to add fodder to the rumors and create a few others. People looked at me with a certain disdain in their eyes and didn't give me a chance.

I wished I could be dressed in better clothing, but this was impossible. Momma did the best she could and kept my clothes clean, but they had been patched and were visibly worn. This meant only one thing to other people: hand-me-downs. My family were the ultimate recyclers. My shoes were not brand name. They were some obscure copycat brand with a circle on them, but no star.

When it was recognized I didn't own new clothes, my social status dropped further than the stock market in 1929. No adult would even consider listening to me. I always stood there quietly while the other students assaulted me with name-calling, accusations and innuendoes. I could not, or rather did not, know how to respond. I felt like some blacks of the pre-seventies era in the Deep South. I received a farce of a hearing or a trial, and then was convicted and punished. I received this only if I was not strung up first by the mob of little children.

I was tired of the fighting and constant double jeopardy I was subjected to. Life had worn me out and I was ready to wave my white flag. I had surrendered anything looking like my rights in this system because the consequences for me getting out of hand were much greater than the other kids. I learned to keep my head down and my mouth shut and hoped I would make it through another painful day. I was in a no-win situation, and I knew it.

I learned it was best for me to stay out of sight as much as possible. When I came home, finished with my chores, I quietly entered the house, grabbed some books from the encyclopedia set, and hid somewhere.

My lack of social abilities had transformed me into an avid reader who lost himself in the pages of those wonderful books. My imagination gave me an escape from a world slowly torturing me because of my color and economic status.

Mine was a terrible place and a heavy burden the world had unfairly placed on my shoulders. My only sins were that I was dark and poor. My only recourse was to read and develop my own reality and books helped me to do that. The books never told me I was too dark or too poor. They only hinted at the legacy of my people and the greatness they once had.

Within the set of World Book encyclopedia's, there was a three-volume section on black history. I read it backwards and forward. Most of the people in those books looked like me. That in itself helped me cope with this crazy society in which I lived.

I was able to calm the sea of madness on which I floated when I was by myself and could read. On countless nights, I fell asleep in the pages of these books, only to be awakened by a noisy old rooster. This signaled the start of another day, and I got up, did my chores, and prepared for school. I hated to go back to a place that had turned into a gulag for me.

Everyone there thought I was legally dumb. My grades were never higher than a "D". Momma received so many bad reports from school that she even contemplated the idea of just letting me work the farm when I became old enough. She felt and I knew this world was swallowing me alive.

One day the school guidance counselor called and scheduled a meeting with her about me. In this meeting, Momma voiced her concerns about my education and my poor conduct and grades at school.

Mrs. Harris, the counselor, suggested I be placed in special education. She said, "It's a lot less stressful there. I assure you, he will learn enough math and reading skills to count his own money and read for himself at an acceptable level."

This sounded good to Momma, and she readily agreed to the program. She wanted all her children to graduate. With me, she was willing to compromise. If I learned to read and write and do arithmetic on an acceptable level, then this was all she could expect from me. If I graduated, it would be great, but she wasn't going to pressure me.

The following day, Mrs. Harris sent for me from my homeroom. She asked me if wanted to try a new class, just to see how well I would do. I was a little apprehensive about the class, but I knew her question was not really a question. It was really a statement meaning, "We are going to place you in this room, whether you wanted to be in the class or not."

So I told her okay, as if what I wanted really mattered. I knew I did not have a choice and sat quietly in the counselor's office waiting for my new teacher. After about twenty minutes a kindly old woman walked into the room and introduced herself as Mrs. Perryton. She hugged me, and we talked for a little while. She then took me to her homeroom.

My day was uneventful in my new class. It was actually great. I found it wasn't bad in special education. I played games all day and was allowed to snack and eat lunch early.

I thought Mrs. Perryton was the best. She actually held a conversation with me like she actually cared. I began to laugh and play because the other kids actually interacted with me in the classroom. School was now fun. I started to do my schoolwork. It was so easy that it only took me a few minutes each day.

Mrs. Perryton was so impressed with me that she thought I should be reevaluated. "John, you are doing great. I need to know the exact level you or on. I have this special test and I want you to take this reading test for me. What do you think about that, John?"

I smiled and said, "Sure." And I was determined to do my best. I wanted to do well on this test because I knew it would please my teacher.

44

I took the quiz and finished in almost the same time as I did with the others. She looked at me in a peculiar manner and asked, "Are you finished already?"

I nodded my head and she told me to just sit down and read a book or something until it was time to go home.

Mrs. Perryton was fascinated with me and left a pile of *National Geographic* magazines and newspapers on the table. She also had on that table a variety of books for people of my age, or more like below because this was special education. She sat at the desk and watched me in a clandestine manner, occasionally peeking around her horned-rimmed glasses. She pretended to be occupied, but by using her peripheral vision, she managed to keep a close eye on me.

I walked over to the table and began gathering books. I rounded up all the *National Geographic* magazines and newspapers and sat down and began to scan through them, looking at the beautiful pictures and reading about exotic places. She probably wanted to jump up and shout, "Eureka!" This being the revelation she was apparently expecting.

She stuffed my test neatly in her desk and leaned back looking at me with an inquisitive gaze. Mrs. Perryton studied me for the next thirty minutes. It ended only when the bell rang, and I exited the building to go home.

Chapter Four: Mrs. Rogers

The next day Mrs. Perryton called me to her desk and gave me a hug.

"John, you did a wonderful job on your test. In fact, you did so well I want you to meet a friend of mine. Her name is Mrs. Rogers. She has her own special class and I think you should take her test."

My face was aglow as I listened to Mrs. Perryton praise. She went on to further say, "Mrs. Rogers gives special tests to determine just how well students are actually doing in school. Would you like to meet her and take her test, John?"

I didn't hesitate and told her yes. If she was as nice as Mrs. Perryton, I would love to meet her.

"However," Mrs. Perryton told me, "she won't be here until Monday."

This was still good news to me, and I was ecstatic about my new situation. My whole life had improved because of my new class. The kids in this room loved to play with me, and life at home was better because my mother made time to spend with me. She actually tried to take about thirty minutes a day, which she really didn't have free, just for me.

Ever since I had been placed in special education I attacked my chores with renewed vigor. They didn't seem so tedious to me anymore. Everything was looking up. I had finally found my niche in this crazy world.

Life was sweet. The other kids could not pick on me, because I was special. If they did and I lashed out, the punishment would be upon them and not me. I had found a safe haven. I finally could say it was all right to be me.

On Monday, Mrs. Perryton's special friend was in the class to visit me. I felt I had to convince her I belonged with my special education teacher. She seemed nice enough. I felt she was even nicer than Mrs. Perryton. I could tell there was something different about this lady from the first moment I met her. I sensed it when she took my gnarly hands and felt the coarseness of them and only smiled.

They were in stark contrast from her soft pale delicate hands. Mrs. Rogers looked at the little hands resting in hers and never commented on the appearance of the volcanic ash that seemed to cover them. Just by looking at my hands she could tell they were tough and strong because they had the appearance of having just poured a slab or two of concrete. I never would lotion them, and the ash always seemed to be present. The dry off-white color aggravated my smooth black skin.

Mrs. Rogers was the second person, Mrs. Perryton being the first, to pretend she never noticed it. She did not make a comment or facial expression to betray her thoughts. I slowly withdrew my hands, yielding only an embarrassed smile, because I had noticed the disparaging contrast in appearance myself.

She gave me a hug to alleviate my anxiety and she asked me if I wanted to go to the public library with her. I agreed, and we took the short walk up town. We talked a little, or rather I talked and she mainly listened. This was a first. Never before had anyone taken the time to listen to me. No one ever wanted to find out what was going on with me inside, and it was an icebreaker situation.

Mrs. Rogers continued to amaze me. She bought me a book about dinosaurs because I told her I liked to read about them. We stopped by the Dairy Queen on the way back, and she bought me an ice cream sundae. She explained to me she had a special class, too.

We walked around talking about everything from what I liked, to what I disliked and she listened to everything I said. This frail-looking lady was very patient and kind. I knew there was something special about her.

She listened as I told her everything about people picking on me, fighting with me and calling me names. A downhearted mood seemed to envelop her as her demeanor changed. She seemed like the type of person to root for the underdog, and I was fast becoming her long shot. She hugged me and told me everything would be all right.

"John, I want to test you, but this needs to remain our secret. I don't want you to tell anyone. This is something Mrs. Perryton and I have worked out between ourselves."

I looked into her face and smiled, thinking the whole thing was great. It looked like I would stay in special education if I passed Mrs. Rogers' test. Maybe I would even be allowed to attend her class as well. I was a misguided young man with no street smarts and could not read the events developing. I never knew if I passed, I would never take another class under Mrs. Perryton again.

It was late in the evening, and the bus was on its way. I had to go back to the school so that I could go home. Mrs. Rogers told me she would be back tomorrow to test me and I should get a lot of rest so I could do my best. I assured her I would and gave her a big hug.

I was having fun. In the span of a month, I had actually met people who liked me. I knew it was for the wrong reason but it didn't matter because it meant I would receive special treatment.

Life at this point was good. My new friend, Mrs. Rogers, was the greatest. She was a wonderful person I felt at ease with. I could open up to her because she actually cared about what I was saying.

At home, the anticipation of it all was eating me alive. I couldn't wait to get back to school to take her test. The night slowly crawled by. I didn't close my eyes at all; if I did, it was only for a brief moment, and I was still up and about without the assistance of the noisy old rooster. I was ready. I did my chores and was the first one at my bus stop. At this moment in my life, nothing could have gotten me down.

At school, the day was going by and Mrs. Rogers had not yet arrived. To say I was a little nervous was an understatement. I began to think she was not coming and had changed her mind. I walked to the desk and asked Mrs. Perryton about our friend. I reminded her Mrs. Rogers was supposed to come to see me today.

She looked down in my face and could see the worry residing there because Mrs. Rogers had not shown up. She rubbed the top of my wooly head and told me she had called and was running a little late. She assured me that she would be there, and it seemed to ease my mind a little.

I was at recess when Mrs. Rogers showed up and had to leave the playground, but I didn't mind. We went into a little room with a small table and four quaint little chairs. The room was cramped and stuffy. The bookshelves lining the wall were stuffed with so many books that no space was left. They were really old. I could tell because they had a funny smell to them. They smelled like the old books in the library that no one ever opened. No one, that is, besides me.

Mrs. Rogers asked me if I was ready and gave me what was becoming her standard hug and kiss on the cheek. She told me my test would be in two parts. It would be a written and verbal test. She gave me the first portion, which was the written part she had made out for me, and I finished quickly. My eyes looked up at her, still shimmering with excitement. They, at this moment, looked as if diamonds were embedded in them.

I had done great. I knew it. Most of the stuff was too easy. Mrs. Rogers had a strange look of disbelief on her face and asked me if I needed more time. I told her no and we prepared for the verbal portion of the test.

I began taking the verbal and immediately did not know some of the answers. I was noticeably agitated and she tried to calm me down by telling me not to worry; I didn't have to get them all.

I bounced back and answered most of the rest with ease. I knew I had missed my fair share, but I hoped I had not flunked. When the test was over, I received Mrs. Roger's customary hug and kiss on the cheek. She told me that was all and I could go back and play.

I was nervous about the test, but went back to the playground and had fun for a while because it didn't matter for now. We then went back to the classroom, and the rest of the day passed rather quickly. I never knew it at the time, but my life had reached a major crossroad. I came home and started working on my chores. My sister, Diane, ran out to the hog pen, saying, "You're going to get a whooping!"

"For what?"

"Your teacher, Mrs. Rogers, just called and she is talking to Momma about you right now."

Her whole statement was confusing to me, and I told her, "She's not my teacher and I didn't do anything."

"Don't tell me, tell your momma," Diane laughingly replied.

My heart sank, and my body felt feeble as I thought back to remember if I did anything wrong. I could think of nothing besides that test. I couldn't be in trouble for flunking it because I was not considered smart.

50

Still I must have done something. I could not think of what but I thought I had a good chance at getting a whooping. I was scared and didn't quite finish doing everything I was supposed to, but I went inside anyway. My siblings snickered as I walked by and my eyes never left the floor. Diane informed me as I walked into my room, "Momma's got to go to the school house tomorrow, and I am going to get the sugarberry for your black ass. We'll see who's special now."

If I had been thinking clearly, I could have told Momma Diane cursed and she would get whooped right along with me. But my own troubles dominated my thoughts, and I had no time for Diane or her harassment.

I crawled under the cover and lay there motionless. Momma walked by, never saying a word. I thought she didn't notice me. My knobby fingers pulled the frayed quilt back to peek to see who was in the room. To my surprise and delight, no one was there but me. The others were outside playing.

I knew me not finishing my chores would mean a double whooping. I would have to put on some extra pants and shirts and hope for the best.

Deep down I didn't want a double because they were the worse kind I could get. I thought about breaking my silence and telling Momma Diane had cursed, and she would go down with me. But I couldn't because I was operating on the principle of out of sight, out of mind. Diane was safe because I was too afraid to talk to Momma, so I held my peace and gave my sister a pass.

I closed my eyes and I could hear Diane counting the licks as my momma struck me with that switch. This was the bad thing about a good imagination. I was able to visualize things, and I remembered almost anything that I came across, including those beatings I received for being bad or when some grown-up said I had done something.

The pain... How I could see and feel the sugarberry switch when I closed my eyes! I mentally counted the little branches Diane broke off to make the switch. Hell, I could smell it. That damn sugarberry switch. It had a smell that was sweet-like in its aroma, but would often turn my stomach because it was a harbinger of bad news for someone. More times than not, it was me that was going to get it.

It was light, narrow to the point of being rod-like and long. It would wrap around my flesh and cut me as if it was a bullwhip. It was a terrible punishment tool for children and as abundant in Brooklyn as the trees were in the woods. The devil must have planted them there himself just so adults could torture their kids.

Anxiety grabbed me around my throat as I thought about that thing in my momma's hands. It would always disintegrate after about two minutes. Those 120 seconds seemed like hours as I received my beatings. The pain I felt and the frenzy my siblings would go into as they tried to count the licks was incredible. They became a bloodthirsty mob that made the torture sessions almost unbearable.

Try as they might to maintain an accurate count of the licks, they could not keep up. They often lost count because Momma was ergonomically efficient at her work, and would never wear out.

She would hit me on her way down and strike me again as she recoiled to prepare for another slash. And when it came to me, Diane would have another batch ready after those tiny limbs wore down to Momma's hands. She would have personally trimmed more of the little branches up and made them into a switch to continue the beating.

I now made a pledge to myself: I would not cry or holler out. Nor would I run away, because the kids gathered around would only bring me in like a fugitive slave. I was determined to remain silent and not give them the satisfaction of whooping and hollering, as I absorbed the self-opinionated, unjust and excessive punishment. I made up my mind I would keep my dignity.

I must have fallen asleep because the noisy rooster was crowing and people were walking about. Uncle Larry was in the living room asking Momma to borrow twenty dollars if she had it. He saw me still in the bed and walked into my room and slapped my leg. He told me the bus wasn't too far off.

Momma didn't say anything to wake me; she just looked at me in a way to make me uneasy. I had never seen her use this facial expression before and could not read it. I did not waste my time trying to discern the meaning of her body language and contortions on her face, and proceeded to do my best Superman impersonation.

I popped up quickly, washed myself off, and got dressed. In the blink of an eye, I was headed out the door to catch the bus. My day had started off badly because I was late the first thing this morning. When I made it to the end of the driveway, the bus was already swaying and bouncing up the road.

There were a few of the kids hanging out the window. They were laughing at me as I chased the bus, pulling steadily away from me. I stopped after twenty yards and cursed to myself, "This is a bunch of bull$%^+! I know he saw me."

I said this to myself, because if anyone heard it and told, it would be a catalyst for a whooping as well.

That sugarberry switch gave me a little extra incentive to sprint up the road behind the bus with adrenaline pumping, determined to catch it at the fork on its way back from Renfroe. For some reason Momma had not whooped me yet. This was worse in my thinking, because I would receive one of the beatings she would let go and build up credit. The infamous double whooping.

She had let a major incident go by without punishing me. If beating me for old and new were her thinking, then I would do everything possible to avoid the incident in which she called her debts in on me. It would not be for me missing school this morning, because I was moving about Mach 5 going up the road. Uncle Larry later joked he saw dirt escape my shoes going about treetop high.

I got there in plenty of time and waited for the bus to make its return trip. In fact, it didn't look as though I had broken a sweat. I looked so fresh after my little jaunt, when my cousins came out to catch the bus, they asked me if Uncle Larry had dropped me off. I smiled a devilish grin and told them I ran up the hill without stopping. They didn't really believe me, because they skeptically smiled and quietly stepped onto the bus.

I was the last one to get on the bus and, it just so happened, it was the last stop before reaching the elementary school. When I bounced up into the bus, it seemed as though everyone was in school today. I had a timid look on my face as I scanned the crowd for any space I could use as a seat. I could tell it was not going to be easy this morning, because there were a few fresh faces scattered among the regulars. The strange faces were probably guests of some of the other students who had stayed overnight.

I walked towards the rear, and the bus was in an uncharacteristic silence. I had never been this far back before. I stopped about two thirds of the way at the only available seat on the bus. Actually there were two seats available, because each seat sat three persons. There was only one person on this seat and he had his head down so no one would even consider asking him to sit.

This morning, the choice was a no-brainer for me. It was either sit with him or stand for about twelve miles. I had already made up my mind what I wanted to do. I was determined to sit after my brisk gallop.

My decision was a major problem and had dangerous ramifications. This guy was "Shotgun" and he was a senior and a bully. He allowed no one to sit with him. No one but his girlfriend, and she was the only person not present. It didn't matter to him that he had the only space available. He was determined to have the seat to himself.

I wanted a piece of this prime real estate this morning. I stood directly over him in the middle of the aisle and quietly waited to sit. Shotgun looked up and laughed. I refused to let him intimidate me and I was determined to wait him out. He then bellowed, "Move on, Little Boy Blue."

He pushed me by clubbing me in the back, and then stood up and kicked me further down the aisle. The bus erupted in laughter.

As quickly as laughter had erupted, a gasp overtook it. Shotgun was in some serious trouble. He had crossed the line. He was picking on a featherweight-type guy, and he was without a doubt the biggest, toughest guy on the block. I gathered myself off the floor to witness four of my sisters wailing away on the burly boy. To my astonishment, Diane, who was the farthest away from him, was the first one on the scene to give the bully some pain. She led the charge like Teddy Roosevelt up San Juan Hill.

I only watched in amazement, too astonished to assist in the fray with my warring sisters. I watched as the bully tried to escape under the seat, only to be outflanked by the other two, who couldn't get clean shots in on him. He took refuge under the seat to get some protection from all those blows.

Those Amazons were not about to let him bail out of the fight. He knew the creed: "If you start a fight, you had better be able to finish it."

He, unfortunately, had elected to start this fight. They were determined to finish it. They initially began kicking at him, but he contorted his body up into a modified fetal position. He defied the laws of physics by doing the impossible and getting every part of his body under the seat.

This feat only caused my sisters' anger to swell. They dropped to their knees to get a better angle. They frantically tried to get under the seat at him by punching and pawing. They acted as though he was some kind of delicacy who managed to get to his burrow. Shotgun remained curled up tight and was determined to wait them out.

The bus finally stopped after about a mile, and the fighting slowly subsided. A withered old man, who appeared to be a descendent of Chiron himself, moved slowly down the aisle using the seats as his guide rail. He clumsily swayed back and forth, as students slid further into their seats so as not to impede his progress.

When he finally made it to the back, he looked at Shotgun with his dimly lit eyes, and then at my sisters. He was the local minister, and he personally knew all of us, and our parents. His authority was never questioned because he personally baptized each and every one of us.

He asked, in a firm but somewhat worn voice, what was going on. The girls filled him in and he quickly resolved the problem by asking Shotgun to stand at the front and bus stop. His wise old eyes then scanned my face, and he smiled and said, "Have a seat, John."

With one arm he hugged me about my shoulders and guided me to my confiscated throne, taking the time to reassure me that I would be all right.

The ride was long and I had time to think about many things on that trek to the schoolhouse. I leaned back on the spacious seat and thought about my momma and the sugarberry switch. I thought of Diane counting those licks out loud. I paused, and a smile crossed my face. Diane actually fought to protect me. She not only fought, but also led the charge that was reminiscent of the Rough Riders. This battle waged in my defense allowed me to acquire Shotgun's seat for today. Somewhere deep down, my sister loved me. The statement she was making seemed to be saying, "I might do you wrong, but no one else will."

I took a quick peek at Diane, who was still fighting mad about the whole incident. Her nostrils were flared and her brow showed its crinkles, as the intensity on her face said she was ready for another round. She stared hard at Shotgun, who appeared to have become comfortable by ignoring her. He wiped the blood away from his neck with his hand. When he finished with that, he flipped his collar up like The Fonz. He was content with ignoring her gaze and continued to stand at his bus-stopping post.

The whole thing seemed to amuse me, as the smile I sported crept into a wide grin. And then the smile seemed to cease abruptly, as my thoughts turned to Mrs. Rogers. Did I do something to offend her? Would she want her book back? I was scared and unsure about what repercussions I would have to face.

It seemed to always be true that whenever there was something pending good or bad, it would take forever to reach your destination. Well, this bus trip seemed about as fast as molasses moving uphill on a cold day. It took an eternity to reach the school. And then it seemed as though it took longer for me to get off the bus.

There was no way that I wanted to face the dilemma my day contained. I moved so slowly the bus driver encouraged me to pick up my pace. He reminded me he had to get the high school students to their destination.

I wanted him to do just that. Leave for the high school so I could get away from this place. On hindsight, it seemed to me it would have been better if I had missed the bus altogether.

My whole day was looking bad. For some reason it just seemed as though trouble was in the air. A brisk gust of air brushed against my face as I took in the scenes around me and finally stepped away from the sidewalk. My feet were heavy and they wanted to defy me, as I made my way slowly across the playground. I didn't notice much because my eyes searched the ground for some rock or pebble to crawl under.

I had already made up in my mind to skip the part where I tried to join in the fun with the other children. I was not in the mood, and I had been through it enough to know I was not welcomed anyway.

I quietly walked by them on my way to homeroom. I paused at the large stepped entrance of the school. Maybe I needed to rest, or maybe I was too scared to enter the building. Whichever one it was, my hesitation afforded me an opportunity to hear an argument going on inside of a little room, perched just to the left of the step. I knew the room too well. It was the principal's office.

There was a spirited debate going on. I didn't want to believe my ears, because I heard a voice that sounded a lot like Mrs. Rogers. I had made up in my mind that it couldn't be. Whoever it was, was doing a lot of fussing and it could not be the mild mannered, soft-spoken, frail white lady I had come to know. I stood there motionlessly and listened as the lady ripped into people. It sounded as though she was defending a student, and it almost sounded as though she was disgusted about something.

"For some reason, people seem to have a problem with this child," she said. "He is only a child. He deserves every opportunity afforded the other kids, and so help me, he is going to have it."

58

The tirade continued, and once she had vented her anger and frustrations to the people inside, she popped out of the room as if she needed some fresh air.

It was Mrs. Rogers. Mrs. Perryton followed closely behind her. These two emerged from the room still discussing the meeting that had just taken place. Almost immediately my eyes interlocked with hers and the scowl on her reddened face vanished. The frown that was once dominant only a moment ago hid itself behind her red cheeks, and she began to smile and beckon me to her.

I moved cautiously toward her and abruptly stopped. Mrs. Bullock and Mrs. Brown had walked into the hallway. They had been in the office as well, and did not look too pleased. They seemed to be talking among themselves about the charges and allegations that had been made and were momentarily unaware of who was in their presence. I stood there and virtually shook in my shoes. I was scared.

Mrs. Bullock's skin appeared to be molting all the time, and the cold air didn't help it at all. Her skin looked dry like mine, but I didn't think white people got ashy. If they did, I never saw it or probably never recognized what I was looking at. Her eyes were green, and contained a scary aura that seemed to radiate from her very essence.

If eyes are the windows into people's souls, then I was definitely afraid to see what was inside of hers, so I avoided her stare at all costs. When she opened her mouth, it yielded a high, piercing harpy-like voice that never had a kind word for me. She was my definition of mean. I never could put my hand on one exact thing, so I simply said it was everything about this woman that I feared. She was one of the teachers that had given me the special chair, in the special corner, in her room. All the woman did was fuss, and I wanted no part of her.

Mrs. Brown, on the other hand, was the epitome of the pretty black woman. She was light or honey-coated, as the kids called her. She appealed to the eye, but not to the ear, at least not to my ear. She had brought me to Mrs. Bullock's attention by her constant criticisms and disdain for me for no apparent reason. She did not like dark people, eespecially my kind of dark, but she was friendly to the white and lighter-skinned black children.

Some say her momma had told her early on not to fool with a dark man. It was said she would not look at one, let alone date one. She was the little devil on Mrs. Bullock's shoulder and always weighed in against me. She radiated a shield that told certain people not to approach her under any circumstances. It was unfortunate for me that I was the type of person her defenses were wired to repel.

Mrs. Rogers sensed something was wrong and began to survey the scene. She watched as I stared at her colleagues in fear. I knew Mrs. Bullock and Mrs. Brown loathed me. Every time they saw me their demeanor changed and their anger swelled. It was almost as if they salivated to get a piece of me. The whole thing seemed like Pavlov and the dog experiment. I was dead meat and they just wanted a piece. They were my personal bullies. They would eat me alive if given half the opportunity.

Therefore, I could not and would not move. Stillness grabbed me and wouldn't let go. I wanted to go to Mrs. Rogers, but I was afraid. I thought if I moved, the two women would notice me. It was as if those two were the pinnacle of the food chain, and I was their favorite prey.

I hoped I was camouflaged into my surroundings because I was petrified. I was a virtual monolith standing there in the open and reminiscing about Mrs. Bullock's screeching banshee-like voice and her piercing cat-like stare. I thought about the chair she had written my name on and placed in the corner.

I remembered Mrs. Brown's aura of disdain towards me, and the unwarranted paddling I always received when I was in her room last year. The way she would get smart with me by sarcastically answering my questions, if I dared to ask her something. But most of all, I remembered how both of them called Momma with lies about me.

They were the two women I had signaled out to Mrs. Rogers as being the source of my lamentations. I now had an idea of what the meeting was all about. I had confided in her my deepest secrets. She had sensed that I was faltering and was about to give up and had decided to pick up my battle flag. The whole scene was really intense.

Somewhere in that slowly developing situation, Mrs. Rogers put together everything that was going on between her colleagues and me. She subtly motioned to Mrs. Perryton, who then walked over and engaged them in a benign conversation. Seizing the distraction of the moment, she walked to the step and hugged and kissed me on my cheek to relax me.

"You okay, John?"

I nodded my head that I was.

"I want you to come and give me a hand getting something out of my car."

I willingly walked with her to her car and was only too glad to do it because it provided an escape from the two wicked women.

We walked a few paces and initially started speaking in small talk. It wasn't anything serious. It was some of the things she had asked before. She went over things like a fine Harvard lawyer, as if she was trying to trip me up or get me to let my guard down.

She asked things like what books had I read lately and did I like sports? Did I watch the news or read the newspaper? It was a leisurely conversation about me, similar in nature to the one we had on our initial walk.

"How are things going for you at home?"

"Okay."

"Did you know your dad, John?"

"No. I don't remember him," I said, looking at her and wondering why she was asking about my daddy again because I had already mentioned he had died.

She then asked, "John, how's your mother doing?"

"Fine."

"Where does she work, John?"

I didn't answer that. For some reason, she had started to ask questions about Momma, as if she was trying to get an angle on her for some unapparent reason.

This line of questioning made me a little uneasy. I looked up at her in the most peculiar manner. The nature and the complexion of the conversation had now completely changed. She no longer wanted to hear or talk about me, but now she wanted to discuss my momma. Remembering what Momma told me about white people, my eyes left the ground and scanned her face, never breaking my leisurely stride. I searched her facial expressions, trying to put her questioning into context. I began to see her in a completely new light.

Momma had warned me they try to be sneaky. She had even conceded the fact they were good at it, too, because they had plenty of practice sitting on their butts with their keen noses in the air, while black people worked all day.

I looked at her nose and saw it had a keen point. My pace began to slow. It wasn't really noticeable, but after about ten or so more steps, I was no longer abreast with her. I was actually a little behind, because I wanted to confirm the point that Momma had made about white people's booties being flat from sitting on their rear end all day.

I pretended to tie my shoes so that my view would be better. I was disappointed. My face yielded a disgusting smirk. All the stuff my momma told me appeared to be true. Their noses were keen and their booties were flat. In my mind, I was basically able to confirm everything my momma had told me about whites and blacks in my nine years on the planet.

I was quiet, besides my occasional "umm humm, yeah" and "no" I gave to her questions. Mrs. Rogers changed the subject, because she sensed I had closed her out.

She asked me how I thought I did on my test. I shrugged my shoulders in a universal "I don't know and I don't care" fashion, not saying a word.

Her voice was only a murmur and was fading fast. It sounded like people trying to hear a conversation from underwater. The two of us were phasing into different planes of reality.

A few more steps and her voice had turned into a foreign muffled language as I contemplated why this white lady had taken an interest in me. My momma had told me, "If they take an interest in you they want something out of the deal."

I didn't have anything she could possibly want that I knew about. All I could think was I would not make a deal with the devil, so to speak.

We reached her car, and she gave me a small parcel to carry. It was light enough. So light I knew she didn't need my help. However, I was glad she did request my services. She did get me away from the two dreadful women, Mrs. Bullock and Mrs. Brown, and I owed her in a big way for that.

On the way back across the schoolyard, I finally found enough strength in my voice to speak again.

"Mrs. Rogers," I said. "Did you call my momma and tell on me?"

"Tell on you about what, John?"

"Nothing."

I thought it was best I shut my mouth. If I kept talking I was bound to say something I shouldn't. I was going to take my momma's advice and just be quiet. She had advised me if I didn't say anything, then they could only speculate.

"They can't get an angle on you," Momma said.

She loved to tell me that a steel tongue supported a wise head. I had not heeded her advice in the past and had paid for it with interest in the canyon.

"A hard head makes a sore behind," I had remembrance of this one too. I was going to start listening now. Besides, I knew Mrs. Rogers was up to something. Diane had already said she had called Momma and told on me.

"That's how these people operate," I said to myself.

We continued on our little stroll, not really saying a word to each other. After a while, I got an itch. No matter how much I tried to remain silent, I couldn't do it. Curiosity got the better of me. After about five minutes I questioned her again by asking if she knew my momma was coming to the school.

Mrs. Rogers thought I was getting at something and therefore decided to put all her chips on the table. She paused, took a brief sigh to gather her thoughts, and said, "John, we have a problem. I called your momma and asked her to come here today because we have something that needs to be resolved. You are a special child and I want you in my class, if you want to be a part of it."

I dropped my head and tried to think. I was having trouble focusing on her words as my thoughts jumbled together. It was apparent I was becoming more stressed and frustrated about this whole thing. It was almost as if my mind was having a syntax error. Try as I might, I could not get my thoughts to be coherent enough to think of anything else to ask Mrs. Rogers or answer her question. I was not good at doing this lawyering stuff and it showed.

My young mind still could not decipher all the things going on around me. What did this lady want? Why wouldn't she go away and leave me alone to be in my new class?

My face was now giving birth to the hostilities I was feeling inside. My lips puckered and my brow furrowed, and I didn't want to talk anymore. I was angry and felt I had lost control of all the circumstances that had developed around me.

"John," she said, touching me on my shoulder, snapping me out of my deep thought cycle. "Do you want to be a part of my class?"

I never looked up; I continued to hide the anger in my face within my chest and replied in a low gruff voice, "No."

"Why not?" the baffled Mrs. Rogers asked.

"I like Mrs. Perryton, and I want to stay with her. I like her room and my friends are there."

This was all I said about the matter. But the savvy Mrs. Rogers knew what I meant. She had started to psychoanalyze me from the first moment we met and had a blueprint on me already. She knew I was saying Mrs. Perryton and those mentally inept kids always played and talked to me. They didn't care what color I was or how well I dressed. They accepted me for being me, making it the best class I had ever been a part of.

She took a deep breath and gave another sigh and said, "John, you can't stay with Mrs. Perryton."

After a moment of silence I asked, "Why not?"

Mrs. Rogers did not get a chance to answer because a loud noise grabbed her attention. It was so loud it actually startled her.

Pressing her hands firmly against her chest, she composed herself. She then scanned the street from which the commotion appeared to have come from.

"It's my momma," I said in a shamed voice, not even looking up the road for the sound.

We did not have a fine car like other people and everyone teased us about it, even the ones who didn't have a vehicle. They told me they would rather walk than ride around in that thing.

We had it so long that I think Momma had sentimental attachments to it because it was Daddy's. She never tried to hide it and always parked in the most prominent spots. I think she was trying to make a statement to us about not being ashamed of nothing we had. Besides, this was Daddy's truck. We went everywhere in this thing, and I knew the sound anywhere as if it was my own dog.

It needed a muffler and a tune-up, at the very least. I also thought it needed setting too--setting on fire because the motor was gone. But I knew Momma didn't care. It had been this way ever since I was old enough to remember, but it usually gathered enough strength to do what had to be done. Besides, it was her work truck. It was her only truck or car for that matter, so this meant it served double duty for us on Sunday.

"A young mind is like wet clay." The kids teasing me, saying they would rather walk than ride in our truck had an impact on me like so many other things they said. When Sunday came, I walked to the church and eventually stopped going.

I managed to stop thinking about the shame I was feeling, and looked at Momma, who was true to form just like her truck. She parked on the north side of the school in front of the main entrance about sixty yards away. The truck had an attitude and refused to cut off. Momma hopped out and did something under the hood and it choked, popped and hissed to a final bow of silence.

66

After her quick operation, she forcibly slammed the hood down, took a quick look around, and squatted slightly to generate lift. She then jumped straight into the air and landed booty first on top of the truck. The impact she managed to generate with her weight forced the latch to catch and securely close the hood. She then grabbed her very large purse and headed across the street.

Mrs. Rogers was taking in the whole scene and appeared to be waiting on this very moment. Once Momma started across the road, Mrs. Rogers proceeded on a journey across the schoolyard to greet her. Her paced picked up when Momma made it up on the sidewalk.

While all of this was going on, I stood there looking at the old truck, wishing I could blow it up and get rid of it as quickly as possible. When my mind snapped out of its daze, I found myself standing alone. I looked up and discovered Mrs. Rogers was no longer with me. She had crossed the schoolyard and was almost to my Momma. I quickly got it in gear and, with elongated strides, narrowed the distance between us. I was trying to reach Momma ahead of the enthusiastic lady.

My brief daze would cost me because there was no way I would overtake her. Mrs. Rogers had already greeted her when I arrived.

I was a little late on the scene and could only listen to their conversation as they discussed me as if I wasn't there. Mrs. Rogers had not given up on persuading me, but she was now reinforcing her position with Momma. She was a persistent person to say, the least.

She lobbied her as if she were a special interest group on Capitol Hill. Their eyes were interlocked, and Momma listened to every word she spoke. Without a waste of any motion or breath in her speech, Mrs. Rogers reached back and pulled me under her arm. This was the first instant in which I realized they knew I was even in the area. She clasped her arms firmly about my shoulders and gave me a firm hug, trying to convince Momma she had my best interest in mind.

Momma listened to Mrs. Rogers tell her how special I was, and how she only wanted what was best for me, without saying a word. After she listened to every word intensely, giving Mrs. Rogers her say, displeasure started to show in her face. It wasn't clear if she was buying what she was trying to sell her on me, but the frustration in her voice was becoming evident as she began to question the over exuberant teacher.

"How can my child be smart when I have been told he is slow or special, as y'all say? How can my child be gifted, when I have been told he is mentally inept?" She took a deep breath and asked Mrs. Rogers, "Which one is he, slow or gifted?"

The inquisitive look on her face was gone. She was staring angrily at the teacher with a defiant pose, in which she rested both her clenched fists on her hips. Being a veteran of the school system, Mrs. Rogers knew this was no place to have this discussion and asked Momma to come with her. They shot across the schoolyard in the blink of an eye. The two of them outmaneuvered the balls and the tumbling kids that crossed their path with ease.

Mrs. Rogers was amazing. She set an extraordinary pace, all along spouting the benefits her class held for children. She never stopped lobbying Momma to allow me to join the who's who among students in the school system.

They took their seats in the little room with the small table and overstuffed bookshelves and I followed them. This claustrophobic room was apparently her office. When we were seated she said once again, "There is so much I want to share with you about your son's potential."

"What's there to know?" Momma shot back, sarcastically.

It was obvious because of Momma's attitude that she believed the former things about me, rather than the latter.

Momma then informed her, "Mrs. Harris has already diagnosed John with a learning disability. It is causing him to act out and become belligerent and disruptive in class towards other students. She recommended to me that John be placed in special education where the pace is much slower so that he could learn to read. Your counselor said if he stayed on the previous course the school system would eat him alive. Is that what you want, Mrs. Rogers?"

As she asked her question she looked at me, reassuring herself that she was doing the right thing, thinking I wasn't playing with a full deck. She was misinformed, but she had already made up her mind that she was going to stay the course with me.

Mrs. Rogers started talking, trying to explain everything, but Momma had started to do one of my numbers and was beginning to faze her out. She only wanted what was best for me and felt she had already done what was best for her anti-social child.

Getting nowhere, Mrs. Rogers calmly reached into her visibly worn leather bag and pulled out an overstuffed manila envelope. She opened the package and proceeded to grab a yellow highlighter that was neatly stuffed into the tattered flap of her old beaten-up bag. She quickly looked over the contents of the folder and began to sort the pages that it eagerly surrendered to her.

Until now, I was really not interested in the scene slowly debated out in front of me. I was impervious to their discussion, until she began to look over certain papers she had separated. She now had my attention. These papers looked like my test. I leaned forward, gazing at the sheets she had arranged neatly in front of her. I was sitting at the far end of the little table and found it hard to make out some of her markings. I squinted my eyes and peered as hard as I could to try to read her writing.

Mrs. Rogers was not saying anything and appeared to be consumed in the task she had undertaken. She quickly scribbled some more things with her highlighter over a few choice selections on a couple of the sheets she had set aside. She moved rather quickly, but methodically, over them. When she finished, she placed them in front of Momma.

"This is your son's I.Q. test and another quiz," she said with great pride. "He needs special education, but not the kind he's receiving. He needs the kind that will challenge his mind and push him forward. He's not mentally inept, Mrs. Johnson. He is actually mentally gifted."

Momma appeared confused as she began to look over the pages Mrs. Rogers had placed in front of her. She didn't quite know what she was looking at, and the veteran educator picked up on it almost immediately. She slid her chair closer to Momma to explain exactly what the pages in front of her were saying.

This drew an uncomfortable look because Momma was already frustrated. The look on her face prompted Mrs. Rogers to explain herself.

"I just want to show you a few things on these papers," she said.

She then began to point out my test scores and the average of my classmates. She broke it down into state and national averages. She then informed her that I was on a 10th grade level. Momma continued to look at the pages in awe. She was flabbergasted that I could possibly be this smart.

"Mrs. Rogers," she said. "Why are his test and homework scores never above a 'D'? Can you answer that? Why is John always

70

into trouble? What's going on with my son?" she asked, as if demanding an answer..

The veteran educator smiled and slid her chair back into its previous position. She was undaunted by this line of questioning because she had been in the educational system a long time and probably had seen and heard it all.

"There are several possible reasons as to what could be going on with John," she said.

She began to rattle off possible theories as to what the problem could be with me.

"Maybe class is boring to him; it's not a challenge. Maybe he is crying out for attention or maybe we as educators have failed him. We have not been able to reach him. But if you really want to know, it's best if you ask John."

When the last statement was made, I looked up from the floor like the cat that had just eaten its master's canary. My slanted soft eyes were bucked, and the expression on my face told anyone watching this gig was up. My con was over.

Momma's eyes focused in on me, and I felt as though the chair I had been sitting in had just been hooked up to about a thousand volts of electricity. To make the situation worse, the look in Momma's eyes told me she was determined to pull the switch.

She asked me in a dry angry voice, "What's going on with you, boy? Why can't you do your work?"

I could not answer because I didn't know why. It was hard to explain. It was not one thing, but a combination of everything. I was having a meltdown. My mind turned to the sugarberry switch. I would get one of those whoopings Momma gave you credit for. The kind where she let you slide, but when she called in her marker, she got you for old and new: the infamous double whooping.

Mrs. Rogers, who had been watching the whole thing, interjected again to bail me out and push the benefits of her class.

"Mrs. Johnson, that's where my class comes in handy. It's a course where special students like John have a curriculum that helps them reach their potential. I am in charge and I am their personal mentor. Students are able to discuss anything with me because I am not only their teacher, but also their counselor. The work they do is on a higher level. They do scientific lab work and reports. They also write term papers and book reports that are turned in to me. My class really pushes and challenges them to perform and reach their potential. The class is for the best and the brightest minds. It not only prepares them for high school, it's the first step in preparing them for college, if they choose to go."

Momma was still skeptical about the revelations about me. She leaned back in the old wooden chair that seemed to moan and strain to support her weight. She looked directly into my eyes as if she was looking for something. The stare-down went on for about five minutes in complete silence. Finally she asked in a monotoned voice, "John, are you smart, boy? Can you read like this lady is telling me?"

I shrugged my shoulders in one of those I-don't-know fashions and contemplated the idea of sticking to my guns and playing dumb.

"Answer me, boy!" Momma roared.

The inflection in her voice seemed to shake me, if not the room itself. Mrs. Rogers intervened again, because she saw how frightened I was and it looked like I was about to disintegrate right in front of her. I was obviously afraid and at a loss for words.

"Mrs. Johnson," she said as she rose from her seat and grabbed an ancient book from the shelf just above her head, "ask John to read this book for you."

It was a thick book covered with dust and speckled with paint from years gone by. It hadn't been opened in so long that it had incorporated the moisture that was in the room. This thing was so stubborn it actually fought to keep the knowledge it contained by refusing to let its pages separate.

Momma forced it open about halfway, and it made the crrrr sound of resistance that is typical with older books like this. She then grabbed the edges of the pages and flipped through them a few times, just to loosen them up.

She quickly scanned through the archaic-looking manuscript. It appeared to be an old biology or chemistry book with diagrams and huge words dispersed throughout the smelly, fungus-ridden pages. She gave the book to me and I proceeded to read it to her quickly and efficiently. It sounded as though I was reading a forgotten language to my momma, who listened in disbelief. When I turned the third page, Mrs. Rogers asked me to stop.

"I don't know what your decision will be about my accelerated program, but he cannot stay in special education with Mrs. Perryton."

She began to gather her things, an obvious signal that the meeting was over and said, "Mrs. Johnson, I want you to think about it, and I will give you a call later in the week for your answer. Meanwhile, I will get John into the counselor's office and arrange for him to take real classes again."

She finished gathering her things and Momma was still pondering what just happened. My confused Momma could not find the strength to move from her seat.

Mrs. Rogers paused for a moment and reassured her the program she was running would be best for me, as she once again clasped me about my shoulders.

She told Momma there were so many things she needed to take care of with me before she returned me to class, and she had really needed to get started. She herded me out the door in front of her and left the door wide open for Momma to leave whenever she liked.

"Mrs. Rogers," I said as we turned the corner. "Do I have to go back to Mrs. Bullock?"

Mrs. Rogers paused and looked me squarely in my eyes and told me things were going to be different this time. She told me if I had any problems at all, to come in and talk with her. She would be at the school every Wednesday, and her door would always be opened for me. She reassured me it didn't matter if I was a part of her program or not, she would still be there for me.

The whole thing had left me a little apprehensive. I was also feeling a little relief too, because I was receiving help from an unexpected source. This white lady had taken a liking to me and I knew I should be a little appreciative. I resented Mrs. Rogers for making me go back to Mrs. Bullock, but somehow I knew she only wanted what was best for me. And if Momma would let me go to Mrs. Rogers' class, then I would go. If I had to go to Mrs. Bullock, I would need a brief hiatus.

We reached the counselor's office and Mrs. Rogers stopped at the door and gave me her expectations. She told me I needed to improve my grades and start to participate in class. I didn't reply. I slid my foot back and forth across the old pine floor, revealing lines of its true luster where my foot had just traced. It was sandy outside and kind of hard to keep the floor shined. The wood was just about worn out, and it had to be dust mopped a couple of times a day. In between times, the dust would gather and conspire to hide the wood's soft sheen. I looked down at the handiwork I was making and refused to look up at Mrs. Rogers, answering instead the floor's plea to be shined. I was doing a pretty good job of removing the dust because the small area I worked on shined nicely, and it was made even more remarkable because all I had were my feet.

I was nervous about everything. I was there with her and at the same time I wasn't. I had been taken to another place mentally and my mind wanted to shut down again. I didn't want to consider anything related to going back to Mrs. Bullock. I was trapped in something like a weird dream where I wanted to wake myself up but couldn't. I could sense everything going on around me but couldn't do anything about it.

Mrs. Rogers took me by the hand to get my attention. She then gave me a reassuring smile. Her teeth were perfect. The smile she gave relaxed me, and I flashed a brilliant smile back at her. She bent over and gave me another hug, and we triumphantly walked into the counselor's office.

The two adults greeted each other in typical adult fashion, grabbed a couple of cups of coffee, and sat down to business. After about twenty minutes into their game planning, their attention turned to me. I remained just at the entrance of the door. They called me forward, and set my school records on the table directly in front of me. The whole scene looked like a war room, as they planned their strategy for my success.

They looked at me, trying to measure my reaction to my file. I took a peek at my grades that were now on display for me to see. The frown, indicating I was not pleased and embarrassed. I put a smirk on my face in which I curled the left side of my mouth up and turned away, as if my grades were too hideous for me to look upon. I did not try to defend my records because I felt I had no reason to. I now believed that Mrs. Rogers thought a lot of my problem was people railroading me.

After this extended strategy session with the counselor and Mrs. Rogers was over, I knew it was time to get down to business. Mrs. Rogers was feeling pretty good about the course they had set for me, and the results it would bring. She smiled, rose from her seat and told me that the ball was now in my court. I had a lot of work to catch up on. She gave her old leather bag to me to carry and we went to get some lunch. Afterwards, we departed for Mrs. Bullock's room.

Mrs. Rogers now talked excessively in the final leg of our journey. I really didn't listen to her muddled voice as it reverberated off the wall. I was more interested in the way the sounds bounced around the room than her words of encouragement. I had developed a nasty habit of tuning people out, and this was what I was doing now. It was my way of controlling stressful situations if people began to lecture me about something I was tired of hearing about.

And as for my benefactor, well, I would have rather had her be as quiet as possible. I had already heard the most important points of her speech. I had other important things to think about. Things like reassimilating myself back into a class that never wanted me. I really couldn't game plan effectively if someone constantly steered my mind in another direction.

With Mrs. Rogers' chattering, the only plan I had managed to develop was to silently walk back into class with my head down and hope no one would notice me.

However, this was not a plausible idea, because that old building always announced to the world someone was coming. Those echoes were terrible and it was the worse place in the world to attempt any kind of stealth technique.

To make matters worse for me, Mrs. Rogers wasted no time navigating the narrow passages or maintaining any kind of silence. She talked constantly to alleviate my fears and reassure me things would be different. She said more on the way to Mrs. Bullock's room than she had said in all our previous encounters combined.

I wondered why she could not tell that I had tuned her out. If I had been paying attention to her, I would have noticed that she had now tuned me out. She was so excited for me and talked so much she turned her chatter into a rambling oration to me on things that I knew must be done.

Even though she was talking, my mind was not on her words. It was on the mere fact I hated this place. I especially hated this wing of the building, which was infamous for causing me so much mental and physical abuse. Why a psychologist or a counselor would ever recommend people go back to face their demons is simply beyond me. My philosophy is to leave the demons behind and get on with life.

Mrs. Rogers' pace had been quick the whole day. I wanted her to slow down, but I figured she had a lot of things to do. She had spent the whole day with Momma and me and had no time to do other things pertaining to her job.

She really didn't mind the inconvenience because she appeared to have a genuine compassion for children, and she loved teaching. She was a person who enjoyed working with and helping children in any way she could.

We arrived at Mrs. Bullock's room quickly, much to my regret. Once we reached the door, Mrs. Rogers gave a knock in the form of three taps in rapid succession, a kind of code, one would guess. After a brief moment, the door opened and the eyes of the class focused on me.

Mrs. Rogers dropped me off as if she was some kind of middle-class working mother taking her child to school. She gave me a hug and a quick peck on the cheek with her typical motherly affection and left me in the care of Mrs. Bullock who was standing in the door watching us with a fake smile on her face, welcoming me back into the fold.

Implementing the only plan I devised, I dropped my head and stepped into the class. My eyes oscillated rapidly, trying to read the expressions on the students' faces and the changes that had been made to the room.

Most of the students wore stoic expressions. I couldn't help but think they would make great poker players. They watched me silently, not saying a word to each other or me. It was a silent stare-down, and I was losing, as always.

I noticed the corner was empty. There was no longer a chair with my name on it. I really didn't know what to expect or how to play my new hand. I claimed an empty desk for myself in the middle of the room, directly in front of Mrs. Bullock's desk. I knew it was mine, because it was the only one available, and it appeared to be set purposely in front of her for a reason. The rest of the empty desks had been removed from the room. I remembered there used to be five or six empty ones spread about, but not today. There were only enough desks for the students to sit, and nothing else. I figured, and I was right, this was my personal new chair.

I took a deep breath and tried to relax. My heart was beating so fast and loud, I knew everyone must have heard it. I was in danger of having it explode under all the pressure. I was so stressed I would do anything to know the Chinese secret of slowing one's heart rate down.

I felt faint. I slumped down in my desk, wanting to put my head down and tell myself this situation was not happening. I was not in this room again. I dared not do this. I did not want anything I did to be viewed as deviant behavior. I knew this type of action would give everyone the green light to start to torment me again.

By now, Mrs. Rogers was long gone and class had resumed. To my surprise, no one mocked me. No spitballs or pencils flew or anything. I watched through my peripheral vision, as a few of the students stole a few quick peeks. They were feeling me out. They were reading the events they had witnessed and weighed them against the rumors they heard floating around the school. They wanted to know if anything had changed or if I had garnered any pull.

I managed to keep my head up and had not noticed my day had turned into a blur. When I glanced at the clock I was surprised to see my school day was about to end. Time was winding down and I couldn't wait to get out of this room. Mrs. Bullock had not yet said anything to me, and that's the way I wanted it to stay. I watched the clock as if it were New Year's Eve and slowly began the countdown until the time the bell would erupt.

Mrs. Bullock apparently had been watching the same thing, closed her book, and asked me to come to her desk. The moment I moved, the bell rang out, and I was almost trampled in a stampede of students heading for the door. I maneuvered through the traffic and stood in front of my new old teacher.

She spoke to me in a kind manner. I assumed this was her way of making a peace treaty. She told me she would work with me to catch up on my schoolwork if I wanted. She also said she wanted to get to know me a little better.

She knew I was suspicious of her so she asked me if I wanted to talk about anything. I shook my head no, and she allowed me to leave to go home.

I silently exited the building and boarded the bus that had just opened its door for us to enter. The bus ride home seemed anticlimactic compared to what had transpired earlier. The ride was noisy as usual, but I was lost in my own thoughts, which drowned out all the noise and conversations going on in the background.

In my mind, I revisited the events of the day. They were all so vivid. I remembered everything, from my uncle waking me, to Mrs. Bullock releasing me for the day.

I focused on what transpired in the middle of all of this. It was the fight my sisters had to defend my honor. This was the real meaning of family. At least that's what I would take away from it.

My problems seemed more urgent than anything in the world at this moment. It seemed as if everything else was insignificant and my predicament was the most critical crisis a person could face. It needed presidential intervention. I knew my ordeal would not make the six o'clock news, but I thought it would make a good story.

In actuality, my plight should have been a news story. Cameras should have followed me around. My situation should never have been allowed to happen because "an injustice anywhere, is an injustice everywhere." But this was just another one of these corny mottos in America, which seemed to have no legitimacy in their meaning.

When the bus finally arrived at my house, I didn't see the old pickup. This meant Momma was not there or the truck had finally gone to the great junkyard in the sky. I quickly did my chores and sat down to read the encyclopedias.

Time disappeared quickly from the clock, and I heard the old pickup truck fussing as it came into the yard. I only saw the dimly lit headlights, because it was now dark outside. I knew it was Momma because of the sound of that embarrassing truck.

She was finally home and I watched her from the living room as she drug herself slowly out of the truck. I barely could see her through the stains on the old pieces of glass in the window, but I knew she had had a long day. She was outside unloading a lot of iron and stuff off the back of that old Chevy C-10. I saw enough to know she looked tired, as usual.

80

I watched the movement of her silhouette, which resembled the Big Foot monster, as she moved pitifully and painfully about outside in the yard moving things about. She finally staggered into the house, made her way into the bedroom, and collapsed on her bed. She composed herself after she managed to get her shoes off, took a deep breath, and told Diane to go get me.

"John," Diane called out. "Momma wants you."

Momma looked at her daughter and sarcastically said, "I could have done that myself."

It really didn't matter. I heard Momma anyway and had already started to make my way towards her room. I was awaiting her summons because of what happened earlier today. I emerged from the living room and ventured into Momma's presence ready to be knocked into the next state.

"Y'am?" I said, in a barely audible voice.

"Why haven't you been doing your schoolwork?"

I shrugged my shoulders and looked around at my sisters who had gathered in the doorway. My attention was especially drawn to Diane, who was grinning hard because she could sense something was about to happen. She had taken the liberty of gathering the sugarberry for the switch and held them up to show me, sporting a devilish grin. Momma forced herself up and closed the door, telling the audience that had gathered to find something else to do.

My mind was running wild. The whole thing was strange to me. However, I could tell there was something different about this interrogation session. My fears subsided because I didn't sense an imminent threat of a whooping.

Momma did not raise her voice. She wanted to listen for a change. She asked questions and they were not rhetorical. I was caught completely off guard. I really had not given much thought to what was going on with me. I stood there with a dumb look on my face, not moving or answering any of her questions.

She could see that her attempts to communicate with me were fruitless. Partly out of fatigue and partly out of frustration, she finally asked me what I wanted to do about Mrs. Rogers' class. She wanted to get it resolved and prepare for bed. No one could blame her. If anybody looked at her, they could tell she was obviously exhausted.

I began to rub my feet across the old floor, tracing the space that the ground always peeped through. I then said in a shaky voice, "I want to go."

"What! Speak up boy, I can't hear you!" she barked.

She was already tired and frustrated with the whole thing.

I summoned a little more bass from somewhere deep within and said, "I want to go."

Momma stared at me in a stern manner and told me she didn't have any problems with it. She also warned me if my grades didn't improve, my butt would go sky high.

She dismissed me from her room. I knew I had just received an ultimatum. I had to improve my school performance or suffer the consequences.

I opened the door and Diane was the only one still standing there. She had not dispersed at all but had only pretended to leave the scene. Apparently she had been eavesdropping. I looked at her in disgust and brushed solidly against her as I walked by causing her to laugh. I didn't feel like reading or anything. I was finished for the night, so I lay on my bed and sleep claimed me.

Early the next morning, I awoke and went about my routine. I knew my life would never be the same. It had changed and I had to come to grips with the new expectations that had been placed on me. I actually paused and opened one of the schoolbooks I told my teachers I had lost. They always knew I was lying because I would miraculously find them at the end of the year to turn them in without having to pay for them.

I glanced through some of the chapters and knew I had my work cut out for me. I had to catch up on a lot of things that had passed me by. I had never read through the books I was issued before, and now tried to familiarize myself with the contents in one of them. This would be a tremendous undertaking. The schoolwork would not be difficult, but catching up on all those missed assignments and readings would be time-consuming. It was a hard punishment for my lackluster school performance, but I felt it was sort of fair.

In a short time span, I had gone from coasting through school, to being placed with the best and brightest minds. I would have to make friends all over again. When I actually thought about it, I knew I had to try to make my first friend--one that wasn't mentally slow--because I had none.

All my life I had been placed with the average or below-average students. Now I was going to be placed with the cream of the crop. So many questions were flooding my mind. Would the Einsteins welcome me as one of their own or snub me for daring to think I could be one of them? Could I do the work? Could I keep up? Did I really belong with them? The answers to those questions and more I would find out later, because the bus was now blowing for me.

What If?

What if we discouraged the development of that one particular mind?
What if it never reached its potential and could have solved problems that plague mankind?

What if years later one of us, or our loved ones had cancer?
What if the mind we discouraged so long ago could have found the cure and the answer?

We ridiculed that little child and the foundation he needed for knowledge was never built,
In our cruel and insensitive moments, we destroyed God's gift.

What if years later we lay dying and we are miserable and weak?
What if we would have aided that child so long ago who could have developed the cure we seek?

Did it really matter long ago what color they were or whether they were cute to us or not?
Does it matter now since we are having chills, but we are sweaty and hot?

We cry out to God for His blessings and look to the heavens above?
God had already given us His blessing, but we refused to show him any love?

We never think about that child that we did wrong, but dare ask God's forgiveness for all our sins.
The angels cry and shake their heads, because such is the folly of men.

Chapter Five: Redemption

Upon returning to the school, I was heckled the moment I tried to intermingle with the other kids. Apparently they had not received the memo of me being considered gifted, because I was treated in the usual manner. I absorbed the harassment and began to slowly back up. To all of my questions, I now had my answers. I was out of my league. I was still not worthy to interact with the other students. How could I be considered an elite scholar?

Without warning, a voice cracked the air. I snapped out of my stupor. A high piercing voice asked, "What's going on over there?"

It was Mrs. Bullock. I was sure I would get it now. Where was Mrs. Rogers? She had promised me things would be different for me this time. Mrs. Bullock looked mad as always, and I felt I was going to be hung out to dry again.

She came over and hurriedly made her way through the crowd. The sea of students parted as if she was Moses himself. The other kids at the center of the controversy started by saying, "John…"

She cut them off quickly, because she had watched the whole thing.

"John what?" she angrily asked.

There was a silent hush over the playground. I stood there watching in disbelief. It suddenly appeared it was not going to be business as usual. She turned to me and asked me what was going on, to give me a say. I dropped my head, and slid my feet nervously back and forth over the red ground, inadvertently drawing circles and lines of all sorts and sizes.

I mustered up enough courage to answer Mrs. Bullock, whose face was riddled with every angry expression known to man.

"I only wanted to play ball, and they told me to leave them alone."

Mrs. Bullock took the ball and asked me to point out the kids who did not want me to play. I nervously pointed to the three culprits and she confiscated the ball, ushering them from the playground and into her classroom. Almost in an afterthought, she turned and tossed the ball to me, and told me to have fun and to play nice. It appeared playtime was over for those three.

I watched for a moment as they were herded into the classroom. My eyes then locked with Mrs. Brown, who had also watched the whole thing play out. The look on her face told me she was not appreciative of the actions of Mrs. Bullock. Those were some of her favorite students, and in her eyes they could do no wrong.

She stood there and watched me for a moment, then silently walked around the corner of the building. I knew she did not like what happened, and I knew I was one of her least favorite students. I did not know whether Mrs. Brown would leave me alone or choose to be a burr under my saddle for the remainder of my ride.

Children are highly intelligent, and some of the craftier ones recognized I had begun to get a little credibility around this place. They were in tune to the events of the previous day, the rumors floating about, and what just happened.

They began to call for new captains, and asked me to be one of them since I had the ball. I had never been allowed to pick before, let alone play. I started the drafting off by picking one of the more popular guys around. Not to say he was the most athletically gifted, but he was well liked.

He quickly made me into a megaphone. I echoed every name he whispered in my ear. I had slyly started playing the political game. I was trying to build alliances and used this moment to try to gain ground into the in crowd. I acted fast so I would not squander any opportunity to gain a little respectability.

Our teams began to separate themselves, and the children who had never given me a chance were about to find out I was one of the more talented players around. This was the first time I had played kick ball with everyone, so it was an exciting time for me.

When it was finally my turn to kick, everybody watched. They laughed when I pulled off my shoes and socks, and pawed the earth with my bare feet. My antics looked like an omnipotent stallion because at this moment I had a certain visible power about me.

I backed up and prepared to greet the tumbling mass of rubber as it rolled quickly toward me. I rushed forward with my adrenaline pumping, and laid into the ball with a war cry of "Kayyy yahhhh!"

The ball escaped my foot with tremendous velocity. The trajectory the ball traveled had never been seen before on the playground. Whether it was the sheer force of impact or the wind that caught it as it climbed into the sky, it traveled over the heads of everyone in the field. The ball continued to travel until it struck the lunchroom wall. It bounced off a third of the way up the building and a dead silence hovered over the crowd. No one had kicked the ball that far before.

I did not have to run, but did anyway. My bare feet dug into the hard red ground, throwing the crushed dirt from my toes high into the air. I moved like an impala around the bases. I didn't stop until I crossed home plate. My team mugged me. They congratulated me on my astounding feat. I was ecstatic. The thought of me being a playground legend crept into my mind.

We continued to play on offense and then on defense. I covered a lot of ground as I tracked down the balls with ease. It was as if a man was playing with boys. The game continued until the morning bell ended the lopsided contest. I had cemented myself in as a player and from now onward would be allowed to play all I liked.

Schoolyards reflect real world situations. Everything happens on a smaller scale, but nonetheless are some of the same things. Sad to say, I was one of the most gifted players in any of the games, but because of my emotional baggage and lack of an amicable personality, I would never be a first overall draft pick.

When the bell rang, we formed a herd and began to gather for class. Mrs. Bullock pulled me aside as I headed up the steps for homeroom. She told me to go to the counselor's office. I didn't know what was going on and didn't care. I was on an emotional high, and began taking everything with a grain of salt and trotted through the building, prompting Mrs. Bullock to shout behind me, "Stop running John!"

I complied and slowed to a leisurely stroll. I started to take in some of the sights in the hallway. The stuff I had never taken an interest in before, I was now starting to observe. Things like the students' art plastered on the wall. Most of the average students' art was presentable, but scattered among them was the gifted students' art.

I could tell the difference between theirs and the average and everyone else's. Theirs was so much better looking and evolved. The talent level seemed to be there for them no matter what challenge they undertook. I wondered why Mrs. Rogers thought I belonged with them.

Nonetheless, I continued through the hallway. I saw my locker and remembered my books were inside the little wooden compartment. I never opened the thing after the first week of school. I never did my homework or read the lesson plans so I never had a need to.

I picked up my lock and knew I could not get into the little safe. I had forgotten my combination and was simply going through the motion. I played with the dial for a minute, hoping the numbers would emerge from a file somewhere inside of my head. But it was not to be.

I gave up rather quickly, continued a little further down the hall, and saw an old rotten tile in the ceiling where water dripped constantly. The water had to have been working on the tile for some time, because there was now a hole in the ceiling that exposed an old cast iron pipe. This school was pretty old, and it had seen its share of history. My momma used to tell me black kids were never allowed to come here. Now that it was run down, it seemed no one minded.

I walked by the principal's office, and I was feeling pretty good. Normally I would stop there, but not today. I kept going through the auditorium, and I could hear my footsteps as they bounced off the wall. The hallways were now empty except for me.

When I finally opened the counselor's door, an impatient and elated Mrs. Rogers welcomed me with her usual hug and kiss on the cheek. She informed me my momma had called and said I could be part of her gifted class. I acted thrilled because I did not want to be anticlimactic, but Momma and I had already decided I could be a part of her program.

As a matter of fact, I never said a word. I never said anything about my doubts of failing or the uneasy feeling I had of not really being gifted. I had to believe in Mrs. Rogers, because I had been conditioned not to believe in myself. I had to believe she would not lead me the wrong way. My journey to scholastic achievement apparently began with her. It was only fair that she was in charge until its finale.

She gave me her supplemental lesson plans. It was a list of remedial classes I would have to take. She was not going to give me a free ride. Work, work and more schoolwork were all I could be about. It was a straightforward, old-fashioned, hard-work-I-did-not-want-to-do game plan.

The whole time I looked at the paper, I wondered, "What have I gotten myself into this time?" I never said it, but I also thought, "How could I have succumbed to doing all this extra stuff?"

I had just given away all my free time and most of my summer, too. I should have held out and probably would have gotten a much better deal.

I now knew I needed a book bag--no, a croaker sack--to carry all the stuff I needed. I thought back to my locker and knew I had to find the combination to that lock or have it cut off. All of these things were running through my mind, as well as me having to set a new standard for myself. I doubted I could do it, and felt I had bit off a little more than I could chew. I thought about Momma and her ultimatum of my butt going sky high. A date with the sugarberry switch would be my consequences of failure.

While my mind explored all these things, Mrs. Rogers hugged and softly kissed me on the cheek once again, leaving a match to the other barely visible crimson lip print on my dark skin. I didn't believe I could do it, but she did. I knew I could not fail. If I failed, then so would she. I could not let it happen.

I scanned the sheet of paper Mrs. Rogers had given me with the additional classes again. I took a deep breath and said to myself, "This is not that bad."

I knew it could have been much worse for me. The classes were dispersed throughout the week, so I would not be overwhelmed. I would just have to get my act together fast.

The whole thing was awkward at first. I stumbled around trying to keep up with my books and assignments due for each class. It was as if I was a colt just trying to walk after birth. Like the foal, the steps I took were difficult, but I had to make them. If not, the predators were at my door ready to devour me.

It was the law of the jungle. The strong survived and moved on. The weak were left to be prey for scavengers. I knew everyone was watching me and would descend upon me in a moment's notice, if given the opportunity. Even with all these things going on around me, I pressed on.

In my struggles to achieve scholastically, I sometimes inadvertently left things behind. Teachers constantly called me back to pick up something. I was lost. The routine things the average kids kept up with, I did not. Things that were essential to the scholarly kids, I often had to try to borrow.

From one class to the next, I had to borrow books, pencils and paper. I was always missing something. I had no sense of composure. If I ever stopped to think, I would have realized everything was probably somewhere in the book bag Mrs. Rogers had bought me.

Doubt crept into my mind again and whispered to me that I could not do it. I would fail. It told me I was out of my league. And I was starting to listen and wanting to cop out. I, always apparently by mistake, would just leave my bag somewhere. It happened so much people must have thought I did it on purpose. Their thinking was right. The old bag was too cumbersome. Deep down I didn't want to be bothered with it or school in this manner.

"John," a voice would call as I exited a door. "Come back and get your bag."

Try as I might, I was not able to outrun the speed of sound. I had become notorious for leaving it behind, and teachers had actually begun to keep an eye on me for such things.

Being one of the most famous students in school was not easy. I was the great experiment, and everybody watched me for any hint of success or failure. The weight of the world, or at least it seemed the weight of mine and Mrs. Rogers' world, was on my shoulders. The pressure that was on me was tremendous as I started to read into people's body language. They just seemed to pat their feet or stare at me in an uncomfortable fashion, wishing I made up my mind on whether I could handle academics or not. They didn't care which; all they wanted me to do was just pick one.

Definitely not used to this scholarly type stuff, I persevered, wishing I could have been the mentally slow John again. It would have been great.

However, I knew I could not go back to being that person, because a couple of people saw something in me. I sometimes wished they hadn't, because I now had no time to myself. My life was more rigid and revolved around my studies.

I worked on assignments at school and at home. In addition to all the extra work, I still had to do my chores. I had no time for leisurely reading of the encyclopedia anymore. Everything had structure and order, and it had to be this way if I was ever going to make up lost ground.

Six months later, after satisfactory progress, it appeared I was finally over the hump and was now getting the opportunity to meet my peers. It seemed Mrs. Rogers thought I had progressed better than expected, and it was time for me to join the ranks of the gifted.

She pulled me out of homeroom and took me to a small building adjacent to the school. The building was right next to the kindergarten building and was not too impressive. I was not overwhelmed at all by the structure, to say the least and asked myself, "Is this it?"

I don't know what I expected to see but this wasn't what I imagined. This was a place I thought was an old storage building. This structure could not be an indication of what being gifted was all about. I thought the gifted would have the finest of everything. I didn't understand how they could be expected to make a Rolex with a hammer and nail.

I managed to hide my disappointment when Mrs. Rogers told me to report for class here, and not to my homeroom on Wednesday mornings. She smiled at me and opened the door to reveal students sitting calmly in their desks, not really saying much to each other.

Everyone there was reading newspapers and magazines, and trying not to disturb their classmates. If they were not reading, they appeared to be looking over homework assignments.

This was not like my homeroom. My homeroom was a zoo. If a teacher was not present, then paper, pencils, and a whole lot of bad words would be hurled about. I knew it to be so, because I was the target of most of their ordnance. I did not know exactly what to make of all of this good conduct. These students appeared to be well mannered as if somebody actually raised them.

I stepped just inside the doorway and quietly took a seat and looked around the room at the other students. They, in turn, looked at me, trying to discover what they could about their new classmate.

Their gaze was not a menacing stare, like the one I received from my traditional homeroom class. It was an inquisitive look of discovery that did not intimidate me. In fact, the look they gave, I reflected back to them as if we were all looking in a mirror.

Mrs. Rogers took a seat at her desk and called the roll. Everyone was present today. Every one of these students was present every day. These kids simply didn't miss school. I recognized a few of their names because they always made the honor roll and perfect attendance. I was finally putting the names with faces that looked familiar. I had seen them around the school, but only when I passed them on the playground or in the hallways.

These were your Area 51-type students. It's like they were top secret. The fact they were meeting here in apparent secrecy told me this program was something that the federal government had to be working on.

Mrs. Rogers asked me to stand up and tell the class a little about myself. She gave me general instructions by telling me there were two questions I should answer in my statement. She told me to tell the class what things I liked to do, and my goals in life.

I didn't know what I liked to do. And I had never really given much thought about my goals in life. I just wanted to graduate high school. That was all Momma ever said she wanted for us.

I stumbled through my introduction by saying, "My name is John Johnson, and I like reading and sports. My goal in life is to graduate high school and to make my momma proud, because she wants all her children to get a high school diploma. As far as what I want to do…" I paused and thought for a minute and then said, "I haven't given much thought as to what I want to do."

I quietly took my seat and looked up at Mrs. Rogers as if I was asking, "Is that enough?"

Mrs. Rogers smiled, and without saying a word, looked at the other students, and one by one they stood up and introduced themselves to me. It was a routine they probably had rehearsed a while.

They told what they liked without much thought or effort. Some said the same as I did as to the reading and sports part. Others ventured off and said poetry, music, and chess, just to name a few. But they all had definite plans about their goals in life even at this age. It was so much more than just to graduate high school. They were saying they wanted to be doctors, lawyers, journalists, and educators. I was impressed as to how articulate and composed they were and felt as though I was in the wrong room. I was quiet and reserved and had a feeling of inadequacy that radiated from my very bones.

Mrs. Rogers looked at me, and the seat I had chosen for myself. It was off to itself by the door. I had never ventured more than two paces into the room. Everyone else's seat was over on the far wall. She asked me to come over and join my new classmates. Reluctantly and slowly, I gathered my things and walked across the room and sat down and listened as she began to discuss the term paper assignment she had assigned to the students. Her inquiry of the paper they were working on was in-depth. I had never heard of a footnote or endnote. What was a bibliography? I didn't know what a term paper was.

Mrs. Rogers concluded this part of her lesson by telling them she would walk them back to the city library for some more research. She was constantly thinking outside of the box for her students. I was impressed with all their liberties and freedoms. These kids were walking all uptown. We were not allowed to cross the street to get the ball! They had it good.

Mrs. Rogers then asked if everyone had brought his or her Coke bottle. There was a rustling of bags and each child produced a Coke bottle. They placed it on their desk directly in front of them. She smiled and began to make the plaster of Paris.

The talented teacher then laid strips of cloth of all colors and textures on a large round table, and then reached into a box and grabbed several bottles of paint and a couple of handfuls of paintbrushes.

She looked at me and smiled, as if to say, "watch this." She asked the class if anyone had an extra bottle for me. All the bags rustled again, and each student pulled out another one. She smiled and said, "Well, John needs a bottle."

All were willing to share their extra bottle. I walked to the first desk and the occupant willingly surrendered his with a big smile. No one at school had voluntarily shared with me before, and this small action said a lot to me.

The art session continued, and I fumbled through my creation. It was a horrible thing that looked spooky and scary. It could not, or should not have been what I was trying to achieve. Mrs. Rogers had specifically asked for a clown. This thing was no clown.

I looked around the room at the other dolls being made and they looked like clowns. They looked like the dolls collectors would buy. If a psychiatrist looked at mine, he would surely conclude I was a disturbed young man. He would probably say my clown exemplified how I felt inside.

Sometimes inner feelings manifest themselves through art. My inner feelings were not too happy. A worried Mrs. Rogers still gave my clown praise, as she praised the rest of the students. The lady was super-smart. I thought she knew all and could do all. She was a hero to me.

The day went by smoothly, and I enjoyed my new class. It was even better than Mrs. Perryton's class. We did interesting things all day long. We ate lunch early and walked uptown to use the city library. There were virtually no arguments within the class. Whenever one would occur, it was quickly resolved with no hard feelings or animosity. This was the good life.

The gifted students all welcomed me readily as one of their own. Some even went out of their way to bring me up to speed on things. They found themselves spending more and more time with me. I had a personality and sense of humor, which grew on them. They found it refreshingly different. They judged me on the content of my character, and not by the color of my skin or economic background.

Somewhere in these events, a fire was ignited within me. The labor of education did not seem like hard time anymore. I took on the persona of my new associates, and failure was no longer an option.

Since failure was not an option, mediocrity became painful. My new desire for learning and excelling at school caused some people who had doubted me to take another look. I found myself impressing the teachers in school who had taken an interest in me from the day that it was revealed that I was gifted.

When I made the honor roll for the first time, it pleased Mrs. Rogers, but it pleased Momma even more. No more calls from the school system about derogatory things. When the neighbors called with their complaints, she now felt vindicated in defending my name.

However, she didn't get too many calls because all the drama ceased. I stopped fighting to hang with the guys who ran roughshod over the community. I operated in a much smaller, smoother ring and was considered a scholar, and loved this distinction.

As I turned my life around, Mrs. Brown stood on the sidelines watching in disgust. She did not like me, and it showed. What was her problem with me? I was just a child and I had done nothing to her. I meant her no harm. Just like the other kids, I thought she was pretty, but unlike them, I dared not tell her.

The things she did to me were terrible. She stood in the hall as I walked by so she could give me an intimidating stare or a dirty uppity look. She was contrary and just plain ignorant. How did she ever become a teacher? I felt she should be psychoanalyzed before she was let back into any classroom.

I was no longer assigned to her as a student, so I did the best thing possible, and simply stayed away from her at all costs. If she asked herself the question, "Why don't I like John?" and answered it, she would have probably chosen to change professions or to teach in a predominately white school.

She was a black racist. Not in the sense of her being prejudiced against other races, but she was prejudiced against the people that others perceived to be her own. Deep down she resented blacks of darker shades and probably considered herself "colored, or other," rather than African anything.

Chapter Six: The Spelling Bee

My performance in school only got better as time elapsed. I gained enough confidence to participate in the spelling bee. Even though Mrs. Brown was in charge, I wanted to participate and win the contest. In some strange way, I thought it would cause Mrs. Brown to look at me favorably.

I was more confident in myself, because Mrs. Rogers had told me not to let anyone or anything hold me back. I was determined to sign up and had all the confidence in the world I would win. Spelling was my strong suit, and I was the self-appointed inside favorite to win it all.

With this resolve in mind, I strolled up to the sign-up sheet in the hallway, and began to write my name. Mrs. Brown watched me for a moment and then smugly informed me it was an after-school event, and there were no buses running late in the evening to take me home. As I began to mark my name out, she seemed to blossom in the disappointment showing in my face.

She turned and walked away with her nose in the air, leaving me alone, totally disappointed, staring at the blot that used to be my signature. My face was bare of any emotions as I tried to pull myself together. I was standing there for the world to see when Mrs. Rogers turned the corner and saw me looking lost in the hallway and knew for some reason I was miserable.

"What's wrong, John?" she asked.

She gave me a hug and kissed me on my cheek, showing her typical motherly concern.

I told her all about my quest of winning the spelling bee and how I was not able to compete because it was an after-school event and I had no ride home. She looked at the scheduled date of the spelling bee and made up a quick lie.

"John, I have to be here late that day and I will take you home, if it's all right with your momma."

My face began to glow when she uttered these words.

She cautioned me again, "Only if it's alright with your momma."

I hugged her tightly, signed up again, and ran down the hall to my class, which prompted her to smile and say, "Stop running in the hallway, John."

I stopped, slowed down, and turned to face her with a smile as wide as the Pacific itself. Still traveling, although backwards, I waved at my benefactor.

Mrs. Rogers had a way of making everything all right and going out of her way to help me, even though she didn't have to. I no longer viewed her as just a white lady; I now viewed her as my friend because she had started to destroy all the stereotypes of white people I had developed.

I wanted her not to have any kids. I wanted her all to myself because I was enjoying her motherly affection. I was thinking maybe she thought of me as her child, but then thought better of it, because there was no way a white lady could look at a black child like that.

When class was finally over, it was time to go home. It had been the last period of the day, and I hurried outside to catch the bus. All I thought about on the way home was asking my momma about the spelling bee, and what she would say.

I arrived at the house and did my chores and even worked on cleaning the yard a little, as well as cleaning my room. This is probably a trait in all children. We do a lot of little extra things to make it hard for adults to tell us no.

When I finished the extra work, I sat down on my bed and started to do my homework assignments. I heard the truck as it fought its way into the yard. It wasn't dark outside and for some reason Momma was home. I didn't really care why; I just rushed to the door to meet her.

She looked around the yard and kind of smiled. She knew what was up when she saw me standing in the doorway. I started off by saying, "Mom--"

She cut me off and said, "I already know, and I told Mrs. Rogers yes. She called and I was home, and I told her you could compete in the spelling bee."

I was delighted and was grinning from ear to ear. I ran to my momma and squeezed her tightly around the waist. She gently pushed me away and laughingly said, "Stop, boy."

I knew she didn't really mean stop because her blushing face told me so. And I latched on even tighter. She felt good inside about me, and it was the first time I had hugged her in years.

She then told me, "Tell your sister I said Thursday she will do your chores for you."

Upon hearing this, I let out a loud hanging "Yeesss!"

This was getting better by the second. In fact, it couldn't have gotten any better, or could it?

About this time Diane and one of her friends came around the corner of the house and Momma said, "Never mind, I will tell her. Poot--" a nickname that Daddy had given her-- "I want you to do John's chores Thursday."

She had to be feeling a little womanish because she said, "John can do his own chores."

Momma, who had started walking up the steps, turned and asked, "What did you say?"

Diane thought about it, and said, "Nothing."

"That's what I thought you said," and Momma continued in the house after finishing her menacing stare.

I stood there mockingly grinning, showing my brilliant smile because I was wrong about things not being able to get any better. They just did.

I knew what I was doing was aggravating my sister, and this was just fine with me. Diane looked at me as if she was looking at Shotgun, and asked her friend, "Why do really black people always have such pretty teeth?"

I said nothing and seemed to grin harder. The smile that I sported at that time could have been used on a commercial for toothpaste, and I could have passed for their signature model.

When Thursday afternoon finally arrived, I was ready. I didn't study or anything. Words were ingrained in me. Momma had unwittingly armed me with an impressive vocabulary. The encyclopedias she had bought had a dictionary set I often looked through just for fun.

The day was going by slowly, but the time for the spelling bee had arrived. At the beginning of the event, I looked around the room, and it contained very few adults. There were a few white ones in the front row, cheering their kids on. I took a deep breath and knew this was it. It was now show time

I never expected to see so few people at a spelling bee. The contests I saw on the news always showed the rooms packed, but that didn't matter to me right now. I shrugged it off because I was there to win.

The contest finally started and it seemed easy enough for me. Initially, I answered most of the words without even thinking hard. Time slowly ticked by, as one by one the other kids dropped out. At five o' clock I looked around the room, and there were only two people left in the contest. It was the principal's niece from the high school, Trina Jordan and myself. The parents and supporters of the other kids had already left the building.

This meant bad news for me. Mrs. Brown and Trina's aunt were friends, and she was even giving Trina a ride home after the spelling bee. This thought made me frown at the two conspirators.

Trina had spelled easy words all day, and I felt I was getting shafted. I had answered tough words from the moment the room emptied, and it seemed to me they were only getting tougher. I was struggling to survive and she kept getting easy words. I felt she had misspelled a couple, but there was no way I could challenge her. Mrs. Brown had said she was right, and we were the only three in the room.

It was 5:15 p.m. and I was already way past tired. Mrs. Brown said, "John, spell <u>diphyodont</u>."

I took a deep breath and tried to break it down into syllables in my head. I had never heard of the word before and knew I was stumped. I started out by saying, "D-i-p-h-i, no wait, d..."

"You missed it, John. Trina, you are the spelling bee winner!"

I looked at her with a certain look of disdain in my eyes. I was angry and wanted to tell her I knew I could spell "bitch" without a doubt, but somehow managed to hold this statement somewhere deep in my gut. I labored to breathe and my face looked like a thundercloud. I was livid. I grabbed my book bag and left the room, disgusted about the whole thing.

I hurried to Mrs. Rogers' office and told her I was finished. She asked me how I did. She knew I didn't win, because it showed on my face. I told her I lost because Mrs. Brown didn't like me. I didn't know why, but she didn't want me to win. I told her it was probably because I was too black for her.

Mrs. Rogers did not know where my accusation came from, but she tried to comfort me anyway. She told me I had to be gracious in defeat as well as in victory. This wise woman told me I had to be even-tempered.

These words fell on deaf ears because I was so upset with Mrs. Brown and the whole spelling bee thing. In my mind I had been wronged, as I had been so often.

For once, Mrs. Rogers seemed not to know what to do or say to make it better. To her, being a white person, she saw blacks, no matter what the shade of their skin, as being Negro. Her view of the world probably broke people down into four categories: white, black or Negro, Asian and Hispanic.

To even contemplate the idea of black on black discrimination was simply unthinkable. Our whole race had been through so much; she could not fathom us discriminating against each other.

She did not know how to advise me on my perceived dilemma because it was alien soil to her. The look on her face told me she wanted to help me, but could not. In her mind, I was probably becoming her child. She had voluntarily taken on the problems I faced, and I was now at the top of her agenda and thoughts. It hurt her to see me in distress. The situation had her stumped, and there was nothing she could do about it.

The ride home was silent, except for the sound of the road whispering through the partially opened window. It seemed to mock me, shouting loudly and reminding me I couldn't do it. The word I couldn't spell seemed to be on the wind circulating into the car. DI-PHY-O-DONT carried on the air and clung to my memory.

I felt, if given the chance, I would have gotten the word right. I had looked it up in the pocket dictionary Mrs. Perryton had given me and thought, "If I had a little more time I would have worked it out."

I knew I would have spelled the word right.

The ride was going quickly. Mrs. Rogers seemed to be driving a little fast. If I stopped thinking of my problems for a moment, I probably would have noticed my mentor really didn't have the time on her hands she said she did.

Nonetheless, I continued to think of myself. It just seemed to me I was the best opportunity for the school to win. Trina was not that smart. The green-eyed monster of jealousy was enveloping me.

Winning the spelling bee was something I wanted really badly, and it escaped my grasp. Why would anyone want someone not qualified to represent them?

This was a mind-numbing conundrum I never solved to my satisfaction. I connected the dots and developed a conspiracy theory that intuition told me was true: Mrs. Brown had to have thought I was too dark to represent the school.

We reached my house, and Mrs. Rogers pulled me gently by my arm when I opened the car door. She reminded me once again I would not always win, and I must be gracious in defeat as well as victory.

I was still cross and I pulled solidly away, and gave a little extra effort in closing the car door. It wasn't really a slam, but a little something additional to show my anger. I was so involved in myself, that I didn't bother saying thanks.

I quickly hurried into the house and never cared to look back over my shoulder at my heartbroken teacher. I wrestled with many things, and I wasn't coming up with reasonable conclusions. This world I was living in was a crazy place, and it seemed to me like there was no justice left.

I made up in my mind to never forgive Mrs. Brown for her treatment of me when I competed in the spelling bee. It would stay with me forever. No longer would I try to win her approval or tolerance. I had come to the conclusion people like her would never like my kind.

I had never done anything to her but admire her from afar. I thought she was pretty like all the other children, but she couldn't see it, or perhaps she did, and didn't want me to think anything like that. It was obvious I was a vermin or something much worse to her. She would just as soon squash me than look favorably upon me in anything.

I struggled with these things, even though I didn't understand them. I couldn't turn to Mrs. Rogers in this matter because she didn't understand either. I knew she could not help me because this was virgin ground to her.

All I thought about was what Momma told me about light or mulatto people like her and how they thought they were superior. From what Momma told me, Jim Crowe was instituted for them too.

The seed of discontent had grown out of control in my heart. And the rest of the time I spent on the elementary and junior high level, I avoided her like the plague. I knew she did not have any use for me.

Mrs. Bullock did not like me, but she hated almost everybody. She was equal opportunity. She did at least start to tolerate me and show me no more apparent intentional malice. I had become more of an anomaly to her. I was someone to be watched and studied at the very least, someone that broke a stereotype.

My bastion of hope throughout his whole ordeal was Mrs. Rogers. She taught me things and showed me that all white people were not bad. Because of her, I couldn't put people in one basket and throw them into a ravine. This would mean I was throwing the baby out with the bathwater.

The lessons I learned from Mrs. Brown showed me because someone was classified as black, it didn't mean they were. I held to my belief of why she didn't like me, but at the same time I really didn't want to believe it.

I surmised whites' dislike for blacks came from ignorance. Black on black prejudice came from stupidity. These were the tenets upon which I had started to build my principle of everyday life and racial interactions.

During this time in my life, some of the things my momma told me about people were proven true. Some were proven false. Nonetheless, my view of the world was shaken. Some of my racial prejudices against others were now suppressed, because a white lady, out of professionalism or love, who could have left me to my own demise, had saved me from the outside world. In so doing, she had momentarily changed my life.

Mrs. Rogers walked me through my elementary and junior high years, and delighted in watching her flower blossom. I would have never made it through without her. She eventually left me, as I embarked on to high school and she followed her husband off somewhere.

Without her, I would have to battle new foes in another realm. The most turbulent years in anyone's life, the adolescent years, were what I had to deal with next.

For now it seemed my life was looking up. I still battled Diane at home, but I had to live with this. It was your typical cat and dog scenario that had carried over since my younger days. I still had my moments and run-ins with the neighborhood bullies as well, but I had learned to deal with them.

When the school system closed out the summer of my seventh grade year, I didn't know what the future held for me. I was going to the new high school. It was a consolidated school only two years old. The student body was going to be larger than anything school-related I had ever seen.

People would not know me. I would be only a number. There would be no gifted class to anchor me, because the only lady who ever taught it was gone. Hopeful her teachings and philosophy were all I would need, I charged into my final summer as an official grade school student.

An Emotional Uplifting

As the days go by and pass like years,
Your strong, and gentle voice drowns away my fears.

Happiness may be near, but for so long, it's been afar,
Yet from out of my dreams, my thoughts, and my prayer, here you are.

Life is so strange with its many twists and turns,
And every day my mind, my soul, my ears for your voice yearns;

Meaningful words you spoke to me and they were coming from your heart.
You never knew how much it meant to me and I embraced them for a new start.

You were an emotional uplifting... in me, confidence you quickly built,
On the mere foundation of your belief that I was an intellectual quilt.

A poem from *Heart Felt Words* by: Teresa Mitchell

In dedication to teachers that like teaching because they love helping children.

Chapter Seven: Summer Work

Momma was working harder than ever to provide for us. In addition to working her farm and hauling iron, copper, aluminum and other recyclable materials, she started her seasonal work on a large plantation-like farm system. She had even gotten me a job. The rest of my siblings turned down the opportunity to work the plantation. Their motto was, "Been there, done that, and wasn't going back again." They didn't want the money and elected to stay around the house.

They didn't share their ordeals on the farm with me. I had asked them why they chose not to work. All they told me was they had enough of working Momma's farm and were not about to venture outside in the heat any more than they had to. To them, working a white man's plantation was nothing more than slave labor. The work was difficult and the wages he paid were too paltry for them to consider.

I jumped at the opportunity to make some money. I did most of the stuff they considered "slave" labor around the house anyway. It was no big deal for me. I just wanted to make some cash for myself.

This particular summer, the sun was in a bad mood. It was extremely belligerent to everybody and everything. It was like an oven outside, and it baked me a few degrees darker, if at all possible. I busted my butt and watched "those" people laugh all day long while we worked in the heat of the summer sun.

Sometimes I wanted to say something, but I knew Momma would have me for lunch. I had a long list of grievances. Among them was the way we were trucked from one part of the farm to another at NASCAR speeds. Another one was their attitude toward us. It was appalling, to say the least. Everything seemed to have a racial undertone around this place, and I didn't like being here.

I quickly resented undertaking the Herculean task, and wanted out of my ordeal after a week or two. Momma was not hearing of it, however.

Bill, "Mr. Bill" as he liked to be called by the help, loved my energy. He raved to Momma that my output was that of two or perhaps three people. He had even given me a nickname. It was a name I wasn't too fond of, though. He had started calling me Rooster. Whatever that meant.

I felt when they gave you names like this, they were really making fun of you or something. It had to be an inside joke. To compound problems, Momma told a friend about it, and Diane overheard her. She began taking the liberty to badger me with the nickname.

"Rooooster, Momma wants you," she would say in jest.

I wanted to fight her every time that word came out of her mouth. It was annoying, and she knew it bothered the heck out of me, and that was fine with her.

The last straw that ended my brief stint on the plantation came at about 1:05 in the afternoon in early July. Until then, the only interaction I had with white people had been limited to their kids and teachers. Their kids were cool, and treated me far better than the black kids. They had not yet learned they were supposed to hate people of different physical features.

The white teachers, except for Mrs. Rogers, seemed mostly indifferent to black kids. They put the information out like they were feeding hogs. If we learned, fine. If we didn't, it was fine too. They didn't care one way or another. They guarded their true feelings and personalities as if they were Vulcans. These people acted as though they were incapable of any emotion of any kind. This was especially true when they dealt with black kids. It was a bad thing to say, but we had better be glad they did.

The situation our family was living in around this area was probably the norm everywhere. We lived in enclaves, and we were no different than anyone else. Momma shielded us as best she could from interaction with white people as much as possible. She didn't want any of us to say or do something that would be perceived as a slight to those folks. Crosses were still being burned and black people were still taken for a ride around here.

I had grown older, and now had a job. It was inevitable that I would meet the ugly face of true racism. It occurred when I backed the tractor up with a load of peaches and turned sharply to get them by the stand. Mr. Bill saw the angle at which I turned, ran over to me and started ranting and raving about me trying to tear up his tractor.

"What you trying to do, boy, break my axle? Are you dumb, boy? Get off my tractor before you tear it up!"

I had already seen the way he spoke with the white boy, Randy, who worked on the farm. It wasn't anything like this. Besides, he didn't make Randy go to the field to shake peanuts, pull weeds, or pick peaches. Randy stayed around the cabin with them laughing it up like he didn't have a care in the world and I resented Bill for this. Compound this with the fact Randy had told me what he made, and it was significantly more than me, and the whole thing smelled like trouble.

I hopped off the tractor huffing and puffing mad and looked at him in his cold, glassy blue eyes. Bill backed the tractor in and told me to get around there and unload the wagon. I did not, and continued to stare.

I was not a man. In actuality I was a boy, but I took exception to this word and the tone it carried instinctively. In those

World Book encyclopedias was a black history section. Between Momma and those books, I knew I wasn't having this stuff.

Bill tried to look through me, but could not. This "boy," as he called me, tried to look right through him. I had not learned I was supposed to fear this white man, and it was evident in the look of fury in my face.

"Rooster, I want you to unload that tractor, and I am not going to tell you again, boy."

I walked around to the back of the tractor, and at the time Bill thought he had put down my mini-insurrection. His tense red face seemed to relax a little. He removed his baseball cap and took his hand and slipped it through his slick sweaty black hair. He was glad the situation had been resolved because he would not have to teach Barbara's boy a lesson.

I was a feisty young man who would not let up and it would not be too easy, much to Bill's surprise and regret. When I reached the back of the tractor, I simply grabbed my thermos, walked over to the shade, removed my straw hat, and took a seat. I then unbuttoned my shirt, making myself as comfortable as possible, and proceeded to take about three big gulps of ice cold water.

Mr. Bill walked over and said, "I will fire you, boy!"

This is what I wanted to hear, and I casually poured some of the cold water over the top of my head and down the back of my neck. I purposely ignored him and the blood rushing to Bill's face told everyone this "boy" had started to get to him.

The situation was still escalating and beginning to spiral out of control. About this time, Momma stepped out of the orchard, and Mr. Bill immediately sent for her.

"Barbara, this boy of yours won't work. You need to talk to him."

She gave some offhand comment by saying, "Rooster is grouchy because he has not eaten, Mr. Bill. John, get over there and unload that trailer, and when you finish, come on over here and eat."

I looked up at her and still did not move. Momma felt she had to do something, and quickly pulled off her shoe. She was brandishing it at me, and making convoluted threats.

I looked at her with her shoe in her hand, and I reluctantly unloaded the tractor. Bill stood back with his chest filled with pride, thinking, "I showed that boy.

I am sure he felt like his great granddaddy must have felt at a time like this. His ancestor was a former slave owner and I had once read how blacks had to discipline themselves if the master said they needed to be punished.

Momma took a deep breath and tried to relax. She probably figured she saved my life, because a black man named Henry had almost lost his only a month earlier over his girlfriend. He had only been with her a couple of weeks, and something didn't seem right about her. Everyone knew her lifestyle and the black men in the community had urged him to leave her alone. They said she was going with white men and she was theirs and nobody else's. The rumor was Mr. Bill was one of them. They always said he didn't like those "boys" in his candy.

Henry did not listen, so he learned the hard way. The way he was beaten was shameful. He was left for dead somewhere in a bloody mess. Henry was big, tough and mean. If they did him like that, Momma probably imagined what it would have been like for me.

Me, I didn't see it like that. I thought Momma showed me up in front of the white man. I resented her for doing this. I didn't feel the danger because of my insulation from the white hate. I always said to myself if I had come up back then, white people would have to pick their own cotton, peaches and anything else they could think of.

I was young and didn't know any better. I probably would have worked harder for free, than I was for the little money I was getting now. The sugarberry switch didn't have anything on the whip.

I admit I didn't know the rules of the game. I had yet to learn that white hate was the most aggressive, cruelest kind. I had never really seen it unleashed, and I should have believed Momma when she told me I didn't want to.

I had seen the face of black hate, and had dealt with it all of my life. I knew how bad it was. I feared its displaced aggression and had no idea it came from being the lowest part of the societal totem pole.

Going home, Momma knew I was mad and told me she wanted me to work one more week, and then I could quit if I chose to do so.

This was probably her way of showing Mr. Bill there were no hard feelings, but they were there, probably on all three sides of the fence. There was no way possible the three of us could not help reflecting upon what happened on the plantation.

After the week was up, Momma was true to her word. I quit and she let David, my cousin, take over my job. He worked the remainder of the summer. I did not ask him how it was going, because I really didn't care. I was just glad my summer job was over.

The work opportunity wasn't short enough for me. I was glad to be rid of Mr. Bill and his damn plantation. I now knew why my sisters had turned down the opportunity for some extra cash. Sometimes no amount of money you make is worth the humiliation it takes to get it.

Somewhere in the summer's heat, I concluded I would never ever demean myself to make a few dollars. My pride was worth more than the little money I would earn to get by. I felt somewhere there was a job that would leave me with a little self-respect. If I did not find this job, then I would be unemployed.

Chapter Eight: Baseball

Toward the last third of the summer, my Uncle Larry approached me about playing baseball, just to give me something to do. He told me how much my daddy loved baseball, and I probably had it in me to play too.

Uncle Larry was a good-hearted man. He really wanted me to play sports because of the benefits it would bring me. I was a loner and he felt I needed to learn to interact with different kinds of people. He watched me as knew I worked all day long on the plantation, and then work at home. He knew how my lifestyle was because he had to live one far worse when he was growing up.

He thought I needed some sort of social life and had made up his mind he was going to give me one. Baseball was the perfect vehicle to get this done. He coached a Little League team and it had developed a little following because they were supposed to be unbeatable. He probably thought, "What better way to introduce John to the world than on a popular Little League baseball team?"

After he talked with me a little about it, I told my Uncle Larry all right, even though I was a little shy about playing. He told me he would pick me up at around 4:30 for my first game. I had never played nor practiced anything that looked like baseball.

Regardless of my lack of experience, I was waiting at 4:30 and casually walked out to meet his truck as it pulled into the yard. The truck was packed with ballplayers and equipment and it looked as though no space was left.

Larry hopped out, bent over, and looked me right into my eyes to try to build some enthusiasm in me. The undefeated coach enthusiastically asked me, "You ready to go, 'Big John'?"

I blushed and looked away. Larry patted me on my back and then grabbed me under my armpits, lifted me up into the air and told the passengers to square up and make room. They slid around, and I managed to squeeze in next to the cab and Jimmy.

There was an uneasy silence on the truck when I was introduced into the equation. It remained that way until Ricky decided he would start in on me again.

"John, welcome aboard. You might be black and smutty, but you're still my little chocolate buddy."

Everyone knew what Ricky was up to. Larry had already warned them some years back about messing with me. He told them he wasn't pleased with the way they bullied his nephew, and if they did it again, they could go play for someone else. There was no one willing to laugh with him, not even Jimmy, and silence gained a foothold on the back of the truck once again.

Moving quickly because we were a little behind schedule, the truck spit out a red plume of dust. We were moving at a good clip and the cloud of dirt mimicked a rocket's exhaust, as it exploded from the tires. The vehicle climbed quickly up and down the hilly roads.

We reached pavement, and traveled another twenty minutes, and he turned off onto another dirt road. On this little country thoroughfare we traveled; the trees had almost turned the road into a path. The branches constantly slapped and scratched at any and everybody. We huddled close together in the bed of the orange pickup truck to escape the aggressive limbs.

Uncle Larry never slowed, and traveled another forty-five minutes on a rough dirt road loaded with bumps that had been created by logging trucks digging into the tough sandy surface. The road was not like the hard red clay dirt roads I was accustomed to seeing around Brooklyn.

Larry had traveled so far that the ecosystem we were in had completely changed. It was now more of a wet and wild area. The air was unusually moist, and the smell of a large body of water nearby told us we had traveled a very long way. The older boys figured we had to be down close to an area like a river, lake or a marina.

We were tired of traveling on the bumpy road and were somewhat restless. The *umph* and *ahh* sounds coming from our lips seemed to insist that Larry slow down.

He did not, as he continued to drive at a very fast pace. Our coach was determined to make it to our destination to give us time to play ball before the sun went down.

Somewhere along the way a pungent odor forced its way into our nostrils and abused our olfactory senses. Some of the guys pulled their shirts up to cover their noses, and others used their gloves to try to eliminate the smell as best they could.

Some of us began to look at the older boys that were on the truck. The look on our faces asked, "Are we there yet?" But the veterans could not tell us anything because they had never been this far away from home before. They had never played this particular team, and they were just as lost as we were.

A few miles farther and we could see a river at the mouth of the road. There were cars and trucks going by where another road apparently intersected. We thought we had to be close to something other than the woods, and to us this was a good thing. Everyone began to look around to see if anyone had figured out exactly where we were. We looked for a store, a sign, or anything we could use as a marker to gather some information about our location.

The odor had become stronger than ever and saturated the air, slapping our nostrils with its stench. It no longer cared to tease us and finally revealed to our senses it was dead fish, and other animals that had been killed or died around the riverbank. The smell was so overwhelming one of the boys asked, "How do these people

live around here, man? This stuff stinks! I will be glad when we get
to where we are going."

In another moment or two, we finally reached a paved road.
The truck made a left, and we traveled until we reached an old bridge
that spanned the Chattahoochee River. On the right side of the road
across the bridge was a line of shotgun shacks. I thought they looked
like the slave quarters that were pictured in some of my books.
These were really substandard houses. I reasoned that these people
must still be sharecroppers.

Uncle Larry, who was a storyteller in the line of Davy
Crockett, said the houses had gotten their name from a dastardly
deed by a white man. He had told us that a rich white landowner was
upset over the production of a black family he had tilling the land for
him. He felt as though he was being cheated, and he shot into the
house at the black man with his shotgun.

He killed him, his wife, three kids, and a dog that was
standing on the porch peeking into an open back door. Hence the
name, shotgun shacks.

It didn't really matter if the story was true or not. Regardless
of the myth, these were the houses of legend. They looked like they
were made of rotting wood in the form of a long box. They had
never been painted. The only stain the wood ever received was from
the beating the weather put on them as they aged. Compared to
these houses, we lived in a mansion.

Just like the paintings in my books, the women were sitting in
their rockers shelling beans and black-eyed peas. The little kids were
hanging off the porch, playing and eating watermelons. We could see
the bend in the river on the other side of the houses, because they
had their doors open, trying to catch a breeze coming in off the water
on a warm summer's day.

This was our destination. When the truck slowed and turned down the steep incline that led down by the shacks, the kids leaped from the porch to run and greet us. They easily outran the old curs that joined in the chase without much effort. They ran alongside the truck in a euphoric state, as though they had never seen guests before.

Uncle Larry slowed his speed because he did not want any of them to get trampled under a truck tire. He was moving so slowly that we could have walked faster than the truck was now traveling. We turned again and were on a straight road leading only about three feet in front of the old houses.

Larry smiled at the women, who returned his smile with a frown. These women looked like they were hard and mad. Some could have been imprisoned with the men and it would not have been a big deal to them. Their whole demeanor told anyone that saw them that they were not as friendly as their kids.

He stopped at the last house on the row and asked about Big Robert Thornton. The women pointed to the bridge where a group of men were standing, fishing, and apparently drinking. We didn't dare get off the truck just yet and stayed safely tucked inside the body, and began to look for kids our own age to size them up before we played.

The only kids we saw were in the group of four-to eight-year-olds that ran to greet the truck. We could not figure out who we would be playing just by looking around this place. Evidently our adversaries hadn't gotten here yet.

Larry called out for Robert, and he yelled back, "I'm on my way!"

The crowd gathered under the bridge seemed to move and splinter apart from each other. Two guys moved with Robert, and the rest fanned out towards a large cow pasture in front of the row of shacks. We were astonished to see the group of guys who splintered off start to throw a baseball.

We looked a little closer and could see chicken wire stretching between two small saplings in the middle of the cow pasture.

"This is the field? Are these men supposed to be our age?" That's what we were asking ourselves.

The so-called children tossing the ball around looked like men. Those guys were huge. They were the boys from down by the river. "The River Boys," as they would come to be known, appeared to be genetically altered.

They were all huge guys, and their women weren't small either. Everything down there had facial hair and looked like men, including the women. They looked as though they had been bred to be big and tough.

Larry shook his head when he saw what we were up against. He told Robert they must have been putting something in their kids' water. He actually thought about asking for I.D.S.

We had never played a team like this before, and those guys looked as if they meant business. They were just as big as Larry, who stood about six feet two inches and weighed a little over two hundred pounds.

They were rugged and even their names told people they were tough. They had names like Crusher, Milk Shake, Bear, Tank, Big Mac, and T-Bone. Their voices sounded deep, and they played with their daddies' equipment.

Our team could barely handle a bat of our grown-ups, and these boys swung their daddy's bats like mop handles. It didn't look too good for our Little League team at this point in time.

Larry didn't say much, because he knew we were in trouble. He was uncharacteristically quiet when he counted up his players and had only nine at his disposal, not counting me. He was now trying to procrastinate a while. A friend was supposed to meet him here with four more of his bigger guys.

After another forty-five minutes and a little prodding from Robert, he knew our time had run out and he would not be receiving any reinforcements. The sun was setting and we had to play. He started to divide the team up based on the other team's strengths.

He told Jimmy, who was his slowest player, he had to go to right field. He was going to try to hide him. The River Boys were mostly right-handed, and by the way they swung their bats they were more likely to pull the ball hard to left field.

Jimmy shook his head, saying, "I can't do it, Mr. Larry. I can't play outfield today."

"What? Why not?"

Jimmy bashfully said, "Naw, not today, coach, it's too many stickers and sandspurs out there for me. I can't do it."

Larry gave him a peculiar look and said, "Boy, you got to go out there, you got on shoes. What's the matter? Are you scared?"

Jimmy dropped his head and pointed towards his shoes. The shoes he wore appeared to be brand new Chuck Taylor All-Stars.

He looked up at his coach and was almost ashamed to show him, but held his feet up to reveal they had practically no soles. He was basically walking on the ground.

Larry began to sweat because he knew he was really up against it. He couldn't ask this child to go out there in that situation. All his guys were not here to give him the flexibility he needed, so he was in a quandary. He looked around and saw me sitting on the old oak log, which was supposed to be the dugout bench.

"John, come here," Larry barked out.

I snapped to and ran over to my uncle.

"Jimmy, give John your glove."

Jimmy did, and Larry told me I would have to play right field. My eyes bucked, and I told my uncle I did not know how to play ball.

Larry looked me squarely in my eyes and told me about how my daddy had never played the game before and had never practiced. They were short a player and needed a shortstop. My dad stepped in, played an error-free game, and hit two home runs to win the game for them, two to zero.

My chest filled with pride as I took the glove and charged into right field. I felt as though I could do it because Larry thought being athletically gifted ran in the Johnson family, and I had to be a chip off the old block.

Once the game started, the contest played out rather quickly. There was not a whole lot of scoring. The game had become kind of a bore to me. No balls came my way in the field, and I was merely trying not to be hit by a pitch when I was at bat. They could have lobbed three pitches up to the plate, and I wouldn't have swung.

The River Boys were throwing so hard, and I was so scared of that ball I almost openly questioned my decision to play. Everyone could see it in my eyes and in the way I acted. This was not what I pictured baseball to be.

They knew they had a patsy when I came to the bat. To show me up and get a few laughs, Milk Shake threw his famed looping lizard. It was nothing more than a wicked curve ball that ran at the batter, and then darted back in for a strike over the plate at the last second.

He threw the ball at me, and I was so scared and jumped so far out of the batter box that the hecklers in the crowd hysterically laughed at me. They kidded Larry about the pseudo-fact I ran halfway home.

It embarrassed Larry, but I didn't care. I just wanted to get my turn at bat over. I didn't want to be hit by the ball because it was as hard as a rock.

More than half the game had passed, and both of our teams combined generated one run. David hit a solo shot, and it looked as though it would be enough for Brooklyn to win. It was the bottom of the seventh, and there were two outs.

I was wandering in too close in right field. I was harassing a butterfly that was flying about my head, and pulling stickers and sandspurs from my jeans. I had not noticed someone had been walked, and Fred had gotten tired on the mound. It only took a moment from us going home undefeated to us losing a game.

There came a big crack of the bat that grabbed my attention. Uncle Larry yelled out, "John!"

I looked up to see a ball hit on a line bearing down on me hard. I zeroed in and broke down at the knees, trying to gauge exactly where the flight of the ball was headed. It seemed to be caught up in a crosswind coming off the river. The ball traveled really fast and mirrored Milk Shake's looping lizard. It landed about fifteen yards past me and bounced deeper into the field. I knew the game was on the line and took off after it. I pulled up shortly after I got into my sprint.

A big bull had wandered onto the field. I was not willing to go and get the ball that had stopped about ten feet from the beast. The River Boys laughed and challenged us to throw them out. They laid down on third base, got up and strutted, did their best imitation of the wrestler Ric Flair, and sat down again.

Finally, they literally rolled over home plate and ended the traumatic experience. They basked in the joy of victory, and for the first time, Brooklyn's hearts dwelled in the sewers of defeat.

They joined me in dropping my head and moping about the whole thing. Somehow we managed to force ourselves over to shake the River Boys' hands.

No one said much on the way home. I felt bad about the whole thing. I had caused my teammates a loss. None of us knew what to say or how to act. They never had to deal with losing before, and it was their first taste of defeat as a team.

Larry could have put a positive spin on the event by telling us how hard we played, and we did well for being short-handed, but he seemed to be taking it harder than we were. He didn't bother to try to salvage anything out of our loss at this time. No one liked to lose, especially when it had never happened before.

It was dark and late when I finally got home. I hopped off the truck, and no one said anything to me, not even Uncle Larry. This hurt me more than all the sandspurs pulling at my skin through my jeans. I moped in the house and barely noticed the truck out of place. If I had looked up, I would have seen the back of a Cadillac protruding from the corner of the house.

I didn't notice a thing because my head was still hung in shame. When I finally opened the door, I saw my momma laughing and talking with a light skinned, well-built man. The two of them were still laughing it up when I walked in.

The man finally caught his breath after a joke, which I neither heard nor cared to hear, and asked Momma, "Barbara, is that little Johnny?"

She said, "Yeah, that's him," and then she asked, "Who won, son?"

To which she fully expected me to say, "We did."

But I shocked her by saying, "We lost because of me," and left it at that.

The man at the table said, "Well, Larry finally lost one, then?"

I had never seen this guy before and was still trying to figure out who he was supposed to be. And how did he know anything about Uncle Larry or me?

When I came close enough to him, he grabbed me by the hand and gave it a firm squeeze. He then told me his name was Sonny and he was my cousin.

I looked over my shoulder and into my room, and saw my bed inhabited by a couple of my sisters. I then looked on the floor by my bed, and I saw that a pallet of blankets had been laid out on the floor for me. It looked like the guy would be our guest, and I didn't know for how long.

I knew the routine and never said a word. I went into the kitchen and there were no leftovers, and I was kind of agitated. Momma noticed my displeasure when I walked by and asked me if I wanted her to fix me a hamburger.

I said, "No, I am all right."

Even though I really wanted one, I decided to do without. The fact that my momma noticed I could be hungry and asked about feeding me made the loss of a meal better.

I made my way into the bathroom to take care of my personal hygiene. I carefully removed the sticker-ridden clothes, and picked the sandspurs and briars off my pants before depositing them in the clothesbasket. I wiped myself off and prepared to get some sleep and tried not to think about our guest that would be residing in my oldest sister's bed.

I lay down and couldn't sleep. I was still beating myself up over the loss. To distract myself, I decided to listen to the conversation taking place in the living room. I had become the center of all the talk since I walked in. Momma had shifted the topic of the discussion to me, her downtrodden son.

She said, "Ole Rooster in there is getting a little spunk about himself. He looked just like Jay when he sat down on the job because he said Mr. Bill fussed at him. Rooster said he didn't like the way Mr. Bill had called him 'boy.'"

And she began to laugh heartily, as she tried to gather her thoughts to tell Sonny about what happened afterwards. My lips crunched together and puckered out as though I had been sucking on a lemon. I now saw where Diane got her backwards humor.

I cringed as she began to tell another story about me and said, "Rooster--"

Sonny cut her off and asked her who had given me this name. She proceeded to tell him about the name and where it came from and finished off some of the details she left out with my run-in with Mr. Bill. She told him how she had to pull her shoe off and threaten "Rooster" to get me to go back to work.

There was a strong chance Sonny didn't find it funny. He was originally from the South and lived with the name "boy" and a whole lot worse. He also felt no one should fuss at anyone on a job. He knew where I was coming from on this point, and he didn't share in my momma's laughter. To him it was no laughing matter. He would have handled it much differently, but he didn't tell her that.

Momma changed the subject because he allowed her to laugh by herself. She then told him she had just managed to buy herself a few acres of land in Cusseta. It had been a dream of hers and Jay's. It was her way of letting him know that she knew where he was coming from, and it was her way of telling him where she was going.

Her innuendo meant sometimes you got to put up with stuff that you don't like so that you can get to where you want to go.

She became a little more direct and said, "I put up with stuff, so that my children won't have to. No matter what happens to me, the house and land will be theirs to do with as they will. And as for

John who don't want to work, he can take his little butt right on up there with his sisters, starting tomorrow, and begin knocking the mortar off those bricks and cinder blocks that I got from the dump. When they finished with that, they can go and help tear down those old houses that Mr. Bill gave me on the backside of the farm. I will need the plywood, floor seals, rafters, and the two-by-fours out of them, because we are going to renovate this house and build a brick house up there on that land. They can start on all of that tomorrow. Since they don't want to work for Mr. Bill, I have found something that they can do for me for free."

They talked a little while longer and Momma excused herself from his company and went to lay down. She had to go to work tomorrow, and she needed her rest.

Sonny stayed up a little while longer, straining his eyes trying to make out the fuzzy images on the box in front of him. It was really hard for him to believe this thing was supposed to be a television set. It struggled to pick up reception, and he gazed hard at the distorted images it was putting out. Soon, he was tired of looking at the fuzz and went to bed as well.

Chapter Nine: The Fourth Sunday in August

The next day we started to work on our new job assignment, and we did our chores as well. Working in Cusseta and not getting paid was still better in my opinion than working on Mr. Bill's plantation. I hated him, and if Bill knew how much, he probably would make me disappear too, like it was rumored he had made so many others. If he didn't make me vanish, he would have made me wished I had. Everyone said Bill was an old-school racist. He would punish a black man if he got the chance.

From Monday on, whether we wanted to or not, we were up every day, working hard and I had not the slightest hint I would ever play baseball again. I never let the first loss deter me from wanting to succeed at the sport. I had failed and looked so bad doing it, that it left a bad taste in my mouth. I voluntarily took up the task of practicing by myself. I had sifted through the books my momma had brought from the dump and found a few on how to play baseball. I read the books and picked up pointers and made a practice field for myself. Even though Larry never asked me about playing again, I had other plans.

I was a driven young man and I was determined to be good at baseball like he said my daddy was. I started practicing immediately after work. I always got home about dark. Through ingenuity, I managed to salvage what light I could to get in some practice. My sessions were short and compact. Whatever particular skill I was trying to hone, I would somehow get it done.

I first attempted to fix my inability to judge a fly ball. This was the big one and it caused us the loss. I bought myself four super-rubbery balls that bounced really high from the store in Brooklyn and laid a piece of plywood against the storage house at a sixty-degree angle. I then took these balls and threw them against the plywood as hard as I could. After they ricocheted off at a sharp angle, I ran under them and made the catch. I practiced hard at this skill and it devoured most of my time.

After I was somewhat comfortable doing this, I taught myself how to use a bat. I took an old broomstick and began to build my hand-eye coordination by throwing my small jack ball into the air and hitting it, always taking the time to look the small ball into my stick. Eventually I became good enough to pick out the exact spot the ball made contact with the surface of the handle.

While doing this, I always tried to hit the storage building so the ball would bounce back to me. If I ever missed, the ball was so rubbery that it would easily bounce into the woods on the other side of the road. If that happened, there was no chance of finding it before the light faded.

I always practiced under the watchful eye of my sister Diane. She constantly watched me for any wrong move, and she was rewarded for her vigilance when the ball inadvertently bounced onto Sonny's smooth ride. It didn't do any damage, but she didn't waste any time when Momma returned to tell her what I did. She didn't bother to tell Sonny because she knew that guy wouldn't do anything. She thought he was too cool.

Taking matters into her own hands, Diane did what she felt was right and reported it straight to the top, without going through the chain of command. She intentionally told Momma right in front of Sonny, hoping that he would frown and show his displeasure. She expected the facial expressions he made would act as a catalyst to ensure I got what she felt I deserved.

When Barbara heard the report, she was warm. She told Diane to go and get me. And that's just what she did. Diane did not call out this time or send my little sister; she went on this mission herself. She approached me and spoke composed and relaxed, so she would not alert me as to what might be up.

Diane said, "John, Momma said come here."

"What does she want?"

"I don't know," she replied. "Go see."

Her plan might have worked, if not for one thing. She did not expect Sonny to argue my case with Momma.

I turned the corner, and Momma apparently had gone from being lukewarm to boiling hot waiting on me. She started in on me almost immediately.

"John, you can't find no better place to play than around Sonny's car?"

My head dropped because I knew Diane had told on me again.

"Can you?" she asked.

I replied in a timid voice, "Y'am."

"Well, I think you need to do just that."

Sonny spoke up and told Momma, "Don't be so hard on him, Barb. He didn't mean to do it. John, you need me to move my car?"

I did not say anything and continued making my way out the door, still sulking about my reprimand. Just as I was about to step outside, Sonny threw me the keys and told me to move the car out of my way. A smile exploded onto my face and I couldn't hold back my joy. I was getting a chance to drive Sonny's car, "the playa mobile," as it had come to be known. Diane's plan had backfired once again. She was not the highly touted CIA operative she thought she was after all. The proxy agent had failed.

After I moved Sonny's prized car, barely missing the storage house, much to Diane's chagrin and Sonny's relief, I then continued practicing. I painted a square bull's-eye on the side of the small shed with a can of spray paint I found lying about in Momma's junk pile.

132

Inside this bull's-eye I painted smaller square rings. When I finished, it looked like a bizarre dartboard.

I then backed up about forty yards and threw one of my bigger balls on a line to test the strength and accuracy of my arm. I did this for two or three weeks. I practiced until it was too dark to see. I did this diligently every day because I wanted to succeed at being a baseball player.

Sonny watched me and saw how consumed I was with practicing. The thing that amazed him most was that I was doing all of it by myself. He wanted to see me do well and often found it hard to resist giving me a pointer or two. He told me that he was a coach in New Jersey and worked with kids for a living. He told me I had potential and he thought it was good that I practiced the way I did.

Sonny had the right profession because he had a sharp eye for talent and a patient hand. He hadn't been here to witness what happened down by the river, so I decided to ask him what would happen to a guy playing for him if he ever caused him a loss.

I gave him the scenario and spilled the beans about what happened. I told him I had messed up big time, and I was determined to redeem myself. I was practicing hard so I would be prepared for one thing, the big game on the fourth Sunday in August after church.

Sonny smiled and winked at me and showed his gold tooth and told me everybody loses. It's what they do with the lessons of a loss that counts.

"You shouldn't beat yourself up because errors are a part of the game. If they weren't, then they would not have a stat for them."

He continued to smile and told me, "I am sure Larry will let you play ball, so if I was you I wouldn't worry too much about that. When you get another chance, just do your best and that's all anybody can ask of you. Now, speaking of church, that's what I am here for."

He stretched and continued to smile at me, as he seemed to reminisce about everything associated with a Baptist church in the South. This particular fourth Sunday was a special gathering event for Brooklyn. It was a religious get-together when everyone came home from all over the country just to go to church. They ate, drank, and had a good time reminiscing. This was why Sonny said he was home. It was his first fourth Sunday in some time.

He said he had not been home since shortly after my daddy died. This explained why I did not know him. He was supposedly my momma's cousin and my dad's best friend, but I only knew my immediate bloodline of first cousins and no further. I wasn't really thrilled to know them and found it hard not to tell them at times. I felt they were just ignorant black folks trapped in a time warp.

Sonny appeared to be different. He talked with me and didn't ridicule me or anyone else under any circumstances. At the same time, he was typical of what I thought light-skinned people to be.

He was considered a pretty boy. He had his wardrobe hanging in the back window on a steel bar that he had jerry-rigged into a closet. The pole ran from one side of the window to the other, and his clothes were neatly arranged on it. I had gotten a chance to peek at the labels on the inside of some of the suit jackets, and the material was silk and various textures of wool. There were several expensive hats displayed neatly in the back window as if they were awards. Sonny had expensive shoes as well. He had all kinds sitting neatly in rows on the back seat. There was also a small bag, which probably contained his socks and underwear he had stashed neatly away on the floorboard between the back and front seat. I didn't

134

know how long he was going to stay. He had been here a while and I suspected he would probably be leaving after the Fourth.

I never was satisfied with developing the skills that I needed and felt I needed more time to practice, but all the weeks and days were now gone, and the fourth Sunday of August was finally here. Everyone was dressed in his or her Sunday finest, and they looked good.

All the men were dressed similar to Sonny, although he was the smoothest there. Each and every man had his wide-brimmed hat with a small feather stuffed in it. They each had a handkerchief folded neatly in the breast pocket of their suit coat, as if it was a military regulation. The shoes were some of the most expensive I had ever seen. They were made of all types of leather, from patent to alligator to regular cowhide. Most wore the shiny Stacey Adams or some other famous brand. The suits were a plethora of colors, ranging from a myriad of pastels to the deepest of earth tones.

Dispersed throughout the range of colors was an occasional plaid or pin-striped suit. These guys were big time. They probably had been saving their money for a while just to buy the wardrobes they were wearing. I found it hard to believe black people could afford clothes on this level.

The women, however, stole the show. They looked as though they had mugged a peacock with the way they had the brightly painted feather plumes nestled around the center of their hats. Their dresses were made of the most vibrant of colors and seemed to hang and caress their physiques as if they had them custom-tailored. They walked about in shoes with the heels so high in them, they were more akin to stilts than pumps. They wore all kinds of makeup, some a little too much of the stuff, and after about an hour in the southern heat, they appeared to be melting in the sun.

Momma took this time to show off, too. However, she was not just another face in the crowd. She pranced around in a chiseled body that did not reveal an ounce of fat anywhere. All her hard work had her looking really nice. She looked to be the queen of the bees that buzzed around this day.

She did not need makeup and refused to wear the stuff. Her demeanor told everyone she was the alpha-female and she still looked good when she was done up nicely. She knew how to strut about in those heels and, like most black women, her body moved with balance and harmony. If clothes make the person, it was the exact opposite on this Fourth Sunday, because Momma made the clothes. She had to be the most beautiful woman there.

At some of her acquaintances' urging, she did what was out of character and spent a little money on herself and took it easy for a day or two. Normally we always came first. With the gentle nudging she received, Momma decided to splurge on a nice outfit for this occasion, and she was intent on getting her money's worth out of it.

She was enjoying herself as she pranced about, intermingling amongst the congregation as if she was Cinderella. She felt and probably knew none of the women around here came close to her. All the hard work had allowed her to keep her figure, and she looked even better because of the way she carried herself.

It cannot be stressed enough, the time of year it was and the geographic location of the region we were in as this scene played out. It was the fourth Sunday in August in the Bible Belt in Georgia, and the heat was unforgiving.

The people had started the day out with fur stoles and three-piece suits buttoned up tight, accented by tight-fitting leather shoes of all colors that were not at all comfortable to the feet.

Everyone acted as though they could not sit down. Not even for a minute, because the whole congregation was happy to see each other. It almost seemed like they were part of a fraternity or sorority of sorts, and their alma mater was the Brooklyn U.

Regardless of the heat, they stayed in their attire the whole day. Only when it was late in the evening and the sun was going down did they begin to disrobe to expose their sweat-filled T-shirts and blouses. At the end of the day the women decided to take off their heels. They preferred the soft feel of the earth and a ruined pair of stockings, to the vanity of looking good.

This whole event turned out to be a fashion show and everyone tried to outdo everyone else. They drove their Cadillacs, Lincolns, sporty Trans-Ams and Mustangs to Brooklyn just to park them by the highway and walk to church. They were obviously used to the heat and had no intentions of getting their cars dirty in the red clay of Georgia. This is where they were raised and they knew all too well of the resilience of the stains the clay would leave behind.

With all this inside information, they chose the lesser of two evils. The walk from the highway to the church was about one hundred yards and seemed well worth the trade.

This was the life. This is what it meant to be black in Brooklyn when people mentioned the good old days. We lived in own little enclave, and the only rules were ours. There were not many white people around at this time. We laughed and had fun and forgot all our troubles.

Everywhere the adults went they had an audience of children behind them. This was perhaps the only time the rule of "children should be seen and not heard" was not in effect, because our voices were the dominant noise in the background of a strident Sunday. When we weren't running around playing with relatives from afar, we enjoyed listening to the adults talk and tell their lies. It seemed to always make us giddy.

Some of us would always watch with enthusiasm the way that the men drank their moonshine just out of sight of the preacher and the deacons. It always seemed to make their day to feel they were getting away with something.

We really didn't know why they were hiding what they were doing, because we had seen the deacons take a drink as well. We also heard them tell a few tall tales. These people were just like anyone else. It was nothing to hear a lie told and them brag on themselves and their children just out of earshot and sometimes to most of the congregation. They also talked about their wives as if they were saints. If they ever sat back and looked, they would see what everyone else saw. Some of the women were not what they were billed to be. They often were found flirting with someone as if it was no big deal. It all looked like a scene out of the movies and they charged a heavy fee to be part of this show because they passed the collection plate around several times throughout the day.

When the grown-ups finished all the showmanship, we changed our clothes and they drove us to Cusseta to let us have a rivalry game of baseball. This was the time I had picked to steal the show. I had no one to pep me up like the other kids. The only thing Momma said was how smart I was and this did not seem to impress anyone.

I was determined to have some glory for myself. I was focused on proving to all who had known my dad that I was a good ball player just like he was. I had practiced really hard and I was ready to put the things that I learned to use.

Chapter Ten: The Big Game

Everyone began to load up, and Larry grabbed the equipment and the kids who did not have a way to the game, and headed for Cusseta. I had never been to the game as a player on the Fourth Sunday of August, and this would be my first. I hopped on the back of the truck with about ten other people. We were the first to leave. Larry intended to get there a little early and give us a chance to warm up. He wanted to show Cusseta exactly what they were working against. The coach wanted to win this game before it started.

We knew Cusseta had heard about our first loss. We also figured they had taken it to heart and were determined to put up a good fight. Uncle Larry still knew he had a good squad and he had never lost to Cusseta, so he intended to show them nothing had changed. He felt, regardless of the blot on our record by the River Boys, we were still better than this bunch of misfits.

People were starting to act as if they started to doubt his team, and it was something he took personally. Momma was one of them. To rub salt in his open wound, she had constantly ribbed Larry so badly about losing he told her to come and see what happened in Cusseta.

Per Larry's request, she had made up her mind to see for herself, and she was finally coming to a game. She rode with Sonny and had a nice time, especially not having to drive her green monster of a truck.

Sonny was laid back as usual and didn't rush to do anything, including driving with any speed. Everybody loved him because of his pretty golden complexion, mellow mood, fine clothes, and fancy car. For people who did not know him and his roots, they thought he was after Momma.

She loved sticking it to the women who gawked after her cousin. Whenever she caught one of them staring at him, she put her arms around his neck or held his hand. She seemed to get a thrill out of the dirty look she got in return for her actions. She would then nudge Sonny and point with her eyes to show him what was going on. Momma would always tell him in a joking manner: "You need to straighten your women, before I have to."

He would always laugh and tell her, "Cuz, you don't have to worry about all that, they can take a number. When you and me came up, I knew whatever you had, I had. That's what family is about."

Momma had never gotten much of a chance to be stylish or relax since Daddy died. She always had to work hard and drive the old truck, and that was a workout in itself because it had no power steering. Riding with Sonny allowed her to do something she had never really had a chance to do in years: relax. She was being a lady, and it was her day. It made her feel wonderful inside. Sonny treated her like a queen and Lord knew she deserved it more than anybody.

The two of them talked in a lot of small talk about any and everything. Even though she had told him about the land she had just purchased, and mentioned in a sweeping generalization the family was still doing well, he still took the time to ask about each individual child once again.

He could tell she did not need anything because it was obvious of how well things were going for her. If it had been any other woman who lost her husband under the same circumstances, he couldn't see her making it. Somehow Sonny always knew in his heart of hearts she would be all right.

Once again she reiterated she was fine and her kids were doing well. He then casually directed her attention to me because he was fascinated with me. She smiled and seemed to pause and told

140

him how proud she had become of me lately and how smart I really was.

"I was worried about him at first," she confessed. "But he came through." She filled him in on my whole ordeal.

Sonny thought this was fine, but he wanted to know about my athletic ability. She had talked about books and school, and Sonny's demeanor and the look on his face told her he was not overly enthusiastic about the books and school part. He had other ideas for me and kept alluding to my physical gifts.

They talked about me a lot. They each discussed me in detail in different areas and perspectives. He told her he had been watching me since he had been here and I seemed to be naturally gifted, strong, and fast, more so than the other kids who held center stage. He asked her if I played any sports at all, to which Momma laughed and said, "He tried and caused Larry their only loss of the season."

Sonny already knew all the details about this because I had told him. He didn't share in her laughter and told her the only thing I needed was coaching. Sonny reminded her that he was a coach, and he knew talent. If somebody worked with me, I could really be special.

Momma kind of parried his suggestion to the side and told him I was fine with my books. The conversation about me was over with those words and Sonny left it alone.

When we finally reached Cusseta, I felt like Laura Ingalls arriving in Walnut Grove. The sights, smell, and the sounds of the place were incredible. As far as I could see down the road on both sides, there were cars. There were pavements and sidewalks around the park. Beautiful young women strolled down the concrete paths and hung around the basketball court watching the young men, who seemed to play a little harder when the girls would call their names.

The smell of barbecue and fish cooking carried lightly on the wind. The whole place was incredible. It seemed like a totally different world than the dusty roads and bicycled rimmed clay courts I was used to.

Uncle Larry found a place to park, and the guys exploded off the back of the truck like the kids down by the river. I grabbed the tools, and the other guys headed for the basketball court. This was unacceptable to Larry, who told them to get down to the field. They thought about defying him because they wanted to stay around the girls, but then thought better of it and complied with his command. They reluctantly walked to the field and began to go to their positions.

I ran to right field and the whole team laughed. There had to be no way Larry was putting me back into the game. No one knew it, not even me, but Sonny and Larry had talked. Sonny wanted to see me play a little in a game. He was the little bird on Larry's shoulder and told him not to give up on me. He told him how hard I had been practicing.

Uncle Larry took the opportunity to immediately test me. He hit a ball out to right field and called out "John!" I nervously tracked the ball down and caught it. Sonny, who was by now at the park as well, seemed transfixed on me, and the raw athletic ability he saw. He nodded his head in approval when I made my first catch.

About this time, Aunt Denise arrived on the scene. She had a big pink Cadillac like the kind Aretha Franklin sang about, and had her own private parking space. She was the manager of the Cusseta Bears. It seemed as if everyone loved this lady and she could do no wrong. She was a tremendous influence on the kids in a positive kind of way.

The people in Cusseta had their homecoming at this time too, and church had just let out. The park was becoming more crowded by the minute. Most of them were still dressed in their Sunday best, and this included Aunt Denise.

She hopped out of the car and pranced around in much the same fashion as Momma, exuding all kinds of confidence about herself. She floated about, shaking hands and hugging necks. She purposely ignored her brother Larry, who said to Sonny just loud enough for her to hear, "My boys will beat hers again."

Aunt Denise eventually made it down to the fence where Uncle Larry stood. He was content on allowing us to practice by ourselves. She walked up and smiled so confidently that he asked her, "What in the world are you so happy about, Sis, another loss?"

He then asked her how could she consistently lose and remain so upbeat about everything. He had heard of good sportsmanship, but them always losing was ridiculous.

Still smiling, she told him it was about the kids having fun and learning to get along with one another. With a twinkle in her eye, she added, "Oh, by the way, my nephew Tim is here and we won't lose today. I am going to unleash him on your Dodgers."

And then she added, "If you thought the River Boys whooped you, just wait until you get a load of my ace."

Larry frowned because he had heard of the kid. People had told him the child played with grown men and was only fourteen. There was no doubt in Larry's mind he was good, but he looked at her with confident eyes and told her, "The Dodgers will not lose to Cusseta, even if you suited those sorry men up to play."

Even though we lost to the River Boys, his Dodgers had revealed their true character to him. He had confidence they would fight for a win no matter what the odds. And besides, he had all of his best players there, and he was not planning on losing two games in the same season. Least of all lose a game to Cusseta.

When the game started, the people who had hung around the basketball courts and parking lots began to move toward the field. They had heard the first loud, exaggerated, extra-emphasized strike call. It was the signal of the main event starting. In no time at all, the baseball diamond was surrounded with a huge crowd.

Tim had not gotten there, and the game quickly reached the fourth inning and Brooklyn was up 7–0. It looked to be the same kind of game as in the past, and the Cusseta crowd wasn't too much into it. They had long ago taken on a sophisticated feel to themselves. They said that it wasn't important for their children to win, but to have fun, play nice, and learn some sportsmanship.

This is what they always said, and this was the line they stuck to as their official slogan. They were apparently conservative when it came to cheering and stuff. They walked around among the Brooklyn parents and fans carrying their message as if they were evangelists.

On this day, these people were about to show the true nature of their emotions. Cusseta had never really threatened to win anything over Brooklyn, because they didn't have the talent. This had been ingrained in everyone from the day the kids started to play ball.

However, this sophisticated crowd had been waiting for the right moment to really get behind their children. The opportunity came to them on this fourth Sunday in August because Tim had just arrived and was immediately sent to the mound to pitch.

He came there, and not a moment too soon for the Bears. We had the bases loaded and no outs. We were about to score more runs. He quickly warmed up and got it in gear and struck the next three batters out to smother the fire.

The guy had a live hard fastball and a whole lot of breaking pitches that were beyond anything that Brooklyn had faced before.

Larry was impressed, but he was not yet worried because we were so far ahead of "those same ole Bears."

He had never seen Tim play before. The coach had heard the boy was good, but he didn't know he was this good. But it didn't matter too much at the time. He was only one person and there was no way we could squander a lead like this.

He looked down the bench and called my name. Sonny looked at Larry and nodded his approval, and with this nod, Larry not only put me into the game, but he sent me to left field this time. It was a bold move my teammates wanted to openly question, but somehow they managed to hold their tongues.

Not only was he putting me into the game, he was putting me in left field. They remained quiet, probably from confidence of our lead, and partially in fear of the benching and scolding they might get.

After my insertion into the game, a rally finally got underway. In the bottom of the fifth, those hapless Cusseta Bears finally mustered some runs. They got five in that fifth and now had come within two runs of tying, and three of the lead.

Tim was still working his magic, and an anxious Larry watched as he struck out the side again to carry them into the bottom of the sixth. He had closed the door on our offense and he was becoming a little nervous. The concerned coach stood on the sideline and pondered his next move. He held firm in his decision to let me play and fought back the urge to pull me out.

I had not had a ball hit my way. I did no worse than anyone else on offense because they struck out just like I did. But unlike my fiasco when we played down by the river, I had begun to show promise at the bat. I had a lively confident swing against their ace, which gave Larry a little more confidence in me. I had actually managed to foul a couple off.

However, it was the bottom of the sixth and Gerald was beginning to be hit hard and we were struggling. It just so happened no balls had been hit my way as of yet.

Larry watched as his ace limped through the sixth inning, and the pressure of the game was building. He did not want to put too much strain on me, but if we lost again and I was at fault, the guys might never want to play with me again.

In the bottom of the seventh, he told me to stay there with him. He was going to let Fred finish up. He had kept his word to Sonny and now he was ready to mail the game home. This was the biggest and last game of the year and Larry did not want to go out on a bad note. Even though he had a misfit desperately wanting to play, he was going to have to do what was best for the team overall.

When he said those words to me, it crushed me. He was the one man that always seemed to give me a fair hand. I was ready and there was no way I wanted out.

Sonny, ever observant, calmly walked over and whispered in Larry's ear, "He's a winner, Stretch."

Uncle Larry looked back at Sonny when he called him Stretch, and he remembered my daddy had given him this name. He had also given him a chance to play when no one else had confidence in him.

"Stretch" was also the name Daddy used to call Larry when it looked like his self-assurance was shaken to pep him up. It was his way of saying, "Get back into the saddle." No matter what happened, Daddy was always in Larry's corner. He was there for him regardless of how much people wanted him to sit on the bench. He was always down with Larry, win, lose or draw, and he knew he owed it to me.

He looked into my eyes and he didn't see fear. He saw a confident intense gaze that Daddy must have seen in him. This look told him I was ready, and he told me to go back out to left field. He then took a deep breath and blew it all out along with any residual air he had in his lungs, and pulled his hat over his head, praying he had made the right decision. He hoped, not just for his sake, but also for my sake, that I didn't fail.

With his hand severely limited, he told David to go to the mound. This appeared to be the worst defensive move he could have unwittingly made. David had never pitched before and the only thing he threw was a hard fastball. It didn't rise or cut in any direction. It just went straight.

His game plan was obviously to overpower the Cusseta batters. But this was a dangerous time to make a pitching change to a rookie pitcher. It was the top of the lineup and this was precisely where we had given up the five runs before.

When Denise saw her brother pull this move, she felt she had him in check and it was about to be mate, and game over. She had been taking her boys to the batting cages just for an occasion like this, and a fastball was all they wanted to see. We had played each other so long she had the scouting report on every prospective player.

Beaming with confidence she called out, "Hey, brother, what's going on over there? It looks like you are confused."

The crowd erupted with laughter and the hecklers became louder than ever. Larry shot a quick comeback to the apathetic Cusseta fans who had never learned to cheer, "I didn't know you guys existed," to which they seemed to get louder.

They felt a win was within their reach and, even though they were behind, the circumstances of the game seemed to favor and embolden them. They had all but forgotten about the message they had spread around about good sportsmanship.

David quickly warmed up and nodded to the umpire that he was ready. He reared back, with his ears jumping and twitching, grunted, and threw the ball as hard as he could.

The ball seemed to sizzle as it headed for the catcher's mitt. It was as hard as he could throw and on a straight line down the center of the plate.

The ball left the plate as fast as it came in. It was a line drive, a crisp single to right field, which seemed to ignite the madness that had been suppressed inside of the Cusseta dugout. They slapped the fence, stomped on the benches, and made as much noise as possible. And then they started a bizarre chant, in which half of them shouted, "Take him out!"

The other half shouted back: "Leave him in!"

"Take him out!"

"Leave him in!"

This went on for a moment, as if they were in an argument of some kind. Then everyone said, "Call the bullpen," as if they had arrived at this conclusion after a poorly held debate.

The next batter, after running the count full, hit a sharp two-hopper to Freddie, the first baseman. He made an error, but managed to keep the ball in the infield. The ball bounced solidly into his chest and squirted away, allowing runners to be on first and second and no one out.

The Cusseta bench, now with the Cusseta fans joining in the fun, started their little ritual once again. They echoed their silly incantation as if they were conjuring up a spirit. They grew more raucous with each pro-Cusseta development.

At this point, Larry swung his entire outfield to the right field shift. It was obvious to him they were having trouble getting around on David and this seemed a logical step. It almost seemed as though Cusseta was waiting on this move.

148

The next batter pulled the ball hard down the left field line on the first pitch. Larry covered his face with his hat. It was over because the fat lady was now walking on stage. There was no way anyone could get to that ball because of his shifting of the outfield.

A cheer erupted from the crowd when the ball left the bat because it looked to be getting close to the end for Brooklyn. Suddenly, and in almost the same breath, a pitiful murmur of a moan covered them.

I had drawn a bead on the ball and moved like a jet to get it. It was obvious to everyone watching I would make a play on it. Aunt Denise implored her guys to run back to the bases.

Larry heard the moan in the crowd and snatched his hat down from his face to see I had caught the ball and had hustled it back into the infield.

Larry managed to take a deep breath because we were still in the game. Feeling a little better about me in left field, he was reinvigorated to coach again.

It was Kelvin's time to bat. This guy had not hit anything hard all year. Larry called his outfield in. He anticipated a double play or a force out at one of the bases if the ball got through somehow.

Kelvin took two fastballs as enthusiastically called strikes, which were reminiscent of the one that the umpire called to start the game.

The wheels in Larry's head started to turn. If Kelvin struck out or popped out, he would have the option to walk Tim and probably load the bases. In his mind it was the best possible scenario. Tim was on deck, but if he got one more out, it would be at his discretion if he got a chance to swing the bat.

No one knew what was going through Kelvin's mind, but his adrenaline was pumping like crazy. This game was getting good.

Never before had Cusseta been so close to us so late in the game. The pressure was on because we knew with one mistake it was over. The Bears felt like all they had to do was keep the pressure on and we would crack for sure.

David threw two fastballs away, and Kelvin showed tremendous patience by not swinging. He managed to hold off on those junk pitches David had thrown to him. He backed out of the box and looked around the crowd, received his encouragement, took a sign from the third base coach, and then he dug his feet back in.

The two-two pitch was a fastball inside tight. Kelvin turned on it, and it was a low blooper-like shot to left field. I broke down, crouching at the knees to try and gauge the flight of the ball. It was carrying on a stiff breeze and mirrored a rainbow's trajectory. It appeared I had not judged the ball correctly because I had drifted in too far. I was now in trouble and turned to run as the crowd erupted in a loud cheer. It was going to be a hit.

Showing tremendous speed and acceleration, I recovered, and at the last minute, I jumped up and snagged the ball and fell to the ground. I rolled over and threw the ball to the shortstop, Eddie, who had by now made it into the field. Eddie then hustled the ball into third base. Once again no runners advanced because they had to re-tag their bases.

Everyone by now was standing almost on the field. The basketball court and the parking lot were empty. It was close to a historic moment for the Bears, and it seemed everyone wanted to witness it.

Tim was at bat and he would put an end to it all if Larry allowed David to pitch to him. He could give Cusseta its first and much needed confidence-building win over us and further pierce our cloak of invisibility.

Tim looked over at Uncle Larry with a taunting grin on his face. He turned and told the umpire, "He won't pitch to me. You can go on and send me to first base."

This smug little boy irritated the hell out of Larry. He called "Time!" and went to the mound and called the entire field in to him. He asked us if we were ready to win. The whole team gave a resounding, "Yes!"

He then looked at his pitcher and asked him, "How you feeling, boy?"

David shook his head to affirm that he was okay.

"David, you are going to pitch to him, son," he told the somewhat shaken guy on the mound.

"It's now or never. Here's what I want you to do. I want you to throw just hard enough for it to be a strike and reach the mitt."

David looked at him in a strange way, as if he could not believe what his coach was telling him to do. Larry told him, "Just trust me, son."

David nodded his head yes, and swallowed hard. He tried to generate spit or some other moisture that was hidden deep in his throat somewhere. Leaving the pitching mound, Larry hit the guy on his rear and told him to take it home.

Sonny walked over and asked Larry, "You're going to put him on, ain't you, Stretch?"

Larry looked at him with a devilish grin and told him, "No. We are going to win by beating this guy. David is going to strike him out."

Sonny found this hard to believe and disagreed with the strategy and told Larry so.

"These kids are fighting too hard to lose on a humbug, Larry."

Uncle Larry just smiled and said, "It's my call, Sonny."

He then walked over and sat in the dugout off to himself and watched Tim standing just outside the batter's box looking over the field, trying to taunt him as if to say, "I am capable of picking the place where I want to knock it out of here." Obviously he had been brainwashed into thinking he was the Babe or some other larger-than-life hero.

The boy was good and he knew it. So many people had told him so, he now found it hard to hide his smug little attitude. He was showboating with flamboyancy never before seen around here, and it just made Larry think he needed to be taken down a peg or two.

The child baseball prodigy stood there for a moment and basked in the shouts of, "Come on, Tim!" "Knock it outta here, son!"

The girls called his name in much the same fashion as they did for the basketball players. If not for the fact their mommas would beat them all the way to the Mississippi River and back, they would probably have thrown their undergarments at him. Tim had his own little entourage and they thought this guy was the best thing since sliced bread and government cheese.

It took him some time to step into the batter's box. When he finally did, he held his hand up for time-out, and began to slowly dig into the dirt to plant his feet. Tim's little ceremony was a little too much for Uncle Larry.

The little routine he was doing prompted him to say, "Come on, boy, let's play ball before nightfall. You know we don't have lights or anything."

Tim ignored him and continued doing what he was doing. Larry looked across the field at Aunt Denise and yelled out, "I got twenty dollars that says he strikes out!"

The crowd erupted in laughter at his offhand comment. "Sis, can I get a bet?"

He badgered Aunt Denise about a wager until finally she gave a hot response.

"If you want to give me your money, I will surely take it, love. Knock it outta here, Tim!"

The first pitch moved about forty-five miles per hour, and the umpire shouted, "Iiiiiiiikkkkke!" As if he left the "Str" somewhere.

It was a called strike and it drew an intense look from Tim, as if he didn't believe the call or the speed of the pitch. It was hard to believe, but the young man could have been trying to intimidate the umpire with his intense stare. But there was no way he could have been this advanced.

There was an eerie silence over the crowd, and Larry leaned back on the bench and began smiling to himself. Tim looked out to the mound with a perplexed look on his face and then over to Larry, who yelled out, "Get it out of here, boy."

Tim didn't know what was going on, but this coach must have lost his mind. He didn't back out of the box or anything and quickly set up again. The second pitch came slower than the first. He swung so hard it generated a gentle breeze.

"Strike twoooooooo!" the umpire yelled out. He had found his "Str" and a few "ooooo's" too. The count was now 0-2, and the Cusseta faithful were shouting encouragement to their would-be hero, who was obviously by now off his game.

Tim thought he would see heat on the third pitch. He backed out of the batter's box and rubbed his hands into the dirt to absorb the sweat on them.

He was perspiring heavily and the dirt was acting as a coagulant on the sweat, which clung to his skin. He rubbed his hands together to relieve them of the mortar-like substance that fell readily to the ground in globs and looked over at Larry, who was smiling at him, mimicking the grin he once sported. Larry yelled out again, "Get it outta here, boy!"

The weight of an entire town was on the young man's shoulders. He stepped back into the batter's box in much the same fashion as before, with his hand held high for time. He dug his feet into the sandy earth and took a deep breath and nodded his head he was ready. He had made up in his mind to set up for the fastball.

David took his time by going through his wind-up and delivered a pitch, which was just barely going to make the plate. It was almost a lob, it moved so slowly. Tim impatiently waited on the pitch and finally swung. He was at least a mile out in front.

"Strike three! Game over!" the umpire yelled out.

David had done it. The team rushed in and picked him up. They carried him about on their shoulders. When I reached the infield, they reached back and picked me up as well. We had won again. Cusseta was never supposed to be able to beat us, and they didn't.

It didn't happen by a blowout like it normally did, but we won. We were just lucky enough to get away with it. We did it and were not ashamed of how it went down.

Aunt Denise was making it to her car in high gear as Uncle Larry slipped up behind her and said, "Sis, you want to take care of your debt?"

The look on her face was of utter disgust and dejection. She had come so close to a win, only to lose with her best foot forward. Larry laughed and gave her a hug and told her they would win one day and to keep trying.

She pushed him playfully in his chest, and then pulled him back and gave him a hug. She reached in her purse and gave him his twenty. She told him she was not going to go anywhere without congratulating her nephews anyway. They both went back to the field to find us.

"Where's my nephews?" she asked.

The two of them found me first because I had gotten off the shoulders of my teammates. I now had the tool bag on my back and was making my way up to the truck.

Uncle Larry walked up behind me and took the tools off my back, and our eyes met again. He really didn't know what to say to me, because he had doubted me; so he thought hard and said, "You played a helluva game."

Aunt Denise smiled and said, "You sure did. I thought we had you guys, but ya'll played ball today."

Still shaking her head she gave me a big hug. She asked me why Larry was not playing me more. I shrugged my shoulders, knowing full well the answer, but I was not about to disclose the real reason to my aunt.

She then said, "I got a uniform for you if you want one." George Steinbrenner had nothing on her.

Larry saw her move coming and wasn't hearing it. He jumped in before I could think about it and said, "You have to leave my prospects alone. He's in his uniform," and gave a solid laugh as he pulled me under his arm.

My uniform was a pair of jeans and tennis shoes and an old beaten up T-shirt. We could not afford the pretty uniforms and cleats like she bought for the Bears. But it really wasn't an issue to us.

It didn't matter how good we looked on the field, but how well we played. This was what Larry stressed in his talks with us as if it was a talking point, and we had bought it hook, line, and sinker.

If you ever listened to Larry, he could talk you into buying some ocean-front property in the middle of the Sahara. He was quite a salesman.

Everyone hung around the field and talked about the game and what could have been. David and I were heroes on this day. We were enjoying our fifteen minutes of fame because the feelings and emotions of the whole day were incredible.

I made an observation. It was just a theory I put forth and would later try to verify. It was simple enough and made sense to me: Everybody glorifies the athletes and their popularity is unparalleled.

I had a taste of it when I played kick ball a few years back, but nothing like this Sunday. I had never had so many people congratulate and seek me out to talk before in my life. The girls pointed, smiled, and waved at me. I felt as though I had just conquered the world.

Everything was becoming clear to an impressionable child. This ball game showed who really held the glory and honor in people's hearts. I knew on the field, on this day, people really didn't glorify the smart people, because most of the smart kids were standing on the sidelines blending into obscurity.

To further emphasize what I learned was the simple fact that, at the park, everyone was there to see their children play. When I competed in the spelling bee, there was nowhere near the amount of people at the school as there was here. That room had been nearly empty except for a few die-hard mothers. It was almost like no one cared about academics like they cared for sports. Here at the park, even strangers were interested in what was going on with the future athletes.

The people around this area of Georgia acted as though they did not really care how many certificates and awards a person won for being intelligent. If a person was not an athlete, then he was almost an afterthought. I began to rethink the whole thing about being considered smart and decided I wanted to be popular, and I had finally figured it out.

This was a dangerous time for me. I had worked hard on overcoming my educational deficiencies. The temptations of popularity were calling me, and it revealed itself in the adulation of people from the oldest to the youngest. The lure of the classroom seemed far away from me on this late summer's day.

Although school was only a week away, I had not given much thought to getting back into my schoolwork. I was caught up in the rapture of my athletic moment. I paused and took another look at the smart kids standing on the sidelines. They had cheered us on as well.

They were my kind of people, but at the same time I didn't want to be one of them anymore. I no longer wanted or relished the title of the gifted child.

Autumn of Change

When the summer ended and the school year began, I was glad to have that chapter in my life behind me. I had a lot to look forward to. The anticipation of going to Bi-County High School was almost unbearable. I thought I had found my little niche in life and was ready for new things. The challenge I was about to face was surreal. I was going to face a whole new set of obstacles, as well as dealing with the ones I thought I had conquered.

The first year here would test me. It would show me what I was made of and what toughness was all about. Would I fold or pull myself forward?

There were another set of wolves gathering at my door and it would take all I had to fend them off. There would be no Mrs. Rogers to save me this time, not just from the packs, but also from myself.

Chapter Eleven: High School

The first day of school was here, and I was up bright and early this morning. My gear was laid out as if I was a soldier preparing for a mission. My attire was a nice pair of khakis with a matching shirt. I wore a new pair of dark brown tennis shoes adorned three stripes resembling bolts of lightning that sported a name from an obscure company probably no longer in existence.

The colors of my clothes complemented each other so well my chest filled with pride when I looked at them. Diane was observing the whole little episode and stood back looking at me with a grin on her face. She laughed aloud when she checked the brand name on the label, causing me to lose my temper. I was angry and snatched my clothes away and called Momma to get some relief from my gadfly of a sister who stung me with her sharp words.

Diane left the room after Momma gave her a stern warning. It really didn't help, because she found it too hard to resist teasing me. She pushed the envelope by continually walking by sniping, giving sarcastic comments on my outfit.

"Look at you with those cheap things," she said. "You wash them one time and you don't have nothing but thread."

I totally ignored her and continued about my business. I bought my school clothes with the money I had earned this past summer, and it was impossible for Diane to do anything that would dampen my spirits. I had worked hard and put up with Bill's crap just long enough to buy my own school clothes and have a little pocket change. I thought the only reason my sister bothered me was because she was jealous.

Nonetheless, with all the drama going on about me, I managed to get ready for school. The bus seemed to be coming to slowly this morning and I was so eager to leave, I began to search the horizon with ears tuned, trying to pick it up on my own special radar. The anticipation of going to the high school had pulled me off the porch, and Diane's provocative comments had now pushed me even farther from the house.

After about five minutes more, I no longer waited by the edge of the yard. I decided to take the walk down toward the end of the driveway. I paced the ground in front of the main road like a father expecting my first child. I was going to the high school on a mission.

The first thing on the agenda for me was to find myself a girlfriend. I was thirteen and in the eighth grade. The puberty bug had hit me hard and I started to smell myself, as the old people sometimes said. At this age, I was going through some serious changes in my life. Being gifted and schoolwork was far removed from my mind.

When the bus finally arrived, I was wired. I hopped into the golden chariot with enthusiasm and vigor and took my time finding a seat. This was going to be great. I was now a high school student whether I was ready or not.

I strolled down the isle knowing the seniors had vacated and a few choice seats were open. I looked at the area called no man's land where all the action happened. It was at the very back of the Blue Bird, and it was a lot like the Old West. The only law in effect was you had to have the power to defend yourself and your girlfriend, if you had one. I was not strong enough to take my place amongst the heavyweights yet, and only dreamed of having my first girlfriend, so I quickly dismissed this area.

I thought about the seat Shotgun once had, but I knew this was a bad business decision because it was prime real estate. It was available, but a senior or an upperclassman would come along and depose me later, and this would make it a strong possibility I would end up without a seat of my own.

Hesitating, putting a lot of thought into my decision, I chose a less appealing seat, which was situated just over a heating duct. It had its advantages in the winter. This may have been the only time because no one wanted it during the summer. It was in the middle of the bus and sat directly over the inconvenient contraption, which meant there was no place to stash my book bag.

I took another look at Shotgun's old seat and I would have really loved to sit there, but since he had graduated a few years ago, it had been passed down from senior to senior. I didn't want the drama with the older boys, and willingly took the seat with the heating duct just for the tranquility it would afford me.

When everyone was finally seated, the journey began. The bus ride didn't seem long at all once we picked up all the children. We quickly arrived at the elementary school, let the little ones off, and continued on. It was an awkward feeling passing the Richmond Elementary School for the first time.

I sat there wide-eyed, watching as the old building disappeared quickly from sight. I had been this way only a couple of times before, so I took in the scene as if I were a tourist.

I noticed just as we were about to leave the town of Richmond, an old oak tree had fallen and was slowly decaying. A crowd of grown men hung out around it with nothing to do. Momma told me the tree fell over dead because it could no longer stand up to the lies the guys told under its branches. It was a pitiful site.

We left the city limits of the little country town and headed for another one. We were on a long empty road with woods on both sides. The bus bounced and rocked around curves and up and down hills as I nonchalantly took in all the sights along the way.

The most prominent thing on this road that I saw was an old dog food factory that had long been abandoned since the railroad no longer visited. The entire area was in economic shambles.

A few miles further into the journey, we passed through Langston, another small city, which was on its way to becoming a ghost town. People were moving away from this area for one reason or another. They said it had something to do with the opportunity to gain jobs and a better life. Others refused to play politics and said it was to get away from the rednecks, who had found a haven in the little communities and would not let them prosper. Their conservative, separatist approach to business had ransacked the entire county. The best and brightest minds, black and white, had chosen to leave.

I could not help but think of my older brother when I saw the small towns. I thought of what he told me about not becoming a victim of my environment. He left to get away from all the negative entities circulating around the rural communities.

Randall, my brother, seldom came home after he enlisted in the army. He wanted nothing to do with this place, nor did I. I had always missed him and often wondered what it would have been like if we were only a couple of years apart.

I looked at the dilapidated structures and I could see how sad the whole situation was. I could see those pitiful buildings barely standing. They were prominently displayed on both sides of the road with people hanging out in front of them doing nothing all day. Anything other than the fate that the buildings or the men standing in front that decorating them had been subjected to would have been better than this slow agonizing death.

The painful sight of the little town passed quickly by and my eyes were almost relieved to see the pine trees again. They now appeared to have become bolder and seemed to be growing almost in the road.

Somewhere in the distance, I saw a clearing in the woods situated on a plateau overlooking a small bluff. My mind snapped out of its deep solemn thoughts and into enthusiasm and vigor. This was the school and I was only a few moments away from becoming a Raider.

The last part of the journey was up a long, steep, winding hill. The bus fought its way against the pull of gravity as the black smoke shot from its tailpipe. At times it looked like it would not make it, but a change of gears and depressing of the accelerator managed to push it over its crest.

Once we leveled out on top of the plateau, I realized I was not ready. I was having second thoughts. I fought so long to gain status at the elementary school that I didn't want to start over. I now realized I had to go back to the bottom of the pile.

It was not fair to me and I was scared of the uncertainty of the whole thing. I was only in the eighth grade and felt the school system had made a mistake by allowing us to attend school with the older students.

I took a deep breath and began to prepare myself for the new experience. The school was still in essence new and held students from two counties. I would not know most of the people I was destined to bump into in the halls, and this is what scared me the most. I looked out the window at the pristine setting and gathered my stuff.

Once the bus stopped, I took a deep breath and made my way out of its open door. I was one of hundreds of new students emerging from the buses, literally lost. There was no faculty contingent there to welcome us into the new high school. There were no upperclassmen to tell us to meet here or there. This is not what we imagined on day one.

We meandered around the yard and finally ventured into the lobby. A bold student walked into the main office and asked the secretary where we were supposed to go. She gave him directions to the gym and said the homeroom teachers would meet us there.

Everyone started to move behind the guy, and I did what was natural and joined the body of students and made the great migration to the gym. I was only one face in a crowd and this felt good to me.

I glanced over the female students to see what they were working with. I looked the ladies up and down as they began to assemble into small groups. I thought of my primary goal for the school year and zeroed in on my target before she could merge with the other females. In my mind she was gorgeous. She was dark like I was and very fine. I looked her over and smiled sneakily to myself.

She had a Geri Curl or a Curly Kit in her hair. I didn't know what she called hers because there were several brands on the market. She wore a ruffled white blouse that sported the stains from chemicals used on her curls to maintain their appearance, and a pair of faded blue jeans. She also wore a pair of Skippy or flat white shoes. She had a gorgeous face accented by dimples.

Her beauty pleased me, but my eyes were glued to what I considered her best feature. I loved her posterior that seemed to jiggle and wiggle. It was something about those tight-fitting jeans that made me simply adore her. Other guys were enticed as well and kind of elbowed each other as we moved down the corridors, trying to decide who would pounce first.

I knew I was up for a challenge because alliances were already being formed to divvy up the girls. A pecking order was being established. If I didn't act quickly I would lose out on the refreshing drink of water walking directly in front of me.

164

It quickly became evident to me that I wasn't the only one who listed getting a girl tops on my agenda. It appeared every one of these little boys' minds had turned to lust at this time.

The most popular guys would have the best of the bunch. I had to move with a sense of purpose to secure my quarry. She was on everyone's radar, including mine.

I picked up the pace and was quickly abreast of her, matching her stride for stride. I introduced myself and asked her name. I could tell she was a little apprehensive, as her voice betrayed her with a barely audible, "Tabitha."

It was so low I didn't hear her reply. I was already nervous and wanted to head for cover, but all eyes were on me after I had made this daring move, so I said, "Excuse me, but what did you say?"

She raised her head from the floor and I could see that she was blushing as she looked me directly in my eyes, smiled, and said, "Tabitha."

At this moment, I was lost. I was in love. Her eyes were so big and round I could see the softness of a thousand springtime daybreaks, which seemed to be absorbed within them. It was obvious she was innately gifted at using them because she batted them with a certain flirtatious appeal that made me melt.

We continued to talk, and both of us loosened up a little as the students continued to move noisily down the halls. We traveled through the cafetorium, a large open space for eating and smaller assemblies.

Our group began to thin out because of the vastness of the room. As we looked around the area, everyone could not help but notice the alpha-males. They were perched upon the stage and were surveying the crowd, deciding which of the girls they would have as their own. These were probably the seniors, who were supposed to have met us at the front entrance of the school. It was obvious they had something better to do.

I was in a class of remarkably beautiful girls. And I had been so bold as to pick one of the best of the litter. One of the seniors pointed at Tabitha as we moved through the huge room. I noticed it and knew I would have a hard time holding Tabitha's attention, but I continued to talk and occasionally tell a joke or two.

We reached the gym and everyone was instructed to have a seat in the bleachers. The homeroom teachers stood up and introduced themselves and called out their prospective classes, starting with 8-5. They continued going backward until they reached 8-1. I was relieved to see Tabitha still sitting beside me. We would be in the same homeroom and share most of the same classes as well.

I looked around and was happy to see all of my gifted friends would be in the class with me. Most of the white ones had disappeared, but it hadn't caught my attention yet. I just felt fortunate to be among some familiar faces in a strange new world.

Even though there was no longer a gifted program, some of us would still be together. This was almost better than I could have ever hoped for or imagined, and I felt I was rewarded with a consolation prize.

Mrs. Wallace rattled off the names of the students who would be coming to her for 8-1. It was a formality, probably to make sure that no one's name was overlooked or in case someone had not heard their name called previously. I was content with my status and as comfortable as one could be with a room half-full of strangers.

After everyone had gathered around Mrs. Wallace, we naturally further divided ourselves up into little clans. I migrated toward the gifted students I knew from the elementary school.

The elderly teacher then gave us a brief overview of the things we were about to embark upon. She calmly stated the itinerary

166

for the day and asked if there were any questions. Since there were none, she told us to follow her. The first thing on the agenda was a tour. It should not have been hard for us to learn our way around this place, although some of us still got lost.

The building was a simple structure built in a square, with a gymnasium adjoined to the west wing. This part of the building plan was nice. The gym was a part of the structure, but at the same time it was separate.

There was a huge opening in the middle of the building not used for anything. In some people's opinion, it was a waste of money on this part of the design. I thought it would make a nice place for the horticulture shop to put a flower garden park, making it the perfect place to take pictures and other things, sort of like the Rose Garden at the White House, which would salvage the wasted space.

I wondered if the state knew what they were getting for their money. Uncle Larry was most critical of the building, saying he would be surprised if the building lasted five years. He was one of the people who help to construct it, and he thought it was done in too much of a hurry. He said it was a shabby job in a best-case scenario.

We paused for a moment when we reached the cafetorium again. In this area, we were once again in plain view of the seniors, who were watching for their young female prey. They were perched upon the stage and surveyed all of us.

I knew Tabitha would be taken. I was really out of my league choosing her. The most popular of the guys was now making his choice. It was too bad for me the choice was Tabitha.

His name was Tommy Tolbert. This guy was the quintessential cool daddy. He was a big-time thug before they ever came into existence in the deep rural South. He was a guy who dressed in the best clothes and wore the best jewelry.

There were a lot of people in the room and a lot was going on. It seemed everyone in the area was talking and all the conversations seemed cluttered together. I focused in on the guy who had his eyes on my potential girl, Mr. Tolbert. I strained my ears as I barely heard Tommy say, "Look at the thump in her trunk. Man, it's playing a tune for me."

Whatever the fascination is about black guys and women's booties is unknown to most, but it is a prerequisite for a woman being fine in our minds. And Tabitha had plenty of it to be as petite as she was. It was one of the things that attracted my peers and me to her, and it snatched Tommy's attention right away. What she had was mesmerizing, to say the least.

Whatever made me think I could drink from the top shelf was not about to let me give up on my pursuit so quickly. Tabitha was one cool drink of water and I knew I wanted her. No, I knew I had to have her for my girl.

I began to ponder ways to offset the balance of power that was about to take place. I was no match for an upperclassman. Let alone Tommy Tolbert. I knew I had to come up with a game plan quickly.

I received a quick time-out when Mrs. Wallace ushered us to our homeroom. I thought back to the scene that had just taken place. In my mind I knew Tabitha heard Tommy's lewd comments, because she was almost point-blank range when he made them. She was not appalled by what he said. It actually seemed as though she was enamored because she smiled like a Cheshire cat. It left me scrambling to come up with a plan, but I was shooting blanks. I therefore decided not to sweat it, and fell back in with the gifted students and she merged with the other girls.

168

The day was going by smoothly and Tommy had not been staring hungrily at Tab seen since early this morning. I had already walked with her to a couple of classes, and I began to think I was overreacting to the events that took place earlier. I spent most of my available time with her and had gone virtually unchallenged. It was as if I had been given a new lease on my romantic life. In my mind, I was close to having a girlfriend and nothing could be better for me than sealing this deal.

I felt I was just a plain fellow. I thought I needed a pretty girl to give me credibility around the school. The first girl I got would probably be the hardest to pull, I figured. After this, I would have a little job history on my resume and there should be no problem in getting another one.

Later, on several occasions I happened to see Tommy walking with his girlfriend. We would pass each other in the hallways and I started to feel relieved. I felt I had been overreacting and began to wonder why I should worry about Tommy.

His girlfriend was beautiful and one of the prettiest, if not the prettiest, in the school. She was honey-coated and just as fine as Tab. I knew all the guys wanted a woman like her. Surely Tommy wouldn't jeopardize Rhonda to be with Tab.

When the school day ended, I walked Tab to the bus. When we reached her bus door, I could sense someone's eyes were on us. We were being watched. I looked over my shoulder and standing in the doorway was Tommy. This guy was stalking us--again. I couldn't believe it.

He stood there and watched as Tabitha stepped into the bus. Tommy continued watching as I sped down the sidewalk and hopped into my bus. Then he slowly turned and walked back into the school. I saw the whole thing and I was worried again. If Tommy wanted her, then Tommy was going to have her. It was the law of nature. Might makes right.

The bus ride home seemed long. It could have been because I was not used to it or I had too much time to think. I was lost in my own thoughts, silently staring at the pines that lined the road. My thoughts at this very moment were of Tab and me. Tommy-and-Tab was part of the equation I was working in my head as well. It is a wonder the people on the bus didn't hear my thoughts because I thought them loud enough for the world to hear. In my mind, I was saying in a sarcastic tone, "Tommy Tolbert, the big-time playa."

I reflected on what everyone said about the guy. "He has such good hair. What a pretty complexion. His folks have money."

Everything he was, I was not. I was so jealous of this guy and his benefits from possessing such "good" traits and the influence he had from his money, it was almost ridiculous.

Tommy actually had never done anything to me, but I had already been through so much with people about color and class. I had even begun to stereotype people based upon the hue of their skin.

In my mind, Tommy was just another over-hyped pretty boy. What could he want with Tab? She was just an eighth grader and just as dark as I was. I was turning things over in my head, trying to find a logical answer, asking myself this question again and again.

"Tab is just as dark as me. What could Tommy want with her?"

It just didn't make sense to me. She looked nothing like his girl Rhonda, who was, for lack of a better description, honey-coated. To him, Tab could be no more than a trophy. She could be nothing more than a conversation piece, another notch on his bedpost, which could only garner him more status with the fellas. In my heart of

170

hearts, I knew I didn't have a chance and it brewed resentment. I knew I was going to get bumped and it was just a matter of time.

I lived through my slow torture for about the first two weeks of school. Every day it seemed Tab slipped further and further away from me. What made the situation worse was there was nothing I could do about it. It was excruciatingly painful for me to watch a relationship never really there die.

Tommy wanted her so I came to the conclusion it would be better for me just to give her space and leave her to him. They had been flirting heavily when she was with me. And it felt at times like he was disrespecting me, sending his little messages by her friends, which caused her to smile and me to frown. There was a respect issue creeping into this picture because I was getting none.

I never told Tab, but I assumed she knew how I felt about her. It appeared everyone could see it, but her. This made the situation more difficult because she didn't seem like the type of person to do this kind of stuff to a man. It had to be a misunderstanding about this whole thing.

Tab was driving me crazy. The looks she and Tommy gave each other were really intense. They exchanged unavoidable, longing gazes that seemed to transport each of them to another place and time. Their gawking at each other was worse for me because she would be walking or standing with me when most of it went down. It was as if she was slighting me, albeit unintentionally.

Tommy, on the other hand, knew what he was doing. He was intentionally trying to make me look bad. At least this is how I interpreted this drama.

I willingly gave Tab a pass from this perceived slight because she was young. Tommy, on the other hand, I wanted to convict and punish, but I didn't know how. I often found myself turning my dilemma this way and then that way in my mind. I was trying to find the solution to a complicated social issue in which I didn't have the formula to plug in the variables.

Chapter Twelve: Respect

It was really affecting me, living under so much pressure. I was going to inevitably burst one day. A physical confrontation between Diane and me was unavoidable. It was destined to happen, and it did one day after the long trip from school.

When we finally reached the house and I exited the bus, Diane was laying it on thick. She followed me closely out of the bus and just seemed to hum her little song in my ear.

"John's got a girlfriend. John's got a girlfriend." She repeated that chorus over and over again. After about the fifteenth time, she said, "Tommy's got John's girlfriend."

When she uttered these words, something clicked inside of me. Rage and frustration took over, and I charged at Diane, who stood her ground. We had been down this road before and she always beat me easily. She was a tall, country, lanky, tomboyish girl who had some serious strength of her own. She always subdued me in a couple of minutes and made me call her momma.

I had hit puberty, however, and this time it was different. Testosterone had caused some major changes in my body. I was now able to look her squarely in her eyes. My voice had developed a low, raspy growl, which escaped my throat as I began my charge. The ground dissipated between us quickly, and Diane's facial expression allowed fear to escape for the first time when facing me. She now noticed my size and the speed at which I moved had radically changed. The encounter didn't last long at all.

I quickly scooped her up when we collided and slammed her to the ground. A cloud of dust escaped the earth as her body crashed into the sand, creating a miniature dust storm. We disappeared in the simulated smoke from the collision and continued our struggle on the ground. When the dust cleared, I had managed to pin her underneath me. After I had straddled her in a full mount, I wailed away for a few minutes before my other sisters were able to separate us.

I stared at them and then at Diane for a moment, not really believing what I had done. I wanted to tell her I was sorry, but pride glued my mouth shut. I gathered my books out of the dirt and silently walked into the house. Nothing more was said about what went down on this day. Everyone just reflected on what happened, trying to digest it all.

I thought nothing much of the encounter except the trouble I was in with Momma, but the fight appeared to consume Diane. She knew the rules of engagement in our primitive struggle had just changed. She now realized she could no longer buffalo me. She had to take me seriously and handle me with a little more respect, or all indications meant it would be another trip to the ground, and a few more knots on her head. With this small scuffle, I managed to usurp some respect from her. I grabbed a bite to eat and commenced with my chores.

No one ever told Momma about the incident, much to my surprise. Diane was far too embarrassed to admit I was now able to handle her. She felt she would keep her dignity, and out of pride she remained silent. The rest of the family was still trying to believe what just happened, and tried to absorb the obvious shift in the balance of power between the two of us.

I knew I was in some serious trouble for fighting my sister. I pretended to be asleep after doing my work around the house. Momma came home and no one mentioned the incident to her. After half the night had elapsed, I came to the conclusion no one was going to tell. I quickly popped up and did my homework, laid my clothes out and got back into bed.

Days passed and the trips to the school had become monotonous. I watched the scenery as the bus rolled along towards its destination. This ride was so boring to me I often fell asleep. I had seen everything on this road a person could see. Sometimes something happened on a farm that would catch my attention; this was not often, though, because there were only so many things on a farm to see. I preferred looking at and trying to count the trees lining the road. There was a good chance I had a running count on the pines down to the last sapling.

My favorite thing about the long, unpleasant ride was getting to the school. I didn't hang out in the halls anymore because I didn't want to see my beloved Tabitha worshipping Tommy.

I learned the possible reason I lost out on her affection by some of the guys who laughed and made a suggestion that I didn't like as to the problem with us. At this age most of us were too young to realize the walls had ears, and the walls were speaking to me. They told me her friends had told her, "Two dark people should never be together."

The pressure was on her to talk to Tommy, probably because he was a better catch. This assumption of dating based on color plagued me, but I just tried to hang in there and weather another storm.

Still without any thoughts or hope for a relationship with Tab, I often reminisced of how we used to chill together. I often pondered our situation and how close we had come to becoming a couple. These were fleeting thoughts, though, because each time she slighted me was a dagger to my heart.

The recourse I chose for myself was to sit in the classroom and go over school-related things I worked on the night before. Mrs. Rogers had taught me many things. Her pet peeve was to be unprepared. At this point, being organized was still the top thing on my agenda. I always checked and double-checked things, just like she told me to do. Besides, it was helping me to forget my sorrows.

I was stuck on Tab and I knew in my heart she liked me. She was just bowing to the pressure of her friends. I no longer talked with her, and eventually I took a seat on the other side of the classroom. If I could have, I would have changed rooms just to be away from her altogether.

When I finally switched seats, it was exactly what her female buddies were waiting on. The roaches quickly moved in. They actually wondered what had taken me so long to get the message. Her entourage hastily surrounded their would-be queen. This turned out to be a major tactical blunder on my part. It was obvious to me when I retreated I became the furthest thought from Tabitha's mind.

A feeling of misfortune had finally come home again. It became worse for me in trying to deal with this. I had willingly ostracized myself; I fell on my own sword to no avail because this action did not end my trauma.

My mind and eyes always seemed to search for her. I didn't know a heart could hurt so much at thirteen. I saw everything happening right in front of me and I was powerless to stop it. It was almost as if a bomb was about to go off and I could neither run far enough to escape the blast or get to it quickly enough to disarm it.

I don't know where Rhonda was in all of this, but Tommy constantly roamed the halls looking for Tab. It didn't take long before the inevitable happened. After about three weeks of this sordid, twisted, flirtatious affair, Tommy broke up with Rhonda and did the obvious: He made Tabitha his new girl.

Her little clique cheered her on as if she had just pulled off the greatest coup in history. She was the first underclass female this school year to steal an upperclass female student's man.

Not just any female and not just any man. She had taken the best of the bunch from the best of the bunch. In those little hoochies' minds, it wouldn't be long before other upperclass guys fell under their spell.

Tabitha had the world at her fingertips. She was almost a deity to them. She received rave reviews on "her man," and about how they were a cute couple. In her friends' eyes, her victory was enticing. They believed before long they would be getting what they wanted also. It would be a just reward in their eyes for helping her to displace Rhonda.

Shortly after Tabitha's coup, the rest of them started to openly maneuver around the hallways with the seniors. The womanish young girls gathered strength and courage from Tab's inspirational victory.

They aggressively hung around the gym, and not long afterwards, started to openly sport the varsity's football player's jerseys. They acted like two-dollar whores who openly bowed to their physical temptations. The guys had followed Tommy's lead and started to date the underclass females: Most of those girls were eighth graders, which they seemed to prefer.

I watched all the developments with a keen eye. I watched Rhonda and the other ladies act cavalier about the whole thing. In fact, they had started to sport some of the underclass guys as if their ex-boyfriends were the furthest thoughts from their minds.

I was so distraught about the whole thing that I went to the most unlikely source for information in the world. I went to a non-paid informant, the want-to-be covert CIA agent, my sister Diane. I broke down and asked the cheap operative what was going on, and she gladly told me some things I didn't want to hear.

"It's nothing," she said. "It's just a thing every senior class does. The senior girls are not that intimate with the guys. They just have them carry their books, and maybe give them a kiss or let them steal a feel, if they are cute enough. Just a little something to play with their emotions and keep them strung out. It's a game."

She then looked at me with an obnoxious grin and broke my heart when she said, "The stupid little underclass hoochie females like Tabitha, they are going to get the bottom knocked out. The guys like that fresh stuff. They will pack them full of all that beef. When they get through with them, y'all can have them back. By then those guys will have taught them a few things, and then they can teach y'all."

She laughed at the range of expression showing on my face as she tormented me with her words. When she spoke these things, all of my hopes for my beloved and me were shattered. It was as if someone had dashed them against the granite rocks of Stone Mountain, Georgia.

And then she added, with the intention of twisting the dagger, "When spring comes around, everybody makes nice and resumes what they had before all this crazy stuff started because it will be class trip time. Don't feel so bad about it. Your girlfriend will not skin you up so bad, you know what I mean?"

There was a storm going on inside of me. I managed to give my face a blank faraway look. If anyone had looked into my eyes at this time, they would have seen the fire raging within me and thought I was going crazy, which I probably was.

I kind of believed Diane about all this switching partners mess. I was ticked off. What was wrong with the senior girls? What were they thinking? Had they gone mad? Would they just turn their boyfriends out to play like a colt in the spring, and bring them back in later? Was this what high school was all about?

178

I saw Diane's prediction unfold. Some of the girls quickly turned away from their schoolwork and it became all about their boyfriends to them.

Tabitha was one of them. She was constantly in the office for being late because she was trying to hang around the gym with Tommy. There was no doubt in anyone's mind she was smart because she was making "A's" on her tests at the beginning of the school year. She tested so well at the seventh grade level she was placed in 8-1. But for right now, she had become a little too fast and started to fall by the wayside.

I didn't know of her academic situation and had all but forgotten about her. I was doing just well enough by myself and had finally written her off. Or at least I should have. This would have been the logical thing to do. I was a little foolish and didn't completely close the door to her.

One morning I was at my locker and someone said, "Hi, Johnny." I was frozen. I had heard the voice of a siren, and whether I knew it or not, I was about to sink my ship. I turned to face the voice, and it was Tabitha, my beautiful temptress. A frog was in my throat and I couldn't utter a word. I finally gathered enough strength to wave my hand in an awkward fashion. She moved very close to me, and I was squirming. Tabitha was flirting heavily with me and I didn't know why. I scanned the crowd and could not find Tommy. I relaxed some, but was still very tense.

"Where's Tommy?" I asked.

"Tommy isn't here yet and I need a little help with my algebra assignment," she said.

It wasn't obvious to me, but it was to everyone else. She was no longer my Tab from the first day of the year. She had mutated into someone or something else.

Tab had matured very quickly, both physically and mentally. Her breasts now complemented her bottom nicely. She had learned to use what she had, to get what she wanted. I was melting as if I was butter, and I quickly surrendered to all of her requests. We slipped into homeroom and I asked, "How much have you done?"

She smiled and dropped her head. Laughing, she looked up and replied, "Nothing."

She had not done anything. There were over fifty proofs that had to be done.

My grades at this time were good. Hers were not. She could not absorb another "F" in this six-week period, or so she said, so she pleaded with me to do her homework. I looked at her strangely because I could not believe what she was asking. I sarcastically asked her if she wanted me to do all of her assignment.

She replied, "Yes," without blinking or smiling. She was serious about the whole thing.

"Tabitha," I said, "the bell is about to ring and our math class is second period. I don't have time to do the work again."

She stepped even closer to me and placed her hand around my waist and pinned me solidly against the wall with her body. My heart was about to leap out of my chest.

"Give me yours, and I will put my name on it. I will look over it and make sure I understand what you have done. If Papa Bear calls me to the board, I can explain how I got the answer. You have an "A" average, and you can afford to take one knock. He drops the lowest grade, right?"

By now there was a noticeable bulge in my pants that I tried to hide with my binder. I felt kind of warm and was panting heavily. I was overly stimulated; it didn't take much to get my mind off and running at this age. I gave in to her request before my heart went into cardiac arrest. This moment I was experiencing was almost like a euphoric torture, and I liked it a lot. I loved the experience I was having, and I knew I wanted more.

I gave her a blue folder I had tucked neatly inside my notebook. I followed her to her desk and stood over her like a centurion as she erased my name and studied my work. She had only been cramming the material in her mind for about five minutes when the bell rang.

I quickly slid into my old desk in back of her as all the students rushed into the room to take their seats. It was a zoo-like atmosphere, as everyone discussed the fourth period pep rally and if they were going to the game.

Debra, Tabitha's new best friend, stood over me because I was in her seat and said rather rudely, "You want to put those buddies to use and move?"

It was a "gotcha" slap at my shoes and this caused everyone in the room to laugh hysterically at her back-door joke. She had just said what everyone else whispered behind my back. My cheap outfits were probably the real reason why Tabitha had turned so standoffish towards me.

Tabitha tried to maintain her composure and not laugh. She couldn't hold it in. She turned to Debra, while still trying to restrain herself from laughing aloud, and told her not to treat me in such a manner.

It was such an embarrassing moment for me. I felt as big as a nanometer as I tried to slither off to my seat on the other side of the room. I had not understood the importance of being in brand-name shoes and clothing. It was now clear why Diane had ridden me so hard about my wardrobe. I fell back into my little clique of scholarly students and put my head down. I felt sick to my stomach.

After everyone took their seats and the late bell rang, Mrs. Wallace called the roll. I kept my head down and wanted to forget about Debra's joke. I could barely hear when my name was called. I don't know how Mrs. Wallace heard me when I said, "Here," after she called my name, because I spoke it directly into the desk without looking up. My intermingling amongst my classmates was at an all-time low this morning. If I could, I would have boarded the bus and gone back home immediately. This had been my most embarrassing moment at the high school I had thus far, and it showed on my face.

The bell rang and classes started. I tried to hide myself within the defenses of my gifted friends as we exited the room. I thought I would be safely enclosed within their ranks and away from the vicious vipers. I was operating on the premise of there being safety in numbers.

As everyone moved down the hall laughing and talking about any and everything, the sound of the steel lockers banging closed echoed through the school. The known couples were pairing up and holding hands. The couples who were discreet and down low hid what they were doing. If anyone looked close enough, they could see it in their eye contact and surreptitious hand waves. The rest of the students stayed within their little clans and moved in tight formations to their destinations as if they were schools of fish. My crew was one of these groups.

I was now more attentive as I moved through the hallways to the conversations in my secondary environment after Debra's joke. The indiscreet discussion seemed to gain focus on me as I walked through various areas. I heard a lot worse than the sampling Debra had given me. It stung my ears to hear the verbal jabs being thrown my way in the background conversations.

Some of the students said I would slip and fall in my shoes. Others said I had on hard-bottom tennis shoes. Even some of the well-mannered students chimed in; they said I dressed like a white boy in my shirt. It just seemed that everybody had jokes, but it was obvious they were not comedians, and their jokes were not funny, at least not to me.

The shoe joke I understood, but the dressing like a white boy joke I didn't quite understand. I didn't know what was wrong with the way white boys dressed, or if it was supposed to be an insult, but I took it as one.

Out of the entire student body, there were only about 120 white people. From what I saw of them, there was nothing wrong with what they had on. They dressed just fine, but as evident by the "janking" or the name-calling that I received, there was something wrong with the clothes I had on.

I took another look at my shirt and noticed most of the white students had on shirts like mine. And again, I still didn't see anything wrong with what I had on. Maybe I would have come out better by just hanging with them.

Most of these minority students stayed off to themselves. The black population far outnumbered the whites. This was kind of strange for a place with only one institution for high school learning in two counties that I knew about. Therefore, I did not know or understand where most of my grade school white friends had gone. I didn't have time to dwell on anything like this because I was under a full assault and just worrying about trying to survive here.

The inconsiderate jokes were getting to me. I was embarrassed and a bit confused. I tried to camouflage myself further in the middle of my friends to hide the shoes and shirt I was wearing, but it was doing me no good. My sneakers were making solid noises as they struck the tile floor. This meant I was like a lightning rod. Even the Area 51 students received the memo to wear brand-name clothes and shoes. Where was I when this information was disseminated?

It was painful to be the butt of everyone's jokes, but I could not do anything about it now. I had gone the cheap way on my school clothes and was paying the price for being frugal. I still had some money left over and made up my mind, or the students made up my mind for me, that I would ask Momma to buy me a pair of Nikes this weekend.

As we turned to come down the home stretch to our first class, Tommy and the other senior cronies were lining the hallway of the main entrance of the vocational wing. They had come here purposely to set up shop. I knew what they were up to because their class was in the gym and it was located on the other section of the building. It was apparent to me and everyone else, they were waiting on Tabitha and her little clique.

As my friends and I approached the area, we remained in tight formation. I was flanked on all sides as if I were the president, trying to hide in the middle of my Secret Service. We traveled slowly and a lot farther behind Tab and her crew.

They left the main body of the crowd and migrated towards their perspective boyfriends. I could not be disappointed because of this. I knew better. I was out of my league. How could I be intelligent and be so dumb at the same time? To associate smart with me was an oxymoron.

I watched helplessly as Tab made a beeline for Tommy, whose gold jewelry was shining so brightly in the hallway it gave off a pseudo-luminescent light. And when I got close enough, I could see her nestled in Tommy's arms, playing in his curly locks with one hand.

He had his football jersey on and she was resting her other hand against his chest, which he apparently could make jump at will. I heard him ask her, "You like the hair, huh? Well, ain't nothing in there but berries and juice."

184

I said to myself, "That punk. He ain't nothing. He knows he's lying with all that activator and other chemicals in his hair."

When we were finally alongside the couples, I turned away because I didn't think I could take one more second of watching this Medusa-like scene. I looked straight ahead, and by mistake, I saw what I purposely turned away from.

It was Tabitha and Tommy's image hugged up all lovey-dovey in the corner by the water fountain. I could see their reflection in the glass of the shop doors, and it turned my stomach. He was palming her booty and the sight of that turned me to stone.

Refusing to stop and trying to forget about what I had seen, I followed my gifted friends to the classroom and we took our seats. They didn't hang out in the hall like the other students. I was now with guys discussing math problems and science projects, and they kept my mind steered in the right direction. I was fortunate to be amongst friends like these.

I managed to calm down and I was fine until the door opened. What I saw drove a stake through my heart. One by one the girls came in, and each one of them had on her boyfriend's football jersey. The sight made me cringe as I prepared myself for what I would see next. What I was prepared to see, I saw, and a whole lot more.

Tabitha walked in with Tommy, his jersey, and his gold chain. It was sickening to me but I had braced myself for this part. What I saw next just destroyed me. Tommy could have walked out with her tongue if he wanted to, because she tried to cram it down his throat before he left the room.

There was supposed to be no kissing at school, and they had stolen this moment to display their affection. I had developed a dogma that I was always the center of everything. And I knew

Tommy was just doing it to torment me. I turned away and hoped the teacher would catch them.

Mr. Bradley was supposed to be on guard duty, but he was out back stacking and sorting lumber. He was out of place as usual as they got away with their kiss.

The way the other students acted when they witnessed it, I could have sworn they had witnessed a Brinks heist being pulled off. The room simultaneously roared, "Wow!"

The girls were high-fiving and yelling out to Tabitha, "You go, girl," and "Handle your business, ain't nobody got nothing on you."

In their eyes Tab was just the smoothest girl around. She had come on the scene and in her first year in high school pulled the captain of the football team under her spell. He was the man everybody wanted and she apparently had him chasing her.

All the guys in the room were impressed as well. Even the gifted crowd was overwhelmed by this astounding feat. It irritated me even more when my friends almost openly worshipped the scene taking place in front of them.

How could they be taken in by the actions of these two idiots? These dummies acted as if they had just witnessed a nuclear bomb going off or a star going supernova. They were apparently just as awestruck as everyone else by the coolness of this gigahoe.

I was steamed and said to myself, "Tommy could have had anybody he wanted. Why is he down here with an eighth grader? What is up with this guy?"

As much as I tried to make sense of it all, my deliberations were not coming up with anything logical. I thought back to what Diane had told me about the seniors and I just shook my head. I knew Tabitha was going to get what she deserved and it was only a matter of time.

186

When Mr. Bradley finally came into the room, fifteen minutes later than he was supposed to, he started the class off by saying, "We are going to discuss safety in the shop area. We are going to talk about keeping the aisles clear of debris and liquid spills. If some kind of liquid is wasted on the floor, we are going to discuss the proper clean-up to prevent slip and fall accidents."

When he said the last part, a low giggling sound seeped from the class. Almost all eyes turned to me. As if on cue, Debra started in on me again by asking, "Mr. Bradley, hard-bottoms are not allowed in the shop area, right?"

He responded by saying, "That's correct, Debra."

She struggled to calm herself down and barely could get her joke out. She laughed so hard I suspected what was coming. Debra managed to pull herself together and say, "Well, you better keep John out of the shop until he gets some more shoes."

A tidal wave of laughter rushed forward and I dropped my head. Tabitha gently elbowed her friend and once again told her to leave me alone, yet she could not restrain herself from laughing and didn't try to hold it in any longer. Mr. Bradley had to laugh as well. It was a pretty good joke. If I hadn't been the butt of it, then I would have laughed too.

I sat there and took all of this abuse and didn't open my mouth. I didn't have time to "jank." I knew it would have broken down into "Your momma this" and "Your momma that," and then I would have to drag her for about a mile. I wasn't beyond hitting a girl with the dark side. I would pimp-slap her butt all the way back to Ottawa, Georgia. I was thinking, "She don't know me like that." I gave her the first joke. She took the second, and I was determined to have the third for myself.

The two of us exchanged evil stares the rest of the period. When the bell rang, I didn't waste time waiting on my bodyguards.

They weren't doing anything for me anyway. I bolted out of the room and on to algebra. I sat down in my seat and waited for class to start. I knew I didn't have my homework and I didn't care.

When Tab made it to the room, I saw what I was getting for sacrificing my homework. She came in with "her man," and didn't even look at me.

She was like a groupie with Marvin Gaye. She swooned all over Tommy. I almost thought I would have to go and get the school nurse for her. She looked like a lovesick pup over this guy. It just made my flesh crawl the way she acted.

Once again, it seemed to me that Tommy purposely looked at me as if to say, "Watch this." He then reached down and grabbed a couple handfuls of what I loved. It just seemed to be like a water balloon in his hands. The way it moved and slipped through his fingers irritated me. She was supposed to be mine. That was supposed to be mine.

Tommy's action caused me to sigh heavily. It caused Tabitha to giggle uncontrollably for about the next twenty minutes. I bit my lip really hard and contemplated slapping the hell out of him. I knew the guy would beat me down, but I wanted a piece of him in the worst kind of way.

Once the stragglers came in and took their seats, Mr. Thomas walked in and the class started. He called for the homework he had assigned. Everyone passed theirs up to the front except me. Tabitha passed mine in, and what made it worse was it didn't even have my name on it. She would be getting credit for my work and all the thanks I received was to have my heart drug through a mound of human refuse. I thought, "How much worse could my situation really get?"

I managed to hold it together the rest of the period without completely breaking down. I avoided more blunt-force insults from Debra, and eventually made it to fourth period.

It was time for the pep rally. Tommy and his cohorts rushed up to the girls to get their jerseys. They then bolted into the locker room to prepare to have their names called out. All of this was supposed to be a new big tradition for the school.

I didn't want to be in the gym or part of the stupid gathering. I felt those guys didn't deserve a pep rally. I didn't think anything could pick their spirits up. Two years ago they lost 63-0 on a good night. Last year they lost 58-3 and fans said they were doing better.

Everyone tried to be optimistic, but they had not won a game since their inception, and all indications were they would not win one anytime soon. The only thing that could possibly pick their spirits up was a forklift, and even that heavy equipment would find it hard to raise emotions that low.

When the student body was seated and the pep rally began, the cheerleaders came out and did their little cheers. The student body stood up and applauded. They then started calling for their football team. They stomped on the bleachers and shouted so loud the noise and the vibrations from their pep rally seemed to cause the gym to shake.

I didn't get up. I enjoyed the shaking of the bleachers, which acted like a therapeutic massage to my body and ego. I was a miserable young man who simply sat there with my arms folded, mad at the world. It was painful for me to be forced to sit there and listen to them reciting the names of the football players. I looked straight ahead and imitated a statue. I neither turned to the left or right. I just wanted this assembly to be over.

When they finally got to Tommy's name, the whole student body stood up and went mad. He was the so-called star running

189

back and co-captain of the football team. Rhonda rushed up and hugged him, and they both dashed out to the middle of the gym.

She was the head cheerleader on the squad and picked Tommy to escort out to center court. When their eyes met, they paused for a minute, and I saw sparks. Not from the two of them, even though they were flirting heavily.

The sparks came from under Tabitha's collar. I wanted to tell her to calm down before those chemicals set her hair on fire. She was fighting mad. Just about as mad as I was when Tommy grabbed what I loved. The look on her face brought me a little redemption. I knew at this moment, she felt the way I did. Hurt.

The next name they called out was Joshua Preston. He was the other captain. He stuck out like a snowflake on coal. He was a white and the starting quarterback for the Bi-County Raiders. He wasn't that good. He was just a token white boy. The way the coaching staff had him billed, he was the second coming of Broadway Joe Namath. The sad thing about it was the only thing that he had in common with Joe was that he was white.

When the 120 minority students heard his name, they stood up and cheered like crazy, as if they were at a rock concert. Playing quarterback was the glory position on the field and the coaches said they needed someone who could think at this spot. It was a derogatory remark aimed at the black athletes on the team.

Most of the black students acted like they didn't know what was going on because they were up cheering, too. Some of the more conscientious students sat down and folded their arms in a defiant pose like me and refused to show the guy any love.

The school was fracturing and there was no unity around this place. The silent protest the small groups of students were having was because the Raiders were a predominantly black school that now sported a white quarterback.

190

The reason the white coaches had said we weren't winning games did not sit well with them. They were upset because they were using code talk, saying they needed a "thinking" quarterback to pull the trigger behind center so he could make some things happen.

The black coaches acted as though they concurred and didn't speak up for the young black quarterbacks. They often moved them to receiver or corner. If they didn't want to do this, they moved them off the team. The attitudes of the black coaches did more to cement in the thinking of inferiority than anything a white coach could do or say.

It was pitiful. They didn't mind telling anybody who would listen they needed a "thinking" quarterback. They went out and actively recruited someone who could actually "think under fire," and the football losses seemed to become worse.

Maybe it wasn't the quarterback, black or white, who was inferior, but the coaching. I don't think they ever considered this as a possibility. It was obvious for some reason their system was not working. People always looked to shift blame when the real problem looked at them in the mirror.

After the pep rally was over and the students began to prepare for their next class, I wanted to watch what would happen between the two lovebirds. I watched as Tab stormed out of the gym, and Tommy quickly followed her. I watched for a moment as Rhonda laughed at them, and then turned to hug her little boyfriend, as he came out of the bleachers to talk to her.

She had just made a statement, and Tabitha didn't like it. If Diane hadn't seen all this play out before, I would have sworn she was a descendent of Nostradamus.

I then did my best Pink Panther imitation, took a shortcut, and quietly exited a side door leading outside and then back into the main hall. I managed to intercept them on the library wing of the

191

building. I watched as the couple quietly entered the back of the stage in the cafetorium.

I casually entered the back door and silently slipped into a small alcove inside the doorway, which led to where they were, and then secretly watched the couple argue about what happened in the gym. They were so involved in their conversation they didn't see me imitating a sleuth. I quietly closed the door so I could discreetly watch the fireworks.

Tabitha had her hands folded and looked mean. I knew at this point she was going to kick Tommy to the curb. I watched Tommy as he tried to pull her close to him. She put out her hand to block this move. She then raised the same hand up to his face and gave him the military halt sign.

Tommy acted as though he thought about smacking her, and I almost left my hiding place. If that pretty boy had done that, he would have had to beat me down because he would have had a fight on his hands. I knew I would have probably lost the fight, but I was looking for any legitimate reason to try to introduce this guy to some pain.

Tommy's little bluff caused Tabitha to take his necklace off and hit him in the chest with it. He didn't try to catch his jewelry, and it fell to the floor. He was still disputing something passionately, talking with his body as well as his mouth. There was no way out of this. I felt that the two of them would surely split up. I saw all I needed to see, so I hurried to get to my class before I was late.

Five minutes passed, and Tabitha still had not come to the room. After ten minutes passed, Mrs. Callaway sat at her desk and started writing. She got up and continued what she was doing an additional five minutes, and still there was no Tabitha. She then called me to her desk and told me to take the disciplinary slip to the office. I knew what it was before she called me: It was a write-up slip for Tabitha being late because she was the only one not there.

I walked to the office, constantly looking for Tabitha on the way. I didn't see her anywhere and casually dropped the slip of paper in a trashcan I walked by. I went around the entire building and then returned to class. I was disappointed Tabitha had decided to do a skip. She had to be crazy. To do this meant an automatic three days in in-school suspension.

I had unwisely covered for her, and I knew I was beyond the all-time doofus mark. I was a dweeb. How could I keep doing stupid stuff like this? She didn't like me and didn't even appreciate me doing anything for her. I sat in my desk beating myself up for the remainder of the class.

I thought I was beginning to lose it. Mr. Bill words echoed in my head: "Are you dumb, boy?"

I nodded my head up and down and said, "Yep" out loud, and everybody in the class looked at me, including Mrs. Callaway. I wished I could take that part back, but obviously I was dumb, and crazy as well.

The bell rang and I headed for my last class. I stepped out of the door and I could see Tabitha coming down the hall. She had her head down, walking with her arms crossed, and she didn't look too good. I made a beeline toward her, and then suddenly stopped.

The reason she walked with her head down was because she still had that heavy gold chain around her neck. If she kept that thing on, then she was bound to have back problems.

She occasionally ran her fingers through her hair, and the activator acted as a cleaning agent to increase the luster of Tommy's rings that she had on her fingers. It was obvious she had not kicked Tommy to the curb. For me to say I was a little disappointed was an understatement. I was not the only one I could think of who was dumb, a doofus and a dweeb. Those adjectives fit her, too.

If I wouldn't get in trouble myself, I would dig the slip out the trashcan and take it to the office right now. I waded to the other side of the hall so a lot of people were between us. I could see she had been crying and my heart was still out there for her. I began to make my way back across the hall to intercept her when Debra popped up. She began to console her and counsel her about her relationship. I was ticked. Debra didn't know what was going on and she was not Dr. Ruth. She should have just minded her own business and kept her mouth shut.

I went to my locker and grabbed all the books I would need for homework the next day. I stepped into the classroom and when class started I just wasn't feeling it. This was a period I should have skipped. So many things were going through my head that I felt as if I was trapped on a deserted island with no one to talk to.

With several issues with Tabitha fighting for dominance in my mind, I also had to wrestle with the thought that I was probably one egg short of a dozen. I wondered why my life had turned so complex once again. After this class was over, I was going to hustle to the bus and try to forget about everything. I was trying to maintain a stiff upper lip. Somehow I knew I had to sustain my composure and just get home.

I sat in class not really listening to the teacher and watched Tabitha and Debra pass notes back and forth. They had to be discussing her relationship. I was cool until both of them looked around at me. I assumed Debra was talking about me and told her I took the slip to the office. This crazy little girl didn't know what was going on and she should keep her nose out of my business.

I didn't know exactly what they were writing on the notes, but I wanted to show Tabitha I was concerned about her, so I picked up my pen and wrote:

Tab, where were you? Mrs. Callaway wrote you up. Are you all right?

I passed the letter up the aisle, praying Mrs. Mayo wouldn't catch the thing. It made it all the way to Debra's desk. It didn't travel any further. The top-secret memo had fallen into enemy hands.

Debra turned around and looked at me and opened the letter with a smirk on her face, and started reading. I didn't know what was up with this girl, but I wanted to knock her head off. She was acting like she was Tabitha's pimp.

I turned away from them and tried to listen to the instruction for the class being given. I was close to going home and glad to have this part of my day almost over.

When the bell rang I rushed out of the room without looking around or stopping. This action by itself made Debra's day. She enjoyed picking at me because I was an easy target and she was learning she could easily rattle me.

While going home on the worst day of my high school life, I didn't feel like talking. I silently stared out the window, not really engaged in anyone or anything. I wasn't even trying to count the trees anymore or see what might be happening on a farm. I reflected on my life and felt sorry for myself.

"Johnson," a voice called out. "You want to play football?" I looked around to see my cousin, Tyrone, who had switched seats with someone and plopped down behind me.

Tyrone said he wanted to play but didn't want to be the only one on the team from Brooklyn. I then took the time to remind him that we were in the eighth grade and were not really high school students. How could we play sports? We were not old enough.

Tyrone told me the coach said it was cool; they were starting a "B" team and would play about four games. People from Brooklyn had stopped playing sports and they wanted to get us back into the act.

"They specifically asked about you because they say your brother and all your sisters played sports. They were all pretty good. The coaches said one of them holds the school's scoring title in basketball. She poured in seventy-three points in one game, before the three-point line. Is this true?"

"I don't know. I will ask her and I will let you know tomorrow. I'll let you know if I want to play then, too."

I turned around and continued doing what I was doing, sulking in my morbid thoughts about my life. Somewhere between here and yonder, I managed to snap out of my daze to hear another one of my cousins picking on my nephew. It was David, and he was going at Rodney hard. I turned around full of aggression and rage from earlier and warned him he had better stop.

"Before you criticize him about his teeth, you should start by criticizing your sister about hers, with her nappy head."

The kids were both the same age, and if Rodney wasn't off-limits, then Angela wasn't either.

This last comment caused the bus to laugh, and David didn't like it at all. He told me, "You got jokes, right? You want to jank? You need to meet me at the bottom of the hill, and we'll see if you want to jank then. We will see how many jokes you got when I put the 'gold glove' on you."

I was looking for a fight and told him, "Don't be late because you just made a date."

196

I intended to take a lot of my rage out on David. He thought it would be business as usual and I would not fight back, but he was going to be in for a shock this time. I was going through problems and was looking for outlets to vent my rage and frustrations and this venue was as good as any.

The whole bus hummed with the anticipation of the scheduled bout. Kids started to call the other people who had gotten off earlier and tell them about what was going down. They acted as though a heavyweight title bout had just been scheduled and they were the promoters.

They gave the reach to me, but the weight and the experience was given to David. He was a year older and had me by about ten pounds. The betting line was probably even or too close to call initially. Everyone said, "This is going to be a good one." The only thing they missed was Michael Buffer.

When I got home, I hopped off the bus and ran into the house. I put my books down and slid on an old pair of Levi's jeans. I was going to use psychological warfare by going up the road with no shirt so I could show off my lean muscular frame. I intended to handle my business with him to get a little respect one way or another.

When I reached the end of the driveway, I turned to go up the road and was surprised to see all the children in the neighborhood walking down the hill with David. They surrounded him like they were his entourage and he was the undisputed champ.

I saw him coming down the street with his hand held up, sporting his gold batting glove as if he was doing a black power imitation. He had bragged to everyone he was going to knock me out with his "gold glove." He had worked his fans up into a frenzy with all his trash talking. They had come to the bottom of the hill to get a ringside seat for this fight.

I walked up the road in a quiet rage; Diane and Betty followed closely behind me. They came to bear witness to the fight as well. They were there in my corner, too, just to make sure I got a fair fight. If I didn't, they were going to even up the odds.

The mob moving with David was becoming restless. It was becoming evident most of the fans had started to favor my adversary. The guy had stirred the masses and had a firm base of support.

All of this stuff was irrelevant to me. All those fans he had really didn't matter as long as they stayed out of my fight. I was determined to get some respect from this guy one way or another. If it meant I had to drag him up and down the road a few times until no skin was left on him, then that's what I was going to do.

When we met, we were two scared combatants standing there face to face. One of us was scared and the other one was glad of it. We stood there for a long time, but never touched gloves to come out fighting.

"You got jokes, right?" David asked me as if he were giving me one more chance to back down.

I was not interested in making a treaty. This was not an option. I yelled out, "I damn sure do, with her nappy head!" trying to spur David on to a battle neither of us really wanted.

We began to circle each other, bumping chest to chest, each of us trying to test the strength of the other. After a few minutes of this, someone yelled out, "Y'all talked all that trash, go ahead and rumble! Damn! I came to see a good fight!"

Jimmy stepped forward and placed a small twig on each of our shoulders and said, "The first one to knock it off is the baddest."

That move provided the spark to ignite a combustible situation as we both reached up and knocked the sticks off, and the fight was on.

198

I landed a flurry of punches to David's head and forced him back into the weeds on the left side of the road. He wasn't really in the supine position because of the angle of the bank. He was more at a sixty-degree angle. I had the presumed champ already in trouble, and the fight had just started.

Ricky, trying to get a little mayhem started, whispered in David's brother Eddy's ear, "You going to help him, right?"

Eddy looked over at the two Amazons, Diane and Betty, and put his best spin on things.

"Naw, he got him. He just got a little lucky."

I finished my good move off by hitting him a few more times for good measure and backed off. I had contemplated the idea of a full mount, but decided against it. David was in a dangerous position because there was a possibility I would not be able to hold him because of the weight difference and would be flipped.

I hopped up, backed away and began bouncing around, telling David, "Come on. You all tough, right? Come and get some more."

If David could have left the scene and saved face, he would have. There was no doubt in my mind he would have taken this option. He had talked so much trash he knew walking away wasn't in the cards. He had to back this one up or risk losing the respect of everyone in Brooklyn.

He walked reluctantly and slowly over to me and had to be thinking, "What on earth have I gotten myself into?"

We began to circle each other once again with the chest-to-chest stuff. I thought the fight was just about over because it was apparent to me I had the guy scared. David wasn't going to try anything else. I felt as though I proved my point and I had my respect from the want-to-be bully. I relaxed some and was about to leave and go home.

Before I could turn and walk away, I was suddenly staggered about two yards backwards. David came up with an uppercut that caught me flush under the chin, knocking some of my skin off, and causing me to bite my tongue. The blow hurt me bad and David knew he had me stunned.

I grabbed my jaw and tensed every muscle I had in my face, asking myself, "Where on earth did that punch come from?"

David had made solid contact with a crushing blow. I tried to compose myself as David held his right fist in the air and said, "Spit blood, sucker, gold glove!"

He didn't follow his good move up, instead he was walking around again as if he was waving the black power symbol, inciting the crowd, who appeared to be going crazy with the punch he had managed to sneak in.

The crowd's would-be champ appeared to be back in control of our skirmish. David knew his punch had gotten my attention and had taken away any momentum I had. The tide had turned and he was now feeling better about the fight. But his failure to capitalize on his momentum allowed me to recoup.

Whether David tried to crack a joke or not, I did have to spit blood, and when I did, I rushed the guy. I took a roundhouse to the shoulder on the way in, but I managed to get the better of the exchange by landing rapid blows to his stomach. At least one shot hit him in his diaphragm, forcing the wind out of him, causing him to bend over and gasp for air. He managed to push me away and retreat a few steps.

While bent over, he saw a rock or perhaps it was a massive dirt clod he picked up and began to chase me with. He intended to do some damage with his improvised weapon and I knew he could throw hard, so if he hit me, I would really be in some serious trouble.

I made a tactical retreat to the other side of the road, keeping one eye on him so that I could try to dodge whatever was in his hand if he threw it, while simultaneously looking for a rock or something I could use to defend myself. I quickly found out my search was in vain. The road had been drug and rocks were usually everywhere, but there were none around today. I quickly decided to dash into the wood line to try to find anything I could use to turn the table.

After searching for a weapon about ten yards into the woods, I reemerged with an old oak limb and began to chase David, and it was obvious this skirmish was beginning to get out of hand.

Diane said, "Y'all need to put that stuff down before someone gets hurt."

Feeling he was outgunned, David threw the object down and most of it disintegrated back into the earth. I looked at him, hesitated, and dropped my limb close to my side. I didn't trust him. If he thought he would pick something up and hit me while I didn't have my stick, then he was crazy.

We slowly approached each other again and David shouted some provocative comments at me.

"Bring your black ass on and get some more of this gold glove. You ugly punk."

I didn't bite, and he then charged me with the intention of trying to spear me. I instinctively reacted and absorbed the impact of his maneuver. I caught him by the shoulders, and, with the momentum he generated, I rolled so that both of us hit the ground on our sides.

The Georgia clay bit into me fiercely, ripping the skin off my bare shoulder, exposing a three-inch gash of my white meat and causing me to grimace in pain. I thought about my decision not to wear a shirt. This was stupid on my part, and if I ever were in another fight, I would make sure I wore everything, including body armor if I had the stuff.

We struggled back to our feet, both fighting like crazy for respect. David was fighting not to lose his and I was fighting to gain mine. With each blow landed, we both regretted our decision about this fight. Maybe this is why in the Bible it says: "Casting lots keep mighty men apart." There was a reason for this wisdom, and I thought it meant keeping David and me apart as well.

The fighting only stopped when Momma made her way up the road. She had heard all the cheering and stuff and had come to see what was going on. Disappointed in what she saw, she ran the kids home and told hers to get our asses back in the yard. Momma scolded all of us who gathered at the foot of the hill to witness the fight. She told David and me that she was disappointed in us because we were cousins. We knew better than that stuff.

It was a memorable battle that happened at the foot of the hill in the early evening hours after school. Both of us had knots and bruises all over our bodies. We both left some skin on the battlefield, but managed to pocket some pain from our fight and take it home with us. I won my coveted respect in Brooklyn this day. And I was happy I had the fight, but at the same time I was hurting so much I regretted the decision to do so. The battle turned out to be no more than a Pyrrhic victory in which I could take no pride.

When I finally made it to the house, I went to the bathroom to assess the damage David had inflicted on me. I took a bath cloth and wiped the dirt out of my bruised chin and spit out the blood, which was steadily accumulating in my mouth. I checked my teeth and one appeared to be loosened a little from the punch David landed when he caught me off guard.

My shoulder stung, as I pressed the cold soapy water against the spot where my skin used to be. I had knots on my head I had not noticed before. It didn't seem like David hit me that many times.

Momma was standing in the bathroom door fussing. She was still pretty hot with me. I told her what the fight was all about and what happened. She quieted down some. She still thought that our fighting was bad, but when she found David was picking on her grandson for no reason, she understood. She always told us family is supposed to stick together. She was actually glad I did get a hold of her nephew.

Since she had calmed down a little, I decided to push my luck and ask her about football.

"Momma," I said. "Can I play football at school?"

She seemed to hesitate, and then asked me who was going to do my work around the house. I told her I would, and explained how I would get it done. Momma told me okay, but if I didn't do my chores, I would have to quit.

Chapter Thirteen: Football

Monday came and I grabbed a pair of shorts and old shirt. I stuffed them in a gym bag on top of my books. Momma had given me permission to play football, and I was going to give it a try. I needed to do something to impress the girls and raise my stock, which was probably the most worthless around the school at this time. I remembered how I gained a little respect when people discovered I was athletic, and playing football was probably my best shot at getting some reverence.

When we finally made it to the school, Tyrone walked up behind me and said, "Well?"

"Well, what?" I asked.

"Did she score all those points?"

"I forgot to ask her because of my little scuffle, but Diane said she did."

This statement was almost like a joke, and Tyrone and I shared a laugh about it because we knew Diane had been known to tell a lie or two. After we finished laughing, I told him I actually believed her. We had both seen her play basketball with the guys and hold her own, so we knew she was good.

And then Tyrone got to what he really meant.

"What you going to do about football, Johnson?"

I smiled and said, "I got my gym clothes in my bag. I'm ready."

I told him to make sure he was out front. If he wasn't, I was going home. We both agreed and parted ways yelling out, "Bet!"

I walked down the hallway toward my homeroom. I could see Tabitha and Tommy leaning in a window. I looked away from them as if something on the other side of the hall had caught my attention and found relief in the fact they were content upon ignoring me.

Walking a little further, I could see Debra and her football-playing boyfriend, Mario, leaning in their window. I wanted to turn around and head back up the hall, but I was determined to see it through.

I had a really bad feeling the closer I came to them and started to walk to the other side of the hall, intentionally looking the other way. It was not so easy this time because these two did not give me a pass.

Mario spotted me coming and began mimicking my steps by striking the window. The imitation of equines he made to accompany the noise indicated he was trying to make my footsteps sound like horse hooves. This got some people's attention and they started to giggle. I still didn't acknowledge him. I kept walking past and headed for the bathroom.

Debra yelled out, "They got the caution sign out, John. Don't fall and break your neck!"

The laughter carried over the hall like drums in a jungle. What was their problem with me? I had done nothing to them. I actually had on a pair of Nikes, and although they were the cheapest kind, they were still brand-name.

I weathered the abuse and it made me more determined than ever to play football. I needed to score some points to raise my stock around this place. I had been beaten so bad mentally I needed one of those fireside chats President Roosevelt used to give to keep the nation on point. I had almost fallen into the category of being a national emergency. It was almost as bad as my days before Mrs. Perryton discovered me, and Mrs. Rogers rescued me. I needed a break in the worst kind of way.

At the end of the day, I met Tyrone at the entrance of the school. I asked him to show me where we were supposed to go. Tyrone pointed to the gym, and we took off across the school lawn, yapping it up about football.

"What position are you going to play?" Tyrone asked.

"I want to play running back like Walter Payton. Man, the guy is smooth. I am going to run that thang just like him."

Just thinking about football put a fire in my eyes. It made me feel stoked at the opportunity to relieve my frustration on someone.

When we stepped inside the gym, we joined the rest of the guys the coach had sitting in the bleachers. He was calling people's names from the sign-up sheet, and one by one they got up and went to the back. They didn't come back out and I did not know where they were going. Finally the coach pointed to me and I stepped into the locker room area.

I began to follow him back into the bowels of the building. The very first thing meeting me at the door was a malodorous breeze. The odor was strong and unpleasant, which caused me to paw my nose momentarily, but I did not frown up. It was a musty scent. A conglomeration of all the guys' body odor, mingled together with mildew and any other smells hiding out in a locker room.

I continued walking to the back of the building while constantly looking around an area I had never seen before. I tried to get a feel for this place, but it seemed like I didn't belong here.

When we turned the corner, the wide hall opened up into a big room with showers and lockers. I saw people in a line at a storage room and the gentle breeze had become a repugnant gust. There had to be a door opened somewhere.

The children had gathered in a makeshift line and were getting their equipment. I took my place at the rear and casually talked with some guys about the team we were forming. Everyone discussed the positions they wanted, and each of us was sizing the other up to try to determine if they had any athletic ability.

The line moved slowly and we were far enough into the room for me to see a spot on the floor where a bright beam of daylight had made itself at home. It was coming through an unseen opening from somewhere ahead of us.

The closer we got to the storage room, the stronger the draft became. I finally discerned the breeze was coming from outside and probably contaminated itself as it circulated around the locker room.

The gust, along with the stink it picked up, eventually greeted visitors whenever they opened the gym door with a big hug. This place really stunk badly. I could see most of the problems with the smell because it was right in front of my eyes. Laying in plain view were old socks, jock straps, old shirts and several other things hanging out of a few overstuffed lockers not worth mentioning.

When I finally made it up to the storage door to draw my equipment, I was glad I was close to getting out of this locker room. I now felt better because the wind blew full throttle and gave me a refreshing burst of much-needed clean air.

I tried on several helmets before settling on one that fit on my head and didn't wobble. I was surprised to see my head was as big as it actually was. It didn't look this big in the mirror. I took a quick peek at the label size and it told me my head was about the size of Newt Gingrich.

The coach gave me a good look-over and gave me some shoulder pads, which were cardboard thin. They were the basic issue and were so flimsy, it almost seemed like I didn't have any on. The pads had the residual smell of sweat oozing from the cloth lining, and of course, added to the bad smell of the room.

Teresa, the coach's assistant, slapped an assortment of body pads on the counter, along with a practice jersey, pants and something referred to as a girdle. She ran the procession of recruits similar to an old army war line.   If I knew the military scheme, it would have been easy to believe we were signing into basic training.

I got my stuff and walked outside in the Georgia heat and toward some of the guys I had seen around the school. I strolled up to them and asked, "What's up?"

They looked up at me and said, "Nothing much, man."

This was a universal question-and-answer we had to greet each other. I took a seat on the curbstone and we tried to assemble our equipment. It was obvious none of us knew what we were doing so everyone put our heads into the mix. After a few minutes we figured out how to assemble the pads and get the gear onto our uniforms.

The hardest thing was to get the jersey over our shoulder pads and the shoulder pads onto our shoulders and the strap latched down.

After everyone was situated we sat around for about thirty minutes waiting on Coach Davis to finish up and come out the door. It was rumored he had never coached anything before, but he had volunteered to help the school out. He was a smart guy and very athletic. He had grown up in the woods just like the River Boys.

The people from Richmond said he still liked mountain oysters. I thought this was disgusting. I didn't believe I could ever eat a hog's testicle. This eccentric man didn't believe in meat from a store and hunted his own. The only store meat he ever consumed had to come from Joe Bob's. Everyone knew Joe Bob raised and killed his own chickens, cows and hogs. Coach didn't believe in eating steroids and things in his meat. He believed in the all-natural way of living.

We stood back and watched him sprint to an open area by the large propane tank. He began stretching and loosening up. It was almost as if he had forgotten us. We were relieved because we were afraid of him. We thought the man was crazy and this little episode didn't help any.

In a sly kind of way, this may have been his method of getting the team's attention. If this was the case, he really didn't need to do anything because everyone was transfixed on him.

He taught physics and had a reputation of being a no-nonsense teacher. He didn't know much about football, or so he led us to believe. We thought he knew the basics and nothing more.

Over the next couple of days he gradually built up a routine, which was mostly mental, until he got the practice sessions in tune with his agenda. After a week of practice we were scheduled to play our first game. He walked us through some exotic plays he had drawn up and then asked, "Is this formation legal? Can we do that?" As if he wasn't sure.

Everyone laughed and then yelled out, "Yeah! We can do that!"

We really thought he did not know the answer himself. He laughed as well and then turned to Marvin Askew and asked in a serious tone, "Why is that legal or why is it illegal? Which one is it, and tell me why."

The young quarterback was lost. An impatient Coach Davis told him, "Go ahead and tell me, son."

Marvin couldn't focus. Coach Davis had caught him completely off guard with his little charade. He couldn't get his thoughts together and it irritated the coach.

Disappointed, he said, "Come on, son, you got to think." And he rapped on Marvin's helmet with his fist as if he was trying to see if there was anybody home.

He then walked us through the basics of telling the legality of formations once again. He went back over exactly what we could do and what we couldn't.

He was frustrated, but had faith in black kids and was there because he wanted to be. It was his personal mission to cultivate the indigenous talent around this area.

After he graduated he could have stayed gone like everyone else, but he chose to come back. He was probably the only faculty member truly offended when the statement about a thinking quarterback was made.

After a week of practice, the team was still off-point from where he wanted to be. To further exacerbate the situation, the first game was tomorrow. These were the plays we were supposed to be running.

He continued his walkthrough, as he chastised Marvin, telling him he had better get his act together. Playing quarterback was more than having a good arm. It also meant you knew what you and all of your teammates were supposed to do.

Not just where they were, but each one's assignment. He told the QB he had to be able to react on the fly to various situations and knowing everyone's assignment was just the beginning. He was the leader whether he wanted to be or not, and had to fill this niche.

We finished our walkthrough and headed for the showers. The young QB was cursing the whole way. He felt Coach Davis had just showed him up and it stuck with him. He didn't appreciate it and felt insulted. He felt he should not have been showed up in front of the team and was going to tell him so.

Marvin didn't say much in the locker room and deliberately kept his chatter down. He was trying to think of the best way to let Coach Davis know how he felt. After thinking about it, he decided the best way was just to come out with it and tell him what he thought about what happened on the field.

He stormed out of the locker room and saw Coach Davis going up the stairs.

"Coach!" he yelled out. "You got a minute?"

Coach Davis asked him if it was important. He told him it was, and the coach told him to come upstairs with him.

"I am really busy, son, and I don't have a lot of time at this moment."

They made it up to the top of the stairs and Marvin got right to the point. He came out with all of his frustrations.

"Coach Davis, why did you shine on me like that? No one else knew the answer either."

The coach took his time and continued getting his stuff together. Then he walked back over to his desk and took a seat. He looked at Marvin and told him to come over and have a sit down.

He became somber and he began to talk with the young man about life and being prepared.

"I didn't shine on you, son. You shined on yourself by not being prepared. You are the quarterback and the leader. If you don't want this responsibility, I will find someone who does. If you think I am going to baby you, then you are wrong. Look," Coach paused and said, "you got to be prepared. If this was life and this was your job, you would be in trouble. You might not have a job. If you put in a performance at work like the one you had on the field today, you might not eat. You understand what I am telling you?"

It was a mind-sobering conversation, which caused Marvin to reexamine his approach toward football. He was just told in a nice way he could lose his job if he didn't tighten up. He was not upset about the conversation. He couldn't be. He left the room knowing it was his fault he was not prepared.

This talk kindled a fire in his belly and he vowed it would never happen again. It now dawned on him, he could have fun with the other guys, but he had to be their leader as well. He had to set an example, and not being prepared was the wrong one.

The next day the B-Team rolled over the Washington County Bulldogs 20-0. The following week we defeated the Red Jackets of Americus County. Our team was on a roll and gave everyone hope for the future.

It seemed everything was going our way. We were young studs and were receiving congratulations and a lot of adulation from students and faculty. It wasn't long before we began to parade around the school like a bunch of superstars and exhibiting a cocky attitude about our success.

In the blink of an eye, the green-eyed monster arrived. The varsity team looked at us strutting about and began to say, "These guys have won a couple of games, and now they act like they have forgotten their role."

They were not too appreciative of our attitudes and let us know about it. It had to be a hard pill to swallow for the varsity because the hum at the school was about the B-Team winning football games and them always losing. The main attraction had lost the spotlight and had basically become a sideshow.

To make matters worse, even thought we were young upstarts, we walked about in our jerseys on Thursdays like we were better than the varsity. In fact, we probably were, but we didn't know we were supposed to act as though we weren't.

With victory came the spoils of war. Several of the guys who had not found themselves a girlfriend got lucky. The girls started chasing us down to gain favor. A few of us had the nerve to have them proudly walking around the school in our junior varsity jerseys.

When Coach Davis saw the little girls with the B-Team's jerseys on, he had to laugh. He told us, "Everybody loves a winner. Look at Paul. Even Paul has a girlfriend."

All the guys laughed but me. I could only muster a smile at this joke. Coach was holding Paul out like he was the most desperate one in the bunch. It was obvious he had overlooked me. Paul had scored and I had not.

However, my situation was somewhat different from Paul's. Paul was out hunting any and everything. He had taken the coach at his word when he told me, "You can walk down the hall and ask fifty girls to be your lady: One of them will say yes."

It had obviously worked for him and he was now happy with his situation. I was not about to try this carpet-bombing routine and had resorted to using smart technology. I was going to get exactly what I wanted and it was Tabitha. I was locked in on her and nobody else. I had to have her. She had consumed my every thought from the moment we met, and my heart was not able to hold one more of cupid's arrows. If I couldn't have Tab, then I didn't want anybody. To me, it was all or nothing, feast or famine. Right now it looked as though I was going to be hungry.

One day I saw Tabitha walking down the hall in between periods. It was almost perfect because my class was in the library. I decided to seize the moment to talk to her alone without Debra looking over my shoulder and quickly and quietly darted out of the side door to set up my ambush. I was going to cross over to the other wing of the corridor to cut her off and fake a chance encounter with her.

I made a right, turned the corner and headed down the hall and was now traveling toward her. Once she turned the corner, our eyes met and my heart began to race. I didn't know what to say. I had on my jersey, hoping it would give me a little prestige. I walked directly into her and simply said, "Hi, long time no speak."

She looked up at me and returned my smile and told me she was sorry she was so distant, she just had boyfriend problems lately, causing me to shake my head and look at her in a discerning manner. She was always having boyfriend problems and I knew the answer to them--it was me.

I licked my lips, trying to moisten them, seriously considering trying to kiss her. I could tell I was far from her mind so I quickly switched the direction of our conversation and asked her if she heard about our play, and success on the field. She smiled and told me, "Yeah I heard about y'all, John. You guys are the future. Look, I got to go. I can't stand here and talk with you because I am already late."

Charles, my teammate, saw us talking and walked out of the library. Charles and I were in the same room and took some of the same classes. The two of us had become friends.

Chuck also knew Tab well because they were from the same hometown. He was a person who spoke his mind. He knew our situation as well as anybody in the whole school. He was tired of seeing me being willingly manipulated.

He walked up and said, "Let the hungry heifer go ahead on, man. She ain't used to a winner. She would rather walk around in the varsity jersey that never won anything, than walk around in yours. It's a shame, your jersey ain't never lost nothing, and you would probably have to shoot her to get her to put it on."

Tabitha frowned and picked up her pace. She continued down the hall. I was kind of warm at him, but Chuck walked up to me and placed his hand around my neck, and told me, "If you knew her like I know her, you would leave her alone. Rule number one, you must never trust a big butt and a smile."

The animosity between the B-Team and the varsity continued to grow. The varsity didn't like our swagger. We had forgotten our place, according to them.

There was so much tension in the air between the two teams, that a pecking order inevitably had to be established. Some of the varsity told us: "If you think y'all are that good, why don't y'all play us? You want walk with a swagger, but you will stagger when we get through with you."

Marvin responded by saying, "Coach won't let us. If he said yeah, we would play y'all."

The varsity guys started smiling and told us, "Leave that to us."

They walked around the corner of the building where the coaches were standing and told them, "The JV want to play us."

The other coaches all looked at Coach Davis, waiting on his reply. He looked at them and said, "You know you guys are a little too big for my boys."

The other coaches had wanted a piece of the B-Team as well and they laughed mockingly at his response.

He glanced over at the other coaches and added, "But if y'all really want to, we can make it happen. We will play a half, and let you guys have a little fun. My kids probably want a measuring stick to test their abilities anyway."

Both teams assembled for a practice, which turned out to be nothing more than a scrimmage game. We lined up and got underway. After a short kickoff return, the junior varsity set up shop and started to go to work. The first play of scrimmage was a simple dive handoff to me.

I was scared, but I broke through the line and was on the second level. I tensed up, bracing for a hard shot from a line backer or a safety, but it never happened. I was surprised the tackling wasn't solid. They only jumped on my back and rode me to the ground. I got up and gained confidence with my solid run.

"This is kind of easy," I said to myself.

The next play was a 44 veer off-tackle. I broke through the line again, but this time I played with more confidence. I kept my head up and found the crease.

Mario slid toward the hole with the intention of meeting me there. He dropped his head to punish me, but he couldn't hit what he couldn't see. With a shuffle of my feet and a dip of my shoulder, I left him eating grass. I broke the run for sixty-five yards and a touchdown. I did a little dance and grinned hard. I found it hard to hold in my emotions as my teammates ran down the field to meet me.

After everyone settled down, we lined up for the kickoff. It was a low line drive kick that Tommy returned for seventy yards. The varsity was in business. They were down on our eight-yard line. The older boys were just going to line up and try to manhandle us. Taking the conservative approach, they tried two handoffs to Tommy.

Each time they tried, James met Tommy in the hole and turned him back. James was the hammer in the heart of our defense. He was one of the crazy River Boys who was already as big as the biggest varsity players.

Facing a lot of stiff resistance, the varsity was forced to throw on third and long. Evidently they hadn't taken us youngsters seriously and threw an out pattern in the end zone. This was the wrong option. Derek had squatted on this play, picked it off and stepped out of bounds.

Coach Davis liked what he saw. He then asked us if we wanted to rattle them. Everyone told him, "Yeah!"

He called a play action, double-tight-end-six-fade to Melvin, our speedy receiver. It worked. Melvin was one-on-one with Chicken Hawk and left him behind easily as Marvin's bomb hit him in stride. The Varsity was now down 14-0 and mad.

I opened my mouth and made an ill-fated statement. Walking back to the sideline, I said aloud, "They look like the B-Team," and laughed.

Mario heard it and began to pass the word around about what was being said. On the ensuing kickoff, Tommy fumbled the ball and we recovered. A mini-skirmish touched off.

The frustration of the game was getting to the varsity. They had wanted and asked for the B-Team, and they were getting what they asked for. They must have imagined the girls not wanting to wear their jerseys, but the B-Team's instead. This would be the ultimate insult.

Things had become desperate for the upperclassmen. They began to throw their weight around. They threw us to the ground and began to bully us. It was apparent they could not win on raw ability and tried to intimidate us to get the upper hand.

The coaches calmed everyone down and we resumed the scrimmage. Coach Davis ran a safe play to get us settled. He was just trying to get our confidence going again. The call was for a 25-belly. I took the handoff and was stuffed in the hole. Mario had popped me and stood me straight up. I struggled for a moment not to go down and was swarmed under by a defensive sea of humanity.

The defense kept coming without an apparent end. Everyone piled on top, way after the play was over. Wave after wave, they kept coming. By the time they sorted through the bodies, they found me with tears coming down my cheek and mucus out of my nose.

Mario had tried to rub the skin off my throat. He had his forearm pressed hard against my esophagus trying to choke me out and possibly break my neck. He was really giving me the business at the bottom of the pile.

I didn't know football got this rough. I struggled to my feet and snatched my helmet off and threw it about twenty yards. I was livid.

"I quit!" I yelled out at the top of my voice and walked off.

Mario had gone too far. There was no way I wanted to play football again for this school. I walked up to the bus and Coach Smith, the head varsity coach followed me, trying to reason with me because I was a prospective star.

He came up with a maneuver I never expected. He walked over and rubbed me on the stomach and asked in his best baby-talk voice, "Is the little baby okay?"

I had to smile because it made me feel I was overreacting and the tummy rub wasn't bad either.

After he was sure he had my attention, Coach Smith became serious and began to talk to me man to man. He told me I had some serious talent and I shouldn't let anybody run me off. The coach stated there was a possibility if we held our team together for four years, we could win a state championship. He definitely saw us winning a lot of games and getting the program turned around quickly. He won me over with our little chat and we walked back to the field.

The other coaches thought it was best to separate the teams before someone got hurt. Coach Davis had taken his B-Team to the other end of the practice field where they resumed practicing among themselves.

218

When the shepherd returned with his wayward sheep, Coach Smith told me to go ahead and rejoin my friends. Mario watched me the whole time. He had bad intentions for me. He wanted to punish me some more. There was no way anyone was going to stop him from getting a shot at me again. He had gotten a chance to give me a taste of what football was really about and he was not through with me yet.

The B-Team practice lasted another forty-five minutes and Coach Davis let us take it to the locker room early. We left the field in a hurry to get dressed and gather our things. The varsity left the field twenty minutes later and found they had the locker room to themselves. We had willingly vacated and didn't want to be around the big fellas because they were in a bad mood. Everyone decided it was in our best interest to let them have a little privacy.

The varsity took their time and had a team meeting once they got in. They talked among themselves about the young upstarts. Mario told them he was going to get him one. He didn't call my name, but that's who he meant.

He quickly got dressed and walked outside. It was almost too good to be true. He saw me running routes and throwing the football around with Marvin. We were laughing and discussing the possibility of getting the program turned around, if we played all four years together.

I told Marvin Coach Smith thought he and Melvin would be good together. He loved his arm and he could see him being the starting quarterback for them, sooner rather than later. And when it came to Melvin, he said the guy had another gear. He had an amazing burst to the ball.

This was good news for Marvin, because he would probably not make him change positions just to let someone who could "think" play quarterback.

I then took the time to ask about James. I saw how hard he had hit Tommy, and the moan that escaped his throat said it hurt him really bad. I saw the discouraged look that took up residence in Tommy's face and the fear he had in his heart because he started to tip when he ran the ball.

Marvin started laughing and asked, "Who? Suicide?"

I laughed and asked, "Is that what they call him?"

Marvin told him, "Those River Boys got some crazy names, man."

We continued to discuss James and I told him I didn't think the guy was playing with a full deck. Then I made a confession to Marvin, "I am scared that guy will break me in half if he gets a good shot on me."

The quarterback turned serious for a moment and told me he probably could because James's brother had broken a bull's neck with his bare hands.

Mario was eavesdropping and overheard the whole thing and walked over and told me, "It ain't him you better be worried about."

He started to stare hard at me. He was the starting middle linebacker and I gave up eighty pounds to him easily.

"It's me," he said. "I will tell you what, why don't you try to make me miss you now?"

He walked even closer until he had penetrated everything that looked like my personal space. I stood still and tried to return his stare, but he was not David.

Mario then took his index finger and put it on my forehead and dared me to move it. I wanted to shove his hand away from my head, but I knew better. The guy would rip my head off.

Mario then pushed his finger forcibly against my forehead, causing my head to snap back and I momentarily lost my balance.

Mario laughed, and then asked me, "What's up? You scared now, right?"

My heart began to race and everything in me told me to fight. I managed to hold his piece because I knew if David made me hurt, then this guy would probably put me in the hospital.

Mario looked at me as though he hated the ground that I walked upon and then said, "Yeah, that's what I thought. You scared. You little black ass punk."

He walked away and I felt humiliated to the point where I could not put a positive spin on anything. I stood with my head down and thought about what just happened.

Marvin watched the whole thing, but he didn't laugh like I thought he would. He walked over after the danger had passed and asked me if I was all right. I was dejected and could only nod my head yes to affirm that I was, but I really wasn't. At this moment I needed a personal pep rally to get my spirits up.

Going home, I was distraught about everything that happened. Tyrone and I were the only two students left on the bus. I looked over at him with crimson eyes. A dried-out salty riverbed had been made from the path the silent tears had traveled. They had been dried up for about an hour, but the tears had managed to leave a lasting impression on my face. I looked as though my best friend had died, and, decided to tell Tyrone what happened. I ended by saying, "I'm through, man. I am not playing anymore. That's it for me. You can keep playing, but I'm through. I had enough."

My cousin couldn't say anything to get me to change my mind because he probably would do the same as I. The odds of me beating this guy were astronomical. If I kept playing, it was inevitable a confrontation would occur again and I would have to fight. I would have to struggle for my life, because as big as Mario was, this is what would have been at stake.

I had time to think about it all night. There was no way I was going to the schoolhouse today. I could not face the embarrassment of what happened yesterday. I figured Mario would tell everybody he punked me out.

I had to come up with something. The day was Tuesday. If I missed today and Wednesday, then by Thursday, things would have gotten so old no one would care.

I decided to stay in bed after pondering the situation and I knew this was my best option. I would tell Momma I wasn't feeling good. It wasn't a complete fabrication. Even if I told her I was sick, it would not be a lie. I was feeling ill in my stomach about the things I was going through.

When the time came to get up, I stayed in the bed. Momma came into my room and told me to get up and catch the bus. I told her I was sick and I didn't feel like going to school.

She placed her hand on my forehead to test my temperature. I didn't feel warm. She looked at me as if I was lying. Most mothers have a sixth sense about things like this, and hers was on display.

The look on her face made me feel uneasy. Momma looked as though she wanted to tell me to get up and get dressed. It was quiet in my room as she stared at me for a moment. I thought she was seriously considering turning down my request to stay at home. Out of desperation, I put on my best act and weakly said, "Momma, it's my stomach."

She pulled the covers down and my shirt up and began to test the temperature and physical feel of my abdomen. She pushed my belly in and looked at me again. She doubted I was sick, but told me to just stay around the house.

When she left the room, I took a deep sigh of relief and pulled the covers over my head. I smiled to myself because I was proud of the hoax I managed to pull off.

222

However, I chose to keep the covers over my head just in case Diane came snooping around, then she couldn't see anything she could tell. This girl told everything. She couldn't hold water if you gave her a pitcher.

When the school bus and truck left, I got up and went about my business. I walked out the door and sat in the yard for a minute. The only thing I saw was a mockingbird chasing a squirrel. This bird chased the squirrel for about ten minutes before it tired of its little game and flew off.

I got up and walked back into the house and turned the TV on. There was nothing worth watching on the tube. I tried to look at *The Price is Right*, but couldn't get into the show. I stood up over the TV, flipping it from one of the four stations to the next, adding more aluminum foil to the antenna and struggling to get a better reception, which I could not.

It was so boring at home. I didn't know what to do, but I knew what I didn't want to do. I didn't want to read. I was almost ashamed to open a book. I couldn't explain to anyone why, but I just wanted to change my image. I wanted to be a thug or a jock, not a nerd.

I had even started to idolize those varsity athletes. Not because they were good, but because as bad as they were, females always wanted to be with them. Teachers often looked the other way when they were involved in bad behavior and they got off light on a lot of infractions.

This is why I started to play football in the first place. I knew it was all about them. They got everything they wanted and I wanted some of their benefits.

One o'clock came and I was regretting my decision to stay around the house. I couldn't talk on the phone because everyone was in school. If they weren't, I didn't have a close enough local friend, which meant I would have had to call long distance and I didn't have the money to pay my bill and Momma would have a heart attack.

A little later the programming turned to soap operas. I didn't try hard, but I couldn't settle on one to watch. It turned out the whole skipping school thing was bad for me. I was in the woods with no one around and nothing to do. Time went by so gradually that it seemed like I was a castaway. To compound my problems the clock was moving so slowly I thought it was wrong. I actually considered looking at the calendar because it seemed like I was waiting on days and not hours.

Finally, I heard the air brakes of the bus as it stopped somewhere up the road. I heard the motor as it struggled to get the bus moving again. I checked the time on the clock and it was four-thirty. About five minutes later I heard the bus coming down the hill so I walked back into the house to continue my charade of not feeling well. I was determined to milk my mysterious illness for all it was worth.

The next day brought the same dilemma. I contemplated the idea of claiming that I was sick once again, but thought better of it. I was tired of being in the woods by myself with nothing to do and no one to talk to but the trees and animals. I wasn't Tarzan, and I had no intentions of trying to be him.

I got up and decided to go to school. I initially thought I should push my act until Thursday and give the incident time to get out of everybody's system. However, there was a good chance that Momma was not going to go for this charade again. I had gotten away with it once and I knew this was all the mileage I was going to get out of this act.

My life was so simple but complicated. I knew I had to go back to school sooner or later and there was no need in delaying the inevitable. I was just going to have to take a calculated risk and endure the anxiety of the moment.

No one knew what I was going through in this asylum and I would not tell because I had to prove to myself I could handle everything. This was my rite of passage and a gateway into manhood.

With all my beliefs about what makes a man, I was still nervous about my choice to return to the forbidden abode because if I misjudged it, then I would have to deal with the ramifications of the humiliation it would bring.

The bus came and I hurried to the end of the driveway. It was a light rain outside. The day just seemed dreary and I had a bad feeling about it. I watched as the raindrops assaulted the bus all the way to the school. When we finally got there, I stepped off into the cold morning air and the wind spit the rainwater into my face.

A cold front was moving into the area. The rain that was on the wind was indifferent and unpleasant as it beat down upon me. The once light rain had now turned into an all-out storm. I hurried to the entrance of the school to take refuge from the onslaught of water, which had turned brutally cold and vindictive.

"Johnson. Johnson." It was Tyrone again. "I need you to stay over."

I looked at him and shook my head and told him, "I don't know, man. I seriously doubt it."

Tyrone really wanted to stay over and told me, "Meet me out front, if you go home, then I am, too."

There was no enthusiasm left in me and I said, "Okay, but man, I am planning on going home."

We parted ways and I turned down the hall by the main office to head for my homeroom. The B-Team had gathered along the wall, and when they saw me and a few other teammates coming, they called us over. We pounded each other's hands and we all asked each other, "What's up?" and everyone responded by saying, "Nothing much, man."

To my surprise, I overreacted to everything with Mario. No one mentioned me being punked out. It was like they were unaware or didn't care. The fellows acted as though something more important was going on this morning.

At first glance, they appeared to be just standing there. All of them seemed to have the same pose in their repertoire. They were leaning either one way or the other and held their private parts as if they needed some kind of support down there. I imitated their routine, trying to fit in.

Even though the fellas said, "Nothing," I knew these guys were playing some sort of game, so I stood there quietly trying to find out what it was and the rules they were going by.

It turned out each tried to prove they belonged in that fraternity they had formed. As certain high-caliber females walked by, one of the guys would dare another one to "pull her."

This simply meant to get her to show a favorable response. The young guys strove for the title "playa." It was how they got their props from the other guys they hung with. The smoother you were with the girls, the more credibility you had.

There was nothing really hard about what they were doing. Their game was easy enough. All one had to do was get a girl's attention, her phone number in her own handwriting, and her, if they had enough game.

There was only one rule to this competition: Don't come back without that number, because if you did, you were in jeopardy of having your membership revoked and being labeled a scrub. Their actions were hilarious and to see them go through their best pimp impersonation would probably be worth the price of admission, if they had sense enough to charge.

226

I quickly came on board, looking for an opportunity to get into the action. The first few days of the competition, all of us worked on our game. We were pounding out lines and getting our routine together. We took notes and found out what worked the hard way. A few of us showed some promise, but we were still a while away from being on the Tommy Tolbert level.

The same day I officially took my place in this organization, it was my turn to prove my worth. I thought no one would call me out so soon, but I was wrong.

Charles had been waiting for the opportunity to put me on the spot and it miraculously fell into his lap. Tabitha was walking down the hall by herself. Charles told me, "Okay, player, it's your turn. Go and pull her."

I was caught off guard and didn't want the challenge. Everyone on the wall was looking at me to see what I would do, so I knew I had to come through. I shoved my heavy book bag into Charles's chest trying to display a cool attitude, and told him, "Hold my bag for a second, and don't let all this knowledge hit the floor."

Charles came back at me and said, "Only a second, John? Is that all you need?"

The other guys laughed and gave Charles a pound for his quip. If I had been thinking, all I had to do was tell the guys Tab was with someone. Everyone knew she was Tommy's girl. This being the case, the other guys would have probably understood.

I could not do this because I was rattled. I took a deep breath and slowed my stroll and started to dap just like I had watched the other guys do. I was dying to know what my buddies had whispered in the girls' ears. I didn't know and there were no books I had read that told me what to say. I had to come up with something original.

I crept up to Tabitha with the coolest stroll I could manage and said in the deepest voice I could muster, "What's up, thickness?"

This was my best Barry White imitation, and it seemed to have picked her spirit up. Tab looked over at me and tried to hold in her laugh. She asked me, "Boy, what's wrong with you today?" while she slowly shook her head from side to side.

I kept a straight face and replied in my normal voice, "Nothing."

I could tell this part of my rap was going nowhere because she obviously didn't take me seriously. I then changed the approach I was using from a frontal assault, to a flanking maneuver.

I asked her what had been up with her lately. She became sad, and shook her head telling me she was just going through some things with Tommy and had to get her mind right. She had to air a few things out by herself and find out exactly what she wanted to do.

I remained quiet after she said this. Even though I knew the answer to her problem, I kept it to myself.

Tab grabbed my wrist and we paused in the hallway and she started to search my face for something and after a moment seemed to relax. The morbid look she displayed didn't last long when our gazes locked. The lights in her eyes started to twinkle again. Her personality peeped around the clouds, which were her troubles, and she said, "You know you always make me feel better."

At first she wasn't looking too good and her body language was awful, but her spirits picked up a little when I tried my little mack game on her. I never wanted to hurt her, and I only meant her well. I figured at this point she didn't look at me the way I wanted her too.

I put away my little BB guns and pondered if trying to breach her defenses was a good idea. At this moment I was in limbo. If I turned around and let her walk on alone, I would look as weak as I really was with the ladies. If I pushed the issue and continued walking with her, I would risk aggravating and alienating her. I was in a Catch-22, a situation number nine thing that no one envies.

I smiled at her and said, "I will let you go ahead and I will holla at you later, when you have a little more time on your hands."

I knew what it meant. The shame of it all was to go back to the wall with my tail tucked between my legs. I started to turn away and she took me by my arm and said, "John, let me talk to you a minute, if you got time."

She had just unknowingly bailed me out. This probably indicated my permanent status. I would be only a confidant to her. I really didn't want to listen to her problems because doing so would only aggravate my own. I also knew I couldn't afford to go back over to that wall empty-handed. The choice was a no-brainer. I was going to give up some of my worthless time for her. So I accepted my role as her confidant and her offer to walk with her. I turned to Charles and yelled over my shoulder, telling him to bring my book bag to the room when he came.

This sounded like a good plan to me, but not to Charles because this meant he would have to carry the heavy bag to our homeroom class. I told him I would holler at him later and started laughing. I felt this served Charles right by putting me out in the street. He would think twice before he did this again.

For a brief moment, it seemed like the first day of school all over again for me. Tabitha and I strolled down the hall together and walked to a window. The eyes focusing on us were cold and callous. I looked straight ahead and Tabitha tried to nuzzle close under me as if I could protect her. It just seemed like she wanted to know what it was like to be under someone who really cared for her.

She began to talk to me about Tommy, and I did my best Mrs. Rogers impersonation and didn't open my mouth. I listened and she vented all of her frustrations about her boyfriend. It was almost like she was confessing to me and treating me as her personal priest. I couldn't do anything to help her but listen quietly to her problems. I could not advise her on anything because I was obviously biased. I wanted to excuse myself from her problems because there was an obvious conflict of interest.

How could I speak badly about the guy without looking like a bitter person? How could I openly support the guy when I knew in my heart he was a snake? How could she confess anything to me and ask for my advice when she already knew my answer?

I stood there listening to all her problems, trying to raise myself above the storm. When she finished with her confession, I did the hardest thing I had to do so far. I told her, "Don't be so hard on the guy. He really didn't do anything."

I had just taken a bullet to my heart because I knew the rules of the game. I knew all kinds of inside information and I felt I had to keep quiet about it. I hated that I asked Diane anything and that she told me everything. Because of this, I could not act as though I was innocent of any information I gave out. I was going to have to chalk it up to the game and let Tommy "loosen her up." I was not going to be a buster.

The bell rang for class and Tommy was waiting patiently by our homeroom door. Mario and Debra were there with him and they checked us out as well.

Debra shook her head when she saw the two of us come up the hall together. She acted as though Tab had just made the worse investment in her life. She was now almost ready to openly question her idolization of her friend. The math did not add up to her. In her mind, twenty of me could not equal one Tommy.

Tommy turned to Debra and whispered something in her ear. She nodded her head, yes to affirm whatever he said. She turned to Mario and hugged him. When she walked off, Mario slapped her on

230

the rear. It was as if he was pepping her up for a special mission. I wanted to laugh at the two of them, but I knew better. Mario already wanted a reason to get me.

I couldn't stand the girl. I just hated to see her coming. She knew she was cute and danced around like she was royalty or something, but like everybody else I had to give her props for looking good, but that was it. This arrogant little girl had her flaws as well. Her booty, on the other hand, was long, and less than voluptuous. It was shaped in the form of a piece of three-quarter-inch plywood. Her body lacked curves and she moved mechanically.

When I walked in the room, Charles was talking to the class clowns and having a good time. I walked Tab to her desk, and then walked over to collect my things from Chuck, who gave me a pound for my operation.

"You smooth, playa."

"Nah, man, not me," I replied, still smiling. I then leaned over and whispered in Charles's ear and divulged to him what almost made him laugh coming into class.

When Charles heard it, he laughed so hard he had to cross his arms. He doubled over as if he was holding his viscera in. It was so amusing to him he felt compelled to tell the guys he was talking to about my joke.

He turned to Gene and told him, "John said when Debra walked into the room, Mario slapped her on the butt and he saw sparks shoot from her rear end from metal-on-metal contact."

Everyone laughed and Debra frowned because she heard it as well. This was not good for me because she was going to tell Mario what I said.

With the joke I made, it seemed to break the ice with the rebels. I now moved to the deep right part of the room to be near them. I was sitting with an uncouth group of students. They had extended me an umbrella of protection from the vipers at the front of the room. Once again, I had left my gifted buddies to try to bridge the gap with the thugs.

The guy Charles was talking to, Gene, was the head of these renegades. He began to school Charles and me on the art of "janking." He lit in on my nemesis, with a bitter zest.

"Debra," he said. "Didn't your momma tell you to clean your kitchen before you left the house and throw that rug under your arm out?"

The kitchen part was an apparent reference to her lack of a perm and the rug part to that excessive hair under her armpit. He was on a roll and had the class clamoring for more. Just like a Roman emperor, he offered the next sacrifice. This was done to my deepest regrets. It was Tab. I didn't think it was cool, but it wasn't being done as a sacrifice to me. It was to appease Charles.

"Look at Tab sitting up there in the front. She thinks she looks good, but don't nobody want a dark and lovely reject model. She has been used up with her dusty black self."

I did not laugh because I didn't find it funny. I managed to smile and this was all that would come out of me. Tabitha had just got through confessing everything that happened when I played hooky and I didn't want it to seem as though I had betrayed her confidence. At this moment I felt as though I was looking conspicuous to her.

Charles and I had found a home with the class clowns of the no-man's land. We were about to learn a valuable lesson: Nothing in life is free. The price we had to pay to hang with these guys was that we had to cut up in class just like they did. Gene pointed up to the front of the room and I lobbed a wad of paper, which landed close to Debra. I intentionally missed her, but it hit close enough to get her attention.

232

She turned around and started to raise her voice so that Mrs. Wallace would hear her and come into the room.

"Gene, ain't nobody playing with ya'll. You need to stop doing this stuff, with your dumb selves!"

She had just put up a miniature tirade, which was not too impressive. Gene looked at her without blinking. His stare was hard and Debra knew if Mrs. Wallace didn't come into the room, her best bet was to sit down before she got knocked down.

The guy was crazy and kind of intimidating. He wasn't that big, but it was not him you had to worry about. The guy had muscle in the form of his brother, who was about 240 pounds of mean. Gene just didn't lose fights. If he lost, his brother won. Most guys would rather not fight him or let him win than face his brother.

Mrs. Wallace did not come into the room like Debra thought she would. She calmed herself down and took her seat. Charles had made a paper football during the commotion and when things settled down again he thumped it up to the front and hit Tab.

She didn't say anything and kept her face looking straight ahead. She was distraught and crying because of the inconsiderate jokes, and now the paper football incident seem to have broken her and pushed her over the edge.

Mrs. Wallace picked this time to come into the room. Debra's ploy had worked. She had been watching from outside the door and she saw the paper fly across the room. She could not see exactly who threw the paper, but she was determined to get to the bottom of it.

"Who threw the paper?" No one said anything. "You guys could have put someone's eyes out. Nobody's going to say anything, right?"

She sat at her desk and began to write. Mrs. Wallace told Charles and me we had picked the wrong day to merge with this crowd and we were going to the office as well.

She called Tabitha up to the desk and told her to take the write-up slip to the office. Mrs. Wallace told all the guys in the back right part of the room to join her.

"I will let Mr. Warner sort through this mess. I have been dealing with you guys cutting up like this the whole year and I am getting tired of it."

Tabitha walked down the hall, leading us behind her like a mother duck. The situation with her and Charles was escalating. Their relationship was strange. No one knew what was really up with them, but Charles still wasn't through antagonizing her. He made comments to the guys just loud enough so she could hear him. He insinuated things, which seemed to put her on edge.

"I told you guys she ain't what everybody thinks she is. I used to talk to her. Ya'll didn't know that, did you? I left her alone because of what she did." He then raised his voice louder and asked, "Ain't that right, Tab?"

I shot him an elbow and shook my head no. I whispered and told him it would be bad if she got to the office and she told on him. She had already been crying.

I didn't asked Charles what was up with him and Tabitha at this time. I didn't want to know. I was crazy about Tab and Charles was the closest thing I had to a friend thus far. I didn't want to get caught in the middle. I hoped Charles would leave her alone, for now.

Charles took my advice, left her alone and got quiet. Tab bit her lip, fighting back the tears. She had her own problems. She was dealing with a guy who sometimes acted as though he didn't want her anymore. He was openly flirting with Rhonda again.

234

It appeared Tab and her crew had lost their swagger. I don't know if it was true or not, but it was rumored they had been giving it up, and acquired a reputation of being easy. A few of her friends had been knocked up and were as valuable to guys as pyrite. It looked as if Diane was right about everything and it caused me to wonder about Tab.

We finally made it to the office and prepared to face the music. Mr. Warner was not in his office and Mrs. Oliver, his assistant looked like she was very busy.

Gene looked around the room and the office was so full we didn't have a place to sit. He quickly came up with a contingency plan that was shot down by Mrs. Oliver.

"I guess we'll leave and come back later."

She barked out, "No you won't either, Gene. You guys will take a seat in the cafetorium and wait on Mr. Warner."

She held her hand out to Tab, who gave her the disciplinary slip and left. She read it, shook her head and looked at us. She singed us with a warm-up speech of what we would be getting next. The regular outlaws were unaffected and most laughed as they walked into the cafetorium so we took their lead and laughed too. The gravity of the situation had not hit Charles and me, but we were in some serious trouble.

Once we were seated in the cafetorium, we saw Mr. Warner coming out of the principal's office in a jovial demeanor. He looked into the cafetorium and saw us sitting at a table laughing and talking. He stopped for a moment and asked us what we were doing. I told him, "We came to see you."

His demeanor didn't appear to change. He told us to come with him. He took a few steps, looked into his office and said, "Whoops, you guys have a seat. I will be with you in a minute."

The look on his face told us it was going to be bad news for everybody this morning. His smile disappeared right in front of us. He was not looking too happy when he saw the volume of students he had to deal with. His office was congested, and it meant it was time for him to get down to business.

Mr. Warner walked into his office, rolled up his dress shirtsleeves and sat down at his desk. He then began to sift through the list of disciplinary slips. He walked into a small room adjoined to his office and started calling people back to the undersized area one group at a time. He closed the door and held a mock court to resolve the problems the children had.

The walls muffled his voice and what he said couldn't have been good. Shortly after his voice went completely silent, everyone heard the echoes of the contact his paddle made on the students' rear ends.

The licks ranged from three to seven. We tried to count them but we couldn't. The assistant principal struck them so hard we could hear them scream out in pain and say, "Wait a minute, Mr. Warner! Hold it for a second!"

At this point we lost count. Once the disciplinarian resumed, the walls once again failed to do their job and suppress the students' shouts. They lost all voice control and the inflection in their cries of agony erupted through office walls again. During the final few moments of the punishment, the licks got a little harder. Charles and I were definitely afraid. If this is what coming to the office was all about, we shouldn't have come.

When he finished his business with that group, he opened the hallway door of the little room. It was a second door, which was usually kept closed, except for occasions like this. The only reason this door was ever opened was to help him quickly dispense the high volume of students who came into his office. For being seldom used, the door was working quite well this morning, because it opened and closed at a fast rate.

Whenever this door opened, we heard the guys tell him, "You dead wrong for that, Mr. Warner."

Mr. Warner always came back and said, "No, you guys are dead wrong. You need to go to class, stop cutting up, and get your lesson."

The students moved in one door and out the next. The whole scene looked like they were products on an assembly line. Mrs. Oliver stood at the door to his main office and gave them a note back to class as they walked by. It was a smooth process they had developed through trial and error.

We were chilling in the cafetorium, but had become increasingly nervous. The licks seemed like they were getting harder and harder. This man should have been tiring, but he apparently had gotten a second wind. Mr. Warner finished with the groups in and around the office, and then it was our turn.

He stepped to the opening of the cafetorium and told us, "Okay guys, you wanted to see me? Come on in and let's see what's up."

He had a smile that would give most people who didn't know him a false sense of security. Most of the guys knew him and they knew him well. There was no misunderstanding on their part. This meant bad news for us.

Mr. Warner sat down at his desk and read the write-up. He frowned when he read the additional comments to the case Mrs. Wallace had written down. He asked us our side of the story. He gave us a sham of a hearing. We were so nervous we somehow managed to bungle our case even though there were no witnesses to implicate us in anything on the paper.

It didn't take him long to come down with his verdict. He took a deep sigh and looked at us. Mr. Warner leaned back in his desk and spoke to us as if we were his children and were breaking his heart.

He said, "Most of you guys have been up here about three or four times a week since school started, for one reason or another. I have put you in in-school suspension and I have sent a few of you home for a while. This doesn't look as though it's doing any good."

He looked directly at Charles and me and sighed. He gave us an intimidating stare and said, "A few of you just came across my radar screen over the past few weeks. I don't know what I can say to get through to you guys, but it's my job to do it, and I am going to try. Come on back here and let me talk to you."

Gene looked at him, shook his head no, and said, "You can talk to me right here just fine, Mr. Warner. I hear you quite clearly."

Mr. Warner got up and opened the door to his infamous torture chamber and said, "Ya'll get on back here. I got too much to do, and I ain't going to be playing games with you boys today."

We all got up and walked to the room with our heads down. The regulars started to muscle each other to see who would be at the top of the line. They wanted to be first. Pushing and shoving, they struggled to get to the spot on the wall where they had to spread them, as if they waited to be frisked by a cop.

Charles and I didn't understand their enthusiasm to get their butts torn up. We stood just inside the doorway, wanting to make a break for it.

Gene muscled his way up first, placed his hands on the wall, and was standing there spread-eagle. Mr. Warner gave him seven quick licks. He opened the door and Mrs. Oliver gave Gene a pass back to class. It was much of the same with the next five guys, which followed.

He got to us and said, "You guys are on a slippery slope. Come on over here and take your medicine."

We looked at each other and fear started to choke us. I lied out of desperation and said, "We didn't do it, Mr. Warner."

"Who did?" he asked.

"We don't know," Charles chimed in.

He looked at us and said, "I'll get you all. That way I will be sure to get the right one."

Charles went next. Mr. Warner took Charles's jeans and pulled them tight and gave them an extra twist at the belt loop. He wanted to make sure the licks permeated across his pants and onto his skin.

He was like a distance runner who had seen the finish line. Even though he was running on fumes, he gave a little extra effort to finish his race. This was probably the reason why the other boys wanted to go first.

Pop, pop, pop, pop and POP! It was four solid licks followed by one long hard stroke, to make Charles think about doing something else to come back to the office. Instead of turning him out to go to class, he opened the door he had came through and told him to wait in the office.

Charles walked by me and I could see the tears in his eyes. The brackish water rolled down his cheek in a steady stream on one side of his face. His eyes were bloody red and he looked and acted as though his mother had just died. He swung his head from side to side in a sorrowful manner and his actions caused the fear in my heart to grow and multiply exponentially.

I swallowed hard and looked at Mr. Warner. I was the finish line. He appeared fresher than ever and had a big grin on his face. He looked almost happy as he told me, "Come on over here, boy, and get your medicine."

I reluctantly stepped forward and looked at the paddle in his hand. It was a paddle Mr. Bradley had made from a big piece of lumber in his wood shop and was about two-feet long. The handle was smooth and round with a leather strap in the taped grip that he used to display the paddle on the wall over his desk. The handle was about twice as thick as a broomstick. The wide part that did the damage to students' backsides was about eight inches wide and had writing all over it that served no apparent reason. The markings scribbled over it were similar to the ones the military used in World War II to decorate their planes.

I debated whether I should take my licks or not. The impatient disciplinarian told me to turn around because he had things to do this morning. I looked at him, and I paused for a moment and thought about telling him, no.

Mr. Warner reached down for my arm to turn me to face the wall and I snatched it away. We exchanged stares for a few minutes. Then I turned around gradually, placed my hands slowly against the wall, and did a vertical spread-eagle like the other guys.

I had not had a whooping in years. Momma had stopped doing it because her philosophy was to ride us hard in the beginning. When we grew up some, this is when she started to talk with us about things.

I stood there and thought to myself, "How could this be? How is it I am standing here, getting ready to have my bottom flattened by a two-pound piece of oak wood?"

I was a fresh face to the assistant principal. Originally Charles and I were supposed to be getting three licks. But with the additional comments that were written on the disciplinary slip about us, it had pushed our licks up to five apiece. My attitude was about to cost me more.

Mr. Warner literally picked me up by the seat of my pants with one hand and then hit me just about as hard as he could with long-stroked licks. POP! POP! POP! POP! POP! POP! He grunted and, POP! It was seven hard long-stroked licks.

Tears filled my eyes, and at this moment, I found it hard not to reach up and slap the hell out of this man. My breathing was heavy and my nose was spread wide trying to catch all the air I could so I wouldn't hyperventilate. This is the moment I made up my mind I didn't like this chump and probably never would.

Mr. Warner was the type of person who didn't really care. He told me to go into his office. Charles and I were the students he had referred to earlier as coming across his radar.

Once we were seated, he gave us a lecture about the company we had started to keep. The assistant principal urged us to part ways with the class clowns. His words had fallen on deaf ears, at least with my ears anyway.

Mr. Warner looked at me and told me I needed to calm down or my attitude would cost me one day. I had completely closed him out. At this point there was nothing he could tell me about anything because he hit me with his paddle. I felt whatever he needed to say to me, he said it then. I paid for my crime and I didn't want a lecture.

I went back to class. The day passed, the rain stopped, and I was not harassed the way I thought I would be. Some of the varsity players made little comments when I walked by, but it was nothing out of the ordinary. I met Tyrone out front and told him I was going to stay. I was not going to let anyone run me off.

We hit the field and started to practice. Soon after that, Coach Smith sent a player down to Coach Davis asking for me.

Chicken Hawk sprinted up to the coach and said, "Coach Smith said he wants to use John for practice, if you can spare him."

Coach Davis called me over and asked me if I wanted to help the varsity out with their practice.

I told him, "No, I don't want to go up there."

I knew that Mario would try to punish me. I figured Debra had told him what I said about the sparks and the throwing of the paper incident.

Mr. Davis told him, "Tell Coach he said no. If John don't want to, I am not going to try to force him into practicing with the varsity."

When practice ended, we waited for our buses to go home. My time of reckoning had come. Mario sought me out. He had meant it when he said he was going to get him one and I was the one. He brought Chicken Hawk with him so he could witness the fight. This was to ensure everyone would know of the beating I received.

Not long after they started their search, the two were rewarded for their efforts when they found me on the other side of the large propane tank, sitting beside my bus. Mario walked up and pushed me upside my head and told me, "I am going to beat your black ass."

Without looking around, I calmly told him, "Look man, I ain't trying to fight you."

Mario was not hearing that and told me, "Don't beg 'cause I don't have no mercy for you."

I knew there was no reasoning with him because Mario was out for blood. I quickly scrambled to my feet and Mario tried to spear me. Instinct and fear took over. I went to another level during the fight. It seemed as if everything was moving in slow motion to me. I performed the same maneuver I had pulled off with David and rolled so that both of us hit the ground together.

I was smaller, and quicker. I slid on top of him and started to choke him. Chicken Hawk ran over and rolled Mario back on top of me.

I was fighting for my life out of the sight of the coaches. Fear had me doped up on epinephrine, and I rolled Mario off me again with strength I had never possessed before, and probably would never possess again in all my life.

We continued to fight, but Chicken Hawk kept meddling in our brawl. He was there as more than a witness and again went over to roll Mario back on top.

Students hung off the bus to watch the fight taking shape right in front of them. It did not look good for me because the deck was heavily stacked in Mario's favor. It was obvious I was on my own. Again, Tyrone was nowhere to be seen.

Just as Chicken Hawk grabbed my leg a third time and began to pull me off Mario, the sound of a bus door opened and I felt like the cavalry was coming. I held my death hold on Mario as Latonya Hamilton evened up the odds for me.

She was one of those big river girls. She rushed out and grabbed Chicken Hawk and threw him to the ground. Her face was contorted and riddled with every angry expression under the sun. She didn't appreciate the double-team taking place on an eighth grade student.

Chicken Hawk knew she meant business because she was an imposing figure standing between him and us like an Abrams tank. Rising from the ground, he saw the large girl looking at him. He looked at her and held both of his hands up as if to say, "I give up," and slowly backed away. He knew for his sake he had better not try anything. If he did and managed to whoop her, those River Boys would have him for breakfast.

Meanwhile the fight continued, and Mario wasn't faring too well. I had now crossed over into a full body mount. I threw an occasional jab and tried to choke him and returned his favor by trying to crush his windpipe. Mario reached up, and out of desperation, tried to gouge my eyes out. He made several attempts to do this, and on a couple of occasions came very close to accomplishing this feat.

"Get up off me! Get up or I will scratch your eyes out!" he yelled.

I got up off him with my vision blurred. I was seeing lines and all kinds of light and darkness in images all around me. I backed away from Mario, trying to focus my eyes and reset myself for another round.

Mario got up, still mad. He wanted to fight some more. The only thing stopping the throwdown was Coach Davis coming out of the gym. He saw all the students gathered around the buses. He made his way through the crowd and stopped the fight. He then took the three of us to his office and wrote us up. He admonished us with a stiff tongue-lashing.

I returned to the bus and a concerned Latonya asked me if I was okay. She turned me around and knocked the grass off my back and out of my head. And then she berated all the guys who stood by and watched as the two older boys tried to double-team me. She was not happy about what went down and she acted as though she wanted to take Mario and Chicken Hawk around the corner herself.

The bus couldn't get me away from the school fast enough. And I didn't have anything to say to Tyrone on the way home. This was the second time he let me down. He appeared to have a habit of disappearing at the most inopportune moments. And right now, I didn't care where he had gone because I felt like I couldn't count on him.

244

When I got to my house I pulled my thoughts together. It didn't take me long to come to the conclusion of what I was going to do. I was going to play football and there was no way those guys were going to make me quit.

The next day on the way to school, I knew I needed some big-time muscle. Jimmy had calmed down a lot toward me, so I decided to appeal to him for some help. I told him everything I was going through. I thought for sure I would receive some assistance because no matter what happened between us, we were still blood.

Jimmy listened to everything I had to say about what went down. He then looked at me and asked, "You ready to handle your business?"

I thought we were going to go and bust some heads and tag-team on Mario and Chicken Hawk so I told him, "Yeah!"

Jimmy was a heavy hitter. He had a big bone structure and I knew firsthand how hard he hit. Jimmy was highly revered as a brawler around the school. He didn't lose many fights and had the reputation I needed to get me a little respect. Athletes and thugs gave this country boy a lot of room.

Who knew what Jimmy's true motives were besides Jimmy? Instead of telling me he was going to help me out, he reached into his pocket and gave me a buck knife. That thing was so big it could have easily eviscerated a man. He showed me just how sharp it was by shaving some hair from his forearm.

He told me, "I want you to go and handle your business. That's what Johnsons do."

He slipped the knife into my trembling hands and my eyes bucked. I was scared, but I put the illegal weapon into my pocket. The bulge this thing created made me think I would get caught for sure. If anyone saw it, they would most certainly know what it was because I was not prominent down there.

I entered the building and turned to come down the hallway, which had become the B-Team's walk of fame. As I approached, my teammates all walked out to meet me and asked if I was okay. They had waited for me to come down the hall to give me my props on how well I had represented myself in the fight.

We were becoming more visible around the school with each passing day. The first wing had become our favorite section of the building. We were here all the time in the morning before homeroom, shooting the breeze.

This morning the guys felt they really had a reason to strut. They were really proud of me and told me, "Man, we didn't know you had it in you."

I didn't either. Regardless of all the congratulations I received, I still knew I was in trouble. There was still the matter of the disciplinary slip Coach Davis had written on us. I didn't want to go back to Mr. Warner's office so soon, but I knew it was coming for sure.

The guys didn't dwell on what happened yesterday, and resumed what they were doing. They were macking the girls walking by, but this morning they gave me a pass. They could tell my mind was still occupied by the trouble I was in because of the fight. The anxiety showed in my face, and the fellas knew pushing up on the ladies was nowhere near my mind.

Their instincts were right. I was so scared. I thought for sure I would get caught with an illegal weapon at school. I knew the bulge in my pants was not my private part and tried to keep it hid with my bag. I was not endowed with that type of hardware. The only thing on my mind was, "How did I end up like this?"

I had read the student handbook and I knew the consequences of being caught with a weapon at school. I could be sent to alternative school at the very least and perhaps expelled. This would mean I would end up like those guys under the tree or in front of those old abandoned buildings--the ones always looking so pitiful when the bus passed them on the way to school every day--if Momma didn't kill me first.

The fellas continued to talk, but my mind was on the knife in my pocket and how best to get rid of it. I heard the buzz and saw the stares in everybody's faces. The rumor of the fight that had gone down yesterday had already made its way around the school and everyone was talking about how scrappy I was.

The thing I dreaded and knew would happen finally came over the PA system, saying:

"Would John Johnson, Mario Armour, and Dexter Reynolds report to the assistant principal's office?"

And the announcement repeated: *"Would John Johnson, Mario Armour, and Dexter Reynolds report to the assistant principal's office?"*

I looked over at Charles and said, "I need to talk to you, man. I need a big favor."

Charles told me, "Sure, whatever I can do."

We stepped into one of the alcoves between the doorways. I turned my back, pulled out the big buck knife, and said, "I need you to hold this for me."

Charles looked at the knife and said, "Damn, you about to mess somebody up, ain't you, man?"

He took the knife from me and stuffed it inside his gym bag and told me, "I got you, dawg. Just make sure you come and get your little toy back."

We gave each other a pound and I left Charles in the alcove and headed to the assistant principal's office. I turned the corner to come down the hallway and saw Debra coming out of the office. She looked at me and turned up her nose and continued going the other way through the cafetorium.

When I reached the office, I opened the door to find Mario and Chicken Hawk explaining what happened yesterday. I took a seat across from them and listened to the rest of their version of the events. When they finished, Mr. Warner asked me what happened at practice. I knew this man thought I had an attitude, and if I had taken my licks quietly, I would not be looking so bad right now.

I began to tell my side in a brief and concise manner:

"I was sitting in the grass by the big tank and Mario slapped me upside my head. He told me he was going to kick my black butt. We started fighting and Mr. Davis came out the door and wrote us up."

The poor man's Columbo expression didn't look like he was buying my version. He acted like a two-dollar crime detective.

"That ain't how it happened, son. I got three people to say it went down this way:

You were picking at Mario's girlfriend. When she walked by, you hit her on the butt and said it was so hard that sparks flew. She also said you were the one that threw the paper at her that morning when all of you guys came to the office. She complained that you had been bothering her a lot, so she told Mario you were picking at her. He asked you about it and you got smart with him and that's what caused the fight. That little lady that just walked out of my office doesn't have any reason to lie. It kind of makes sense to me how all of this might have developed. Son, I am going to give you three licks for feeling on Debra. I am going to give these guys five licks for fighting. They can't just go around beating folks up like that. There are ways to handle everything. Y'all come on back here and get your licks."

He took us back into that little torture chamber to the left of his office and dealt out his punishment. He really didn't hit us hard. It was something firm to get our attention, but I didn't like being

248

punished, especially when I didn't do anything but defend myself. I began to think it was elementary school all over again.

I walked out of Mr. Warner's office looking like a thunderstorm. The other guys laughed about what had just gone down. But I didn't find it funny.

Mr. Warner sent me to the left and then the other two guys right. He smiled as usual with that stupid grin, and said, "Don't ya'll come back to my office."

I simmered as I walked to my homeroom. I was fighting hard to keep a straight face. I told Charles I would get "that" from him when the bell rang. I didn't want Debra to see me with it.

I was ticked off and it took everything I had not to go up there and hit her with some dark justice. I wanted to pimp-slap her, the kind where I left a bad taste of knuckles in her mouth. She had no business telling a lie like that on me. The only thing that saved her was I knew I could not afford to go back to the office so soon.

I told Charles what happened on the way to our first-period class. I then said, "Let me get 'that' from you, Chuck."

I opened my bag, let Charles slip the knife in, and immediately I took that thing back to Jimmy. I didn't want it and I knew I could not afford to be caught with a knife at school.

However, I thought I still needed help. I thought about asking Diane, but decided I had to walk this mile by myself. I was beginning to backslide by internalizing things again. I felt that I had to be a man and repeated my creed of not being a tattletale. I had also made up my mind that I would not let any of those guys run me off from playing football.

Days went by, and one afternoon at practice, a scenario went down almost the same as before. Coach Smith sent someone down to ask Coach Davis to use me. Instead of saying no, I said, yes, and hustled up to the Varsity end of the practice field.

When they saw me coming, the guys looked at Mario and said, "He do have a pair, Mario."

Coach Smith still wanted me to run the football for him. He was looking for a spark to jumpstart his struggling offense. He set the guys up for a drill using an offensive line against a defensive line. The objective of the drill was zone blocking up the gut and let the runner pick the hole to daylight. On the other side of the ball behind the defensive line was a middle linebacker. That player was my "good friend," Mario.

Coach Smith told me he needed me to run hard between the tackles. I told him I understood and set up five yards deep in a makeshift single back formation. Coach Smith blew the whistle and handed the ball off to me.

I ran up to the line and saw the penetration by the tackles. The middle linebacker had plugged whatever daylight was left, so I bounced the play outside and ran up the sidelines. Coach Smith told me, " No, son, not like that. You got to run between the tackles. Let's try it again."

Again we ran the play, and again it was the same result. I was not about to go up the middle. I knew why Tommy was getting killed. Those guys could not block. They acted as though they didn't want to block. They never blocked Mario and I felt it was a conspiracy to get me. I said to myself, "I ain't getting killed for nobody."

Coach Smith came over again and told me I had to run hard up the middle. A few of the other coaches saw my unwillingness to do it. They told Coach Smith, "He ain't ready for varsity yet, Coach. He's too scared. He might get hurt."

Coach Smith shook them off like a pitcher would do a catcher and said, "He might be scared, but he's fast. Come on, Big Gun. Run that thing up in there hard. There is a linebacker and a corner sitting on the outside ready to take your head off. Keep it inside tight."

We tried it again and again it was the same thing. I was determined to bounce it outside. It made some of the coaches frustrated. They schemed to teach me a lesson about the linebacker and cornerback being out there waiting on me.

Unknown to me and to Coach Smith, they sent Chicken Hawk and Yak into the action. When Coach blew the whistle, I rushed up to the line and again tried to bounce it outside.

This time the corner and the linebacker Coach Smith warned me about were there. Chicken Hawk went low and took my legs and I went airborne. Yak, a short, stocky backup middle linebacker went high and tried to decapitate me. They performed a modified version of the Road Warrior's doomsday device wrestling move.

They crumpled me up like a sheet of paper, and I lay there motionless on the ground. The coaches came over and checked me out. I wasn't dead; I was still breathing, although barely moving. They asked me what was wrong and I told them I had hurt my back.

They motioned to a group of guys to come over and take me off the field. Two of the linemen who failed to block for me walked over and caught me under my armpits and pulled me over to a pile of tackling dummies. They laid me down and everybody resumed practice without once thinking about me.

I was writhing in pain and it hurt me to move. I watched the team continue to practice, and I knew I had become an afterthought to them. When practice concluded, everyone finished their wind sprints and hustled to the gym. I looked around to see if anyone was going to help me off the field. There were no volunteers for the job and even the coaches had started to leave.

I struggled to my feet and limped to the school as if I was Quasimodo. I cursed aloud to myself all the way to the gym and didn't care who heard it.

When I made it into the locker room I barely managed to get out of my equipment. I struggled to the bus, lay down on a seat, and didn't move anymore until I got home. That was it for me. I had enough. I made a pledge to myself not to practice or play another game of football for Bi-County.

Chapter Fourteen: Retained

Months went by, and my back had gotten better. The football season was long over and the B-Team had built ourselves a true friendship. We had been at our game of sweating the girls for a while. Some of us sharpened our skills to the point where we passed the test with ease. I was not one of them, however.

Those select few often continued down the hall, telling our crew they had just left on the wall, "I'll holler at you guys later. I got something to do."

Those were the guys who would be, without a doubt, the heirs apparent to Tommy Tolbert. No one knew what they were saying to the girls, but they had them grinning from ear to ear.

Charles saw Tab coming down the hall and elbowed me to get my attention.

"There go your girl, man."

I shook my head and said, "She ain't mine, man. That's Tommy's girl."

We both laughed and stood there and watched her for a moment. She was having trouble getting through the sea of students carrying her book bag because her belly was full. Tab had a little crumb snatcher on the way. She was loaded down and laboring just to get to her locker. It was a pitiful sight.

Tommy walked by with Rhonda and didn't look Tabitha's way. Tab looked over at us and we both looked away from her, as if we were trying to pose for some cool picture. Our demeanor was reminiscent of James Dean. When we did this, Tabitha dropped her head.

I still watched her out of my peripheral vision and I knew the look she had on her face anywhere. It was a look of a person being bludgeoned to the point they wanted to give up on everything. I knew the look well, because I had virtually made it famous. I used to be the poster child for it.

I felt it was kind of my fault she was in her predicament. I could have passed the information on to her that Diane had given me, but I didn't want to look like a hater. It wouldn't have mattered anyway, because she would have probably said I was lying about the whole thing.

My heart went out to her. I came off the wall and asked her if she needed any help. She smiled a sheepish smile and told me, "No. I am fine, John."

She was a prideful person and didn't want help from me because she figured it was pity. Tab saw the antics Charles and I displayed when she looked at us. She really didn't have time for games.

I reached up and took her book bag off her shoulder and said, "Come on, I got you. We still friends, right?"

"We still friends." She needed to hear these words more than anything. If she knew how I would have responded, Tab might have collapsed into my arms.

Since she wasn't sure, she just waddled beside me to her locker. She had made so many mistakes and it was killing her. She had done what her friends wanted and most of them wanted nothing to do with her now.

There were only a few people left willing to deal with her, and occasionally I was one of them. Events at this point in her life were complicated. She had gone from one of the most popular girls in school to one of the least thought of.

The weird thing was I wanted to chill with her, but I was kind of standoffish. I acted the way she had acted toward me earlier. I liked her company, but was afraid of what people might say.

254

Public perception to me now was just as big as it was for her at the beginning of the school year. However, for all my caring, I had gone through a metamorphosis of my own. I was sneaky and mannish. I seized the opportunity to do anything I wanted to do.

I wanted to keep Tab close, not just because I still liked her, which I really and truly did, but for other reasons as well. I was a devious young man who sensed she was vulnerable. She was trying to latch on to anyone for emotional support and probably still wanted me to be her priest or confidant.

Initially, I acted as though I would fill this niche and still be that for her. I eventually moved to my original seat behind her, after Debra deserted her. It was almost sad to see that rat leaving a sinking ship.

Tab didn't know it, but I was trying to learn the game. She should have pushed me away. I was an opportunist, a carpetbagger. I had mutated into the biggest rat of them all.

The things I did were much worse than deserting her. I knew all of her weaknesses because she had confided in me about everything. I found it easy to play with her mind because of the inside information and the emotional state she was in.

I used everything against her and eventually started giving her a false sense of hope of there being a chance for us. This was the farthest thing from my mind. I was thinking nothing like this. I was trying to find myself while dealing with my own hormones. I was still a child and I didn't want to be tied down to nobody else's baby.

Tommy had "loosened Tab up." He had scorched her and I was through with any kind of official romantic interest in her at this time. If I were to even think of chilling with Tab, all the fellas would tell me I was getting "sloppy seconds" by taking "Tommy's leftovers." I couldn't let this happen.

The only good to come out of the whole thing for her was she immersed herself in her books and a graph of her grades indicated she had started to improve again. Her attitude had completely changed and she was doing her schoolwork.

She made the big change in her life because she had two people to worry about, and this sobered her up quickly. Gone were her wild, flirtatious ways and carefree days of breaking boys' hearts.

It sounds cruel, but he wasn't even claiming her child. I didn't know if it was Tommy's or not, but I knew it wasn't mine. I wasn't even trying to be caught up in the mix. I still talked to her for the benefits of groping her. Not only Tab, but also almost anyone else I wanted at will.

I was doing childish things because I was far from mature. The whole thing was a game to me. It would make my day and I would laugh like crazy if they turned around and swung at me. As agile as I was there was no chance they would hit me.

Some of the girls just shook their heads and went on about their business and passed it off as "John being John." Others reported me to the office, and Mr. Warner either sent me to the torture chamber or in-school suspension. He had talked to me until he was blue in the face. He had whooped me so much he had developed carpal tunnel syndrome, and this was the funny thing about it to me. I was winning because he was walking around with a splint on his hand.

I had personally taken on the task of wearing him out. The torture chamber didn't bother me anymore because I had been back there so much the skin on my rear end was about as tough and thick as a rhino's hide. It was an adaptation my body had made to deal with all the paddling I received.

In-school suspension wasn't too bad for me, either, because most of my buddies were there. Just like inmates in prison, we often found ways around the teachers assigned to guard us while we carried out our sentence.

Most of the renegade types like I had almost become, but was striving hard for, actually began to like it better than their normal classes. Too much classroom time meant we would only find too many bad things to do, and would only end up in one of the two little rooms again.

We were written up so much it was like a revolving door between the classroom, the principal's office, and the suspension room, which seemed to contain most of the same people all the time. We had a bad reputation and we wore it as if it was the Congressional Medal of Honor.

I hadn't thought anymore of the warning that Mr. Warner had tried to sell me on his guilt-by-association theory. I was having too much fun doing things people used to do to me. I had become corrupt in my actions and my philosophies. Maybe there was something to Mr. Warner's theory after all.

All of my schoolwork was suffering and my gifted friends seemed like complete strangers to me. I was one of the most infamous students around the school. I had become notorious for the controversy always seeming to surround me. I no longer wasted my time trying to deny allegations, because most were true. Many people called me rotten and terrible and this gave me the excuse to cut up a little more.

I had fallen so far from grace, that if Mrs. Rogers could see me, it would have made her cry. All the time and effort she put into salvaging me, and now I was willingly throwing it all away for apparently no good reason. My grades had fallen from the highest of highs to the lowest of lows.

School was about to end and I had managed to create the reputation I had craved. The bad thing was I didn't know if I had passed or not. To me this was the worst thing about my predicament.

I hoped I had, for my sake. If I didn't advance, how was I going to explain it to Momma? She had complete faith in me. There was no way anyone could tell her I had a rap sheet at school a mile long, and more bad grades than sand on a beach.

To maintain secrecy of my failures, I started to sign my own card as my grades went into a freefall. Over the last few years, I had done so well she assumed I was still on a high level.

When all my siblings came up to get their report cards signed, she had not noticed my card was missing. She really felt I was the last child of hers, outside of Margaret, who would fail. I had set such a high standard for myself, my mother had long since abandoned any thoughts of me going astray again.

When the school year ended, I limped into the summer under a cloud of doubt. It was a 50/50 chance whether I passed or failed. I took solace in the belief the school system would pass me along as it had done before. Especially if I were borderline advancing to the next grade as I was now. I thought there wasn't anyone who should have a problem with someone like me going forward. Even with this hope, I still dreaded the day my report card came from school to pronounce my standing for the year.

A couple of weeks after school let out, judgment day was finally upon me. My siblings and I were in Cusseta working on the house the family had almost finished. I was pushing a wheelbarrow of concrete around back to finish the deck when Momma came up. She had a lot of mail with her and had begun to casually sort through it. One by one she went through her kids' report cards.

I suspected what she was looking at and wanted to run away. I was still wrestling with a gut feeling I had failed, so I dipped quickly around the corner.

All of my fears coalesced when Momma had a flashback. The lightning that exploded within her eyes and the thunder that became her voice told me I was in trouble.

"John! Come here, boy!"

I took some of the cement I had in the wheelbarrow and rubbed it all over my body to give the perception I had been working hard. If that ploy didn't work, I intended to use it as body armor for what I knew was coming.

"John, don't make me call you again. You had better get here, and I mean quick!"

I stepped around the corner of the house with my head down because I knew what she wanted. There was no doubt about it when Momma saw me she wanted to knock me into the next county.

My mind shut down. My journey to her seemed like it was taking forever. It was becoming apparent I was going into a state of shock.

She looked at me as I drug myself slowly across the yard. Unwilling to wait until I made it to her, she asked at the top of her voice, alerting everyone to my dilemma, "John, how in the hell did you stay back?"

Taking Control

Without the intimacy of love, my life's been in a drought.
Chasing dreams, coming to forks, and choosing the wrong routes;

So many times I have made the wrong choice, and now my life's a mess.
Those decisions were mine, I'm guilty, I plead, "No contest;"

To defend myself, I ask for just one chance to explain.
How I am taking control of my life and there's going to be a change;

I have managed to dream again, and look forward to tomorrow,
A brighter future for me, with no room for sorrow;

I have redirected, adjusted, and focused myself well,
From the words I speak, it is easy to tell;

That I know what I want and I know what I need,
To be happy in this world and to succeed;

I have got to stand up, be counted, and take control of my future,
And accept the fact that in life, nothing is for sure.

A poem from "Heartfelt Words": By Teresa Mitchell

Sneak Peak

Sherri's Song

Sherri,

I love you. Never before have I met a person whose heart has the warmth of a rainbow's glow. All my inadequacies and doubts you wiped away with a simple smile that was so genuine that a thousand springtime daybreaks pale in comparison. Everything about you is surreal; it's almost hypnotic and magical. Since I have met you I have been living a fairytale. I never want this to end because I am living the greatest love story of all time. You can make my dreams come true by saying, "Yes," to me. It would be the answers to my prayers and we can continue with happily ever after and forever more. I love you now, always, and forever,

Paul

I slowly closed the letter and bit down on my bottom lip and I reminisced about the days when Paul and I were dating. I often found comfort in opening the old shoebox filled with love letters and reading from the folded pages the words from days gone by. He always had a loving heart, and I always opened those letters he used to write to get that special feeling again. I was still in love, even though things had changed so much for us since he had been laid off.

My husband, Paul Thomas had been out of work for over a year. To make matters worse, his unemployment payments had dissipated a long time ago. The economy was dragging and unemployment was a reality to him. The stresses of daily living were working on his mental psyche. He felt a desire and a need to re-invent himself in his dramatically altered world. Mentally bankrupt after being downsized and trying to pull his life back together, he needed an outlet, because we had lost everything, except each other.

Finding nothing in the newspapers, and being turned down at job after job had finally pushed Paul into a stupor. The only thing keeping him from fading into a complete comatose state was the mere fact that he had a wife that needed him, or at least that's what I always told him.

I had been shouldering the lion's share of the load around the house for some time. Even though Paul had obviously given up, I remained optimistic with gentle words of encouragement and a superwoman's mentality. I was determined to stand by my man because I remembered the house with the large backyard, the walks in the park, the late evening sunsets, the romantic dinners and him kissing me gently, awakening me on a Sunday morning for a breakfast he would have made especially for me. Those were the good times we once shared. I had faith in him and thought with a little nurturing, he would pull himself together and we would regain it all again.

I had promised to love and cherish him always, through good times and bad, for better or worse, till death do we part, and I meant it. Anything he said he wanted, I tried to get for him. One evening after I came in he suggested we try to get a computer to help him in his job search. We had been forced to pawn the one we had when he first lost his job just to put food on the table and help with a few of the bills.

As he made his suggestion, Paul looked spry and had a bounce in his step I had not seen in a while. I thought I had my Paul back. The computer was going to be a strain on our meager budget, but if it put sanity back into our marriage, then it was worth it.

Weeks passed and we managed to find what we were looking for at a garage sale, but without a bank account or a credit card, that meant no internet. My frustrated husband began to slip back into a vegetative state. He lounged around the house and was always in a bad disposition. Daily life seemed to be wearing on him and adding turmoil to our tenuous marital relationship. It would seem that lack of financial abilities does this to a marriage quicker than anything imaginable.

After purchasing the computer, we were running low on food and I told him, "Paul, we need some grocery."

The sound of my voice seemed to irritate him as he walked into the living room and turned on the television. I was feeling perturbed that he had ignored me and I went after him. Determined to have him at least acknowledge me, I said in an inquisitive calm voice, "You didn't hear me? I said we need some grocery"

Paul turned to face me and snarled, "Where am I supposed to get the money. Bitch, you go buy some."

My mouth swung open and remained fixated into that position. The sound of the word "bitch" echoed in my ear. My yellow complexion was displaced with a crimson hue at the words I heard coming from my husband. Paul had never cursed me before, and calling me a bitch was something he had sworn he would never do.

I looked at him, still in shock and replied in a disgusting tone, "I could have gotten some food if I hadn't bought that computer."

I walked out of the room to try to gather my composure and let my mind absorb what I thought I heard him say. Still not wanting to come to grips with the words I knew came from his mouth; I paced the floor trying to gather my self-control. I was still pulling myself together after finally taking a seat at the kitchen table. A few moments later I returned with a boiler and the sound of "**dank**," echoed through the house.

Paul clutched the back of his head and rolled off the couch and curled up into the fetal position. My attack was premeditated and vicious. I intended to live up to the definition of the word 'bitch'.

Seizing the opportunity that had presented itself to me, I sprang over the couch onto his back and straddled him. Snatching his hood back to expose his flesh, I swung wildly with my nails. With each swipe I made, I removed skin to expose his white meat, which was quickly saturated with blood. I went into a frenzy, causing as much damage as possible while he was off guard.

"I got your bitch," I yelled out.

I was so angry I had no intentions of letting up and he was doing a poor job of protecting himself as my nails dug deeper and deeper into him.

It didn't take long before Paul's anger erupted somewhere beneath a shallow surface of his suppressed feelings. His pent up aggression exploded into physical force as his frustration became channeled at me as he decided to go on the offensive. He already resented me for the things I wasn't able to do, but he resented me even more for my impudent act.

Coming up with everything he had in him, I went airborne and flew back over the couch from where I so daringly had leapt. Paul was in hot pursuit. Almost the moment I struck the floor he was on top of me with a cat like quickness. He rolled me over so that he could pin my shoulders to the floor with his knees. Snatching the phone off the coffee table, he broke the end of the line that seated the cord into the phone jack, and then smacked me in the forehead. He was really trying to hurt me. He improvised and turned the cord into a weapon to strangle me and cut off my air supply.

The situation had turned potentially dangerous. Paul was losing control. Leaning close to my face he was spitting, trying to get his words out in a hurry.

He asked me, "Bitch you got the nerve to scratch me? What in the hell wrong with you?"

I could not answer him because I was merely trying to maintain consciousness. A person I thought I knew and loved was denying me the precious air every human needs to maintain life. I was fading quickly but I still fought to hang on. I was succumbing to oxygen deprivation and about to slip into that alternate dream like reality. But it would not be easy for me. Paul let the cord go and backed away from my face. He was monitoring my vital signs by staring into my glazed eyes and had watched my pupils as they started to retreat back into my head.

With me gagging for air, he then started slapping me. Tormenting and keeping me cognoscente, he had no intentions of allowing me to pass out and find comfort in my unconscious state.

He continued feeding me pain by working on my shoulders; driving his knees forcefully against them causing a causing a deep throbbing sensation in my tender joints.

I was hurting. His head was so close to my face we recycled each other's breath. My situation had just turned dire because his carbon dioxide supplanted the oxygen my body so desperately needed. To make matters worse his breath was hot, and I felt like it pushed the temperature in the room to extreme levels. I was now in a full-blown emergency. Struggling with everything I had in me, I managed to turn my face away from him so I could breathe a little better.

I knew what he was doing with his knees, but it was nothing more than a nuisance as I worried about more important things like living, and continued to gulp in the much-needed oxygen. That's all I could do. My husband had knocked all the fight out of me and I just lay there.

With my body paralyzed by his weight and in dire need of relief, my mind became heightened and started to take in everything including a familiar odor that polluted the room. It was the scent of my favorite cologne I had bought him when we really couldn't afford such luxury items. The stench was lodged in my nose. He smelled as if he had showered in the stuff and it became repugnant to me as it rode the air that cascaded rapidly down my throat. Never again would I ever want to smell that sweetness that was now a vile stench.

Paul was now in full torment mode as he punished me for things I had done and might do later. Our small one bedroom wooden framed house became a gulag and it seemed like an eternity before he decided I had enough and started to rise off of my dejected body. He shifted his weight forward so the pressure from his knees increased the strain on my shoulder joints again, causing me to groan in considerable pain.

He paused, showing his dominance in a dog like fashion, daring me to move. My blurred vision could not focus and I saw multiple images of my tormenter staring down on me from just above her head.

Suddenly, after he hovered over me for a moment, in almost a move of disdain he gave me something to remember the incident by. With a closed fist he smacked me solidly against my forehead, causing it to collide violently with the floor, making the "thump" sound with its impact and then ricocheting weakly back into the air.

The angry man got off me and checked the laceration he had received in our scuffle with his hands. They stung. The broken skin and bloodstains mingling with his white hoody served to remind him of our encounter.

He now felt better about being unemployed because he would not have to go to work and explain to everyone what he had been through. I would not be so lucky. I would have to conceal the damage my 'loving' husband had inflicted on me as best I could and make up an explanation for the marks I was unable to hide.

Paul, walking out of the room after restoring order to his house looked back at me while still on the floor sobbing loudly, and threatened me saying, "Bitch if you ever put your hands on me again, I am going to hurt you bad."

Throwing his head forcefully from side to side in a sorrowful manner, my husband continued into the bedroom with nostrils flared, trying to calm himself down.

During this reprieve, I managed to pull myself off of the floor after the imminent danger had passed. I struggled into the bathroom to try to pull myself together. I hurt all over my body. My skin was now marked with deep dark bruises and my forehead was swollen with a nasty gash where the phone had cut me. I was in bad shape and could not stand to look at myself in the mirror and gradually slumped away from it.

I shrank until I was finally on the floor and unable to go any further. I then started searching for an ounce of solace somewhere within the white tile.

I could not find it, and anger exploded from within me and I yelled out, "Paul! I am going to tell Momma! I am going to call *her and tell her you put your hands on me! You don't put your hands on me! You dirty bastard!"*

Paul was still game and yelled from the bedroom, "Tell the old ho, and tell your pappy too. They will get the same thing if they come messing with me."

I was despondent and reminded him of the promises he had made to me when we were dating.

Somehow finding the strength to raise my voice even louder over my sobs I told him, "You said you would never curse me or call me a bitch! You said you would never hit me! You a punk! You want hit a man with your sorry ass!"

Paul surfaced from the bedroom and peeped around the corner of the bathroom door. He had just about had enough of me. My indifferent husband looked at me and smirked, "You maybe right, but I hit your ass."

ACKNOWLEDGMENTS

I would like to thank God for never deserting me in my times of need. Your love is everlasting, and your blessings are boundless. I would like to thank my momma, who stayed with me, and comforted me through all of my problems. You have been the greatest Mother on earth, to sacrifice so much for your children to achieve. You realized the importance of education, and you poked and prodded me to learn. I would like to thank my brother for being there for me, even when everyone else doubted me. We have always been close, and no one on earth shall ever break our bond. Most of all, I would like to thank my God once again and many times more, because through you all things are possible. You knew me from the womb, and loved me. You know me as a sinful person here on earth, and have made the choice to stand by me. There is no doubt in my mind, you will know me when I leave this place, and comfort me when I cross over to the other side.

Tonie Short